W9-BXX-737

BRASS

BRASS

HELEN WALSH

CANONGATE U.S.
New York

Copyright © 2004 by Helen Walsh

All rights reserved. No part of this book may be reproduced in any form
or by any electronic or mechanical means, including information storage
and retrieval systems, without permission in writing from the publisher,
except by a reviewer, who may quote brief passages in a review. Any
members of educational institutions wishing to photocopy part or all of
the work for classroom use, or publishers who would like to obtain
permission to include the work in an anthology, should send their
inquiries to Canongate U.S., 841 Broadway, New York, NY 10003.

First published in Great Britain in 2004 by
Canongate Books Ltd., Edinburgh, Scotland

Printed in the United States of America

FIRST AMERICAN EDITION

ISBN 1-84195-484-5

Canongate U.S.
841 Broadway
New York, NY 10003

04 05 06 07 08   10 9 8 7 6 5 4 3 2 1

I go hunting, beneath bodices and thin attire,
The divine back below the curve of the
    shoulders . . .
I recreate their bodies, burning with fine fevers.
They find me absurd . . .
And my savage desires fasten on to their lips.

                                        Arthur Rimbaud

                    To Kevin,
                    With love.

CHAPTER 1

Millie

We turn onto Upper Duke Street and the view sucks the breath from my lungs.

The whole of the city is aglow and the Liver buildings, brightly drenched by the rising moon, reign magnificently in a cloudless sky. I snatch a quick glance to see if she too has been seduced by the vista but the eyes are paralysed by some chemical excess. She's at least three or four years younger than me – a child in the eyes of the law. Yet she wears the spent constitution of a woman who has lived, breathed and spat these streets out all her life. There's mixed blood in her face too, the dark complexion suggesting the Mediterranean while her narrowed eyes hint of the East. It's a good face – awkwardly composed but pretty nonetheless. It doesn't belong to these streets.

We head down towards the Cathedral which pierces the night like some majestic foreboding, and she lopes off ahead, creating enough distance between us to show we're not together. At the graveyard gates, she swings round and instructs me with the flat of a palm to hold back. I watch her elfin silhouette slide down some steps and without warning, dissolve into the petrol blue night. I doubt she'll return and I'm pricked with a mild spur of relief. The effects of the beak and the booze are fast ebbing away now and there's elements of the old me lurking in my subconscious, urging me to turn on my heels and flee.

The night spits her back into focus and she's standing before me again. Skinny legs and fat breasts. Coal black hair pulled fiercely into a high pony. I swoon.

She swings an arm in a beckoning arc and I follow, down a flight of uneven steps, through a dark stubby tunnel and out into a sprawling graveyard. For one lucid moment, a spasm of terror jolts my heart as I anticipate what looms ahead but as we veer down towards the right of the Cathedral which now towers high above us, the brilliance of the moon finds us and all danger is neutralised in the serum of desire. Randomly, she selects a grave, which is located at the remotest corner of the plot. It's flat, wide and practical. She removes her clothes with a routine agility. She's serviced a hundred other punters on this very slab of timeworn concrete though I guess I'm her first female punter.

'I don't do fish,' she said in a coarse Toxteth accent, 'Norra done 'ting round 'ere girl.'

And she was right. I'd scoured these streets, this city, relentlessly in pursuit of brass on many a drug-fuelled bender and only twice had I struck lucky. However, once I assured her that *she* didn't actually have to do anything. Just remove her clothes, *all* of them, and let me indulge myself, she began to crumble. I produced a fifty and she surrendered.

★   ★   ★

She lies back and the shock of the slab juts her nipples out and arches her slender back. Her breasts are large and intrusive. At odds with her pubescent framework. She has the hips of a twelve-year-old. I run a hand across the width of her navel which is hard and sticky and gleams in the moonlight as if lightly smeared in Vaseline and lower my mouth to her breasts, sucking hard at her dark nipples, manipulating them to solid black bullets. Her skin tastes of stale, salty sweat. Cheap body lotion and spent chemicals. Pungent and almost unpleasant. It drives me on.

'Look at your tits,' I whisper, 'Touch them.'

She does so, reluctant at first but wanting to be urged on. I slip an arm around her small back and flick my tongue across her flat young tummy.

'Do you like that?'

She doesn't answer. I raise my head to find her eyes roaming in their orbits. Her mouth is slack, lopsided. A stream of spittle trails her chin. I prod her hard in the navel and she protests with a dilatory flinch.

Impatient now, I part her legs which are coloured with fresh bruises. I slide a finger inside. She's dry and stiffens at my touch. For an instant, I feel I should stop, I should turn on my heels and run. But as my mouth falls upon her cunt and the smell of rubber smacks me in the face, I resume my role. Guiltlessly. As a punter. With a stiff tongue I press down hard on her clit and with short purposeful strokes, I slowly massage her to life. I feed in another then another finger and her resistance gives way to minimal yet compliant thrusts. My movements become more forceful and her juices gush freely onto my face. The body arcs upwards and outwards and holds up there as she strains against this pleasure.

I slide a hand in my trousers and seek my cunt.

The beak seems to have temporarily robbed its walls of all sensation but my clit swells beneath the clammy nest of my palm. I manipulate myself hard and selfishly, the whore becoming nothing but a body. A cunt in a magazine. My climax is powerful but as soon as those crackling shortwaves subside I'm overwhelmed by the impulse to abscond. I feel sober and awkward. I remove my hands from her body, which are lathered in our sweat and wipe them on my hips. She props herself up, fuck-faced and shining with the stench of her latest trick and stares into me. The face is no longer drug dead but wide open with questions. Her eyes stare out, large and fright-ened, giving me a glimpse of the girl behind the whore. She makes to speak but the words evaporate on her lips. Half of me wants to take her in my arms, the other, despises her. Once more I take in the child's eyes, the woman's breasts. I force a valedictory smile and sprint off across the graveyard, spurred on by that unique tingling and euphoria that follows orgasm.

Back on Upper Duke Street, I feel the rush of the urban glow once more. It's still early and there's a whiff of excitement in the air as taxis bundle life into the core of the city. I *love* Fridays. There's an infectious delirium that Saturday nights fail to deliver. Come 8 o'clock, the streets of Liverpool are heaving with studes, schoolies and nine to fivers, all drunk on the freedom of the weekend, trying to stretch the night out forever.

I'm meeting Jamie at 60 Hope Street, less than a hundred yards from the spot where I picked the whore up. The idea of walking through her patch again unsettles me so I take a circuitous route, down along Rodney Street and back up pulsating Leece Street, already writhing with bodies. The moon is behind me now, a big yellow balloon lingering on the skyline, slowly blinking the stars awake. Next full moon, I'm gonna perch myself on top of a hill – Frodsham or Wales. And get stoned. Just me and that big old moon. If I had a car and a smoke, I'd be tempted to fuck off right now, resist the lure of the city, but it would be impossible to mellow out with all this going on. Absolute torture in fact. The stifling heat of the day is only just cooling and it's the start of the weekend and the excitement of it all is sweeping the city like lava. I love this feeling. I love it.

Jamie

Shite! I'm late and that'll be her on the mobie now so I'm just letting it run on to answer. Can see her now, by the way. She'll be sat there at the bar with that half irate, half betrayed gob on her and she'll be going:

'That's thirty minutes he's robbed me of. Thirty minutes I could have spent down the Blue Bar checking out the honeys.'

Ah, I love her madly though I do, bolshy little waif that she is. She's like a sister to us. Seven spanking years of history we've clocked up. That's a third of her life and a quarter of mine. And we've been through some bad shite me and Millie. Oh aye. Stuff that would've torn most friendships like wet paper. But me and her, it's only made us stronger. Invincible like.

Has to be said though, can be a nasty piece of work at times, lil' Millie.

Aye, she can be fucken merciless she can. You don't want to be getting on the wrong side of Millie O'Reilley.

This cabby's pure doing my swede in now, though. Having a fully-fledged domestic on the mobie, he is. Mad fucken Somali accent screaming into this brick-sized mobie he's got. Beads of sweat oozing from his shiny aul' head. Fucken car stinks of dead animals. It does – whole thing reeks badly and I just want out, now. I winds the window down and thrusts my head out, gasping on the smoggy summer's air as if it were an inhaler. He swings round and removing himself reluctantly from the brick-like contraption gives us this big mad glower.

'Put the fucking window up la! I've got the air con on.'

Air con, by the way! This shed must be twenty-thirty years old.

He returns to the wheel just in time to see that the lights have turned red but crashes em anyway and carries on hurling obscenities into his 'phone. I ignore the cunt. The windows are staying down. But I don't want to be getting into no nonsense with the Somalis, mind you. That's one group you're best leaving alone. Fight one Somali and you're fighting the fucken lot of em. That's how it is. It's not so long since Sean had to bite that lad's face off before he'd slap the floor. He's a mad cunt Sean, used to box for England under 16s and that, but this Somali lad would pure not go down. Hit him with all sorts Sean did, but the lad just carries on and that. 'That the best you can do?' and what have you. And then, once Sean loses it and bites a chunk out of his face, he's got the whole fucken barmy army of em on his back. Tell you la, you're best just avoiding it. He's only an aul' cabby, end of the day, but I'm not fucken rising to him. And the other thing is, I don't want to be soiling my new Jil Sander kecks. Lil' Millie is going to pure love these kecks by the way. Pure fucken class, they are.

We're coming up past our aul' flat now at the top of Parlie and this big surge of nostalgia sweeps all over us. I'm like that, me you know. I'm proper sentimental. I fill up at things like that Buena Vista Social Club. Fucken too much that is – when that Ibrahim Ferrer's walking round New York. Pure fucken gets you right there it does. Slays me, stuff like that. Always has done – good films, books, tunes that take you back, whatever. Dunno, la – I'm just like that. I still gets all dewy-eyed when I see that cobalt blue door and the mossy windowpanes and the skeleton of our Billy's first car sat there in the yard. Amount of times I had to fucken kip in that car. It's only a few years ago and that, but I can't help myself – I already feel last about it. I feel like it's gone all that. I feel as though we've lost them times for good.

It was happy days back then. Me, Sean and our kid, living like fucken kings. It were all down to Sean of course. Our Billy were signing on and I was spunking half my wages from Fords on that joke night school.

But Sean, he were pure rolling in it and he made sure that we all enjoyed the fruits of his labour. The fridge were always jammed full with ale and classy grub from Tezzies and Marksies. Not that we ever ate none of it. Our time was split fair and square. Half the time we was getting high, the other half we was coming down. The perks of Sean's new career extended to muchos class A, and in the two years we lived together, he must have plied us with enough gear to feed the whole of Garlands of a Saturday night. There were no protocols or anything where the consumption of gear were concerned. Oh no. And we'd think nothing of dropping one of a Monday avvy. Sean was the worst. Got so's he'd have to snaffle a line or two 'fore he read the sports pages of The Echo. Pure dependence or pure indulgence la? It's a miracle his liver is still intact after all that. And his head for that matter. There was hardly a morning back then that Billy and Sean didn't wake up with the taste of old copper in their mouths and their hearts drumming in their ears. And if I hadn't've spent most of my nights at college or up in my bedroom grappling with Keats and Hardy, I would've well gone under. Even then, though, I'd still come and find em when I was done, not wanting to miss nothing, still wanting mine like an idiot. Match nights, I was pure putty. Sean'd pop his head around the door around half-five-six, just as I was plunging into an assignment. He fucken knew it and all too, knew I didn't want no distraction. But he'd be stood there waving a ticket and a bag of beak at us and that'd be that. I was putty.

★   ★   ★

He's always been a lady's man, Sean. Still is by the way, but more so back then. Fucken effortless and all, he got himself a fan base bigger than Boyzone's. The flat were always chocker with exquisite fucken birds with flawless complexions and polished accents that he'd picked up over the water. Fucken *loved* him, they did. Thought he was the real thing. Of course none of em looked twice at myself and our kid. But I was just made up to sit with em and soak it all in and that. He had this aloofness about him Sean, which time seems to have diluted a little. I used to think it were manicured like, that it was all for show, something for the ladies and that, but maybe there was more to it.

He always has been a moody cunt, Sean, and we never really had any idea back then how deep he was getting in. Even when he were eckied up he kept his thoughts on a harness. Gave nothing away, Sean. Just used to sit there, mute. Them dark expressionless eyes of his impervious to the euphoria that would flush his cheeks and rattle his jaw.

Looking back though, I was a pure hypocrite where Sean was concerned. I half knew how he was making his dough, but I would never let myself dwell on it. My mind just sort of overrode it. It was Sean, my mate, just a lad what I grew up with. And I was more than happy to help him spend it. Oh yes. But not now though. Now, I *always* go fifty/fifty with Sean, and I don't accept freebies off him no more. Least, only the random line now and again, and even then I always feel obliged to buy him a drink and that.

So I knows full well what's going down in Flynn-strasse. But did I put up a fight when he offered my Missus a job in one of his salons? Did I fuck. Why would I?

It's a proper fucken legit business and she's a beautician, end of the day. She's doing what she's always wanted to do. Happy as a twat down that salon of his, lil' Anne Marie. Goes to work with a spring in her step and comes home beaming like a kid. I've said it. I'm a two-faced cunt. My bird works for Sean Flynn and I look the other way. I try and think of him, and us lot, how we were back then. How we was when we met Millie.

Magic times to be living through, they were. The club scene were raw and unearthly. It had a lingo of its own and those who spoke it were bound by a shared secret that welded us together like glue. It went way beyond anything you'd known. Way beyond comprehension. It was more than a deviation from my working week. It was more than just escapism. It was a way of life. When they closed down the State in 1991 after all that trouble with the Ungis, a part of us shut down too. It was only a matter of months before they reopened but it was gone la. All that energy, that arcane magic, gone. It were full of aul' heads, desperately clinging on to a memory. Trying to make sense of it all. And they couldn't. Tragic it was. I still see some of them faces, drifting round town. Casualties of their own youth that never recovered from the fact that history had robbed em of somet they'd devoted their lives to. And will they fuck let on? Blank us they do. Pure burns my head out when I sees some face from back then and they're not having it. Fills us with the same kind of tristesse that I gets if I runs into an ex who really meant something. Pure madness that is. How you can get so close to someone and let em delve so deep into your soul. Take em to them far remote places and let em run amok and explore every little crevice and hollow 'til there's nothing left to unearth and you're pure spent and exposed. And then one day you're just strangers. All that history and intimacy just hanging in there by a flimsy thread of memory.

The State though la, gives us goosies just thinking on it. That's where I met the little scamp. Lil' Millie O'Reilley. Oh aye – that was her. Pure front, even then. Pushes her way to the front of the guezzie – no money, by the way, no I.D and no fucken patience or tact or manners, neither. Just bang at it she were. Proper trying to blag her way in. This bolshy lil' waif. This beautiful fucken kid with rain-slicked-hair and big mad liquid eyes, trying to skank the doormen with that husky little voice of hers. Had it been a year before, then her looks alone would have guaranteed her the VIP treatment, but the club were under close scrutiny by then and a thirteen-year-old dying from an overdose would have been the final curtain.

So, anyway, when it dawns on her that her performance is getting her fucken nowhere, it's onto Plan B and her eyes well up and she starts pleading with em, spieling em this rueful little number about how she'd dropped a pill half an hour ago and were coming up fast and strong and needed to be in there with the music. And if they don't let her in, she'd have a bad E and pure go mental and end up in some loony bin and they'll be bang to rights for fucking up a beautiful young life. What? Fucken hilarious la! Billy's in stitches, and me, I'm half starting to well up. I've said it – I'm a sentimental cunt.

Good as she is, Millie, there's no way these fellas on the door are letting her in – not now she's told em she's on an E. And now they're doing that thing that grocks on the door like to do. They're having a shite night emselves so what they want best is to fuck someone else's night up, too. Specially the young girls, weirdly. We all know what all that's about, by the way. And these knobheads, they starts trying to grab her and saying let's call the busies and what have you. So me and our kid says we know her from by ours and we takes her by the arm and all three of us bolts right off into the night – her grinning like a skate, me wondering what the fuck we must look like, sharking off with a bird that's barely reached puberty. And I'll tell it again. There was nothing shady about it you know, *nothing* that was in any way thingio. Pure spur of the moment it were. Spirit of the era and that. That's what you'd do back then – Us and Them. The Billy Bunters and the doormen. And anyways, she was a kid, Millie. She was a proper little girl, right down to her braces and ponytail. And she had that nervous undefeated energy that unworldly teenagers have. She'd kill us if she heard us say that. Thought she was it lil' Millie did. Even then – even with her braces.

We don't want to risk getting K.B'd from another

club and we can see she's slumping into a sledge so we starts walking back towards the flat. What we're thinking is — we'll play some tunes and make her a brew and that, sort her a Joe Baxi. But before we've even reached the Blackie, the three of us've glided into one of those gorgeous drug-fucked conversations which you never want to come down from. At thirteen and a half, she was lucid and funny and cynical as fuck. Full of fucken insight, lil' Millie — way too clever for her own good. But she still saw the world with that kidlike simplicity, too. That unblinking naivety that stemmed from having good and protective aul' folks. And growing up in a decent area. You could just see it from talking to her. She was from a place where bad things don't happen. That stoic fucken self-assurance la, it don't come from fear, that. It comes from never having to worry about nothing.

We stayed up and talked all night. I'll admit it — we was buzzing of her, me and our Billy. And when Sean come in and seen how young she were, he just half nods and that, grunts and goes upstairs. He knows us too well. He knows there'd be no funny business going down.

We dropped her off the next day and she blubbed like a baby. Made us all swear that we wouldn't write her off as some ecstasy cliché. When we woke up, we were going to remember this as something real, something good, not some strobe-lit fling. That the plans we made for the future would not perish before the crushing onslaught of the inevitable comedown. We all swore we'd meet for a drink at The Belvedere — mine and

Billy's local from when we was kiddies round there – that following Friday. Did she fuck turn up, mind you. And in fairness, even though we never said nothing, I think we was both that little bit relieved, me and Billy. What was we starting here, end of the day? Where was it going to go – a binding friendship with a kid? So for them six months, that's exactly what she were – a strobe-lit fling but one which shone on in my head like a big bright fireball. Then, six months later, one November morning, she produced herself at the door, gurning her kite off and acting like she'd only been gone five minutes. Like she's just nipped out the all-nightie for juice and Rizlas and that.

'Coming to catch sunrise at the Docks,' she goes, just like that.

And apart from the fact that dawn's dissolved into daylight more than four hours ago it's fucken teeming down! Big mad storm brewing out across the Irish Sea and creeping up on the city like some malevolent fog. I puts my coat on anyway and plunges out into that bitter winter morning, hungover and wretched but with my heart romping in its cage, happy as hell. You don't think of friends in terms of chemistry but there's some-thing between us, la. There's some powerful magnetism at play that's got nothing to do with sex.

So we've sat in silence for hours that morning, just staring out into the sea with the wind slamming in off the river, bang into us, feeling it full force. We've sat there watching it conjure up a storm, teeth chattering to fuck, pair of us staring out in pure awe as the storm finally hits and lightening cracks across that big black

Mersey sky. I could've been swept away and tossed to my death for all I cared that morning. I was so fucken happy. That moment with her – that was the pinnacle of that whole eckie period. It was pristine and immovable and I knew that moment could never come again. And when I was falling asleep that night this lovely warm swoon crept over us – the kind you gets when you're a kid, when dark nights start kicking in and you know there's stuff to look forward to like Bommie night and Halloween and Crimbo. And for me, that special something was Millie. She'll tear us to shreds when I do finally get there, tonight.

Millie

He's fucking late. Jamie's always late when he's been at hers. She drops her knickers just as he's walking out of the door, on the supposition that if she sends her man out sexually gratified, he can spit in the face of temptation. Cute, but incredibly naive. Doesn't matter how big a grin your fella's wearing as he walks out of the door – fresh fanny is fresh fanny at the end of the day. And she's still nauseatingly paranoid about Jamie and I, or *James*, as she calls him, our man-and-girl friendship. This, I just can't fathom, seeing as though the plaster of our friendship was cast four and half years before she lumbered onto the scene and started rationing the time we spent together. In the past, when Jamie's had girl-friends, we've always remained as thick as thieves. We're impenetrable us two. We can withstand anything and the reason for that, if she'd just open her eyes and see it, is that we don't fancy each other. She should embrace

15

it, the tube-bronze tart, but instead she's trying to break it. Jesus! It's not so long since the pair of us would suffer withdrawal symptoms if we let the day expire without speaking to each other. Now, days lapse into weeks. Months even. That conniving tip rat managed to keep us apart for the whole of June this year. Dragged him off to some two-star sunny scouse paradise in Marbella and drained him of all his savings.

Jamie wears his emotions like a clown and I know for a fact that he enjoyed that holiday as much as I'd enjoy wanking my Dad off. Even the prospect of sex on tap was but a paltry compensation and I'm sorry but no way in the world is that bint an imaginative lover anyway. I know for a fact that she doesn't suck dick and boy did she lose the plot when she stumbled upon his stash! You don't just stumble on Jamie's stash by the way. It's sandwiched between a pile of Auto Marts and old phone directories in a storage cupboard in the yard so she must have gone rooting which makes her fucking nosy as well as frigid. And because of that selfish bitch he had to forgo our annual pilgrimage to Amsterdam this year. He said it was a financial impossibility but I bet it was her jutting the bottom lip out. In her monolithic outlook, there is something sinister and threatening about friendships between men and women. Apparently we have 'latent' desires for each other. Latent! She doesn't even know what that means. She's robbed that from Cosmo or Ricky Lake, the daft bitch. And I really *hate* the way he refers to her as a model. He always has to slip that little reference point in. As though staggering down the catwalk for a few poxy local fashion shows can somehow justify that she paints digits for a living.

Another twenty minutes lapse and I'm still loitering at the bar; sandwiched between two fat suits and silently debating my third JD which will either soothe or exacerbate this ball of anxiety swelling in my gut. Usually when I've a been a glutton with the beak, a couple of stiffs is all I need to calm my ticker down and stop my mind from rambling and lets face it, I've been here a thousand times before and I *always* pull through. There's been occasions when I've done treble the amount I've done tonight and my heart has beat so violently that it's felt as though it might smash through my ribcage and like I say, I always pull through. It's nothing to get worked up about but I can't deny that there is something sinister about the way I'm feeling. Maybe it's just the austerity of the surroundings, all calculated minimalism, accentuating the need to feel and appear normal. Or it might just be that the gear was cut with speed. But there's this nasty, negative feeling squirming through my system. No point dwelling on it though, best just to keep your head clean. Trouble is, you can't pre-empt the onslaught of a panic attack. Not when it's drug induced. There are no alarm bells. It just engulfs you in one powerful sweep. Putting it into perspective though, I had three bumps before I left the house, a tiny one in the taxi on the way into town and a couple in the toilets about five minutes ago. That's not even half a gram. Doesn't warrant thinking about. People don't OD on half a gram of beak.

Fuck's sake Millie. Get a grip. Order yourself another stiff and get a fucking grip!

Jamie

I'm pulling up outside 60 Hope Street now and if the truth be known, I'm not that fussed on the gaff. End of the day though, it's one of Millie's favourites and I haven't seen the waif in days. She practically lives in here. I can't help myself though. I'm on okay dough at Fords and all that, I'm no worse off than any other wannabe cunt in here but it's the same thing every time. I do – I half crap myself as I walks up these steps. Half feel like some cunt's running his eye over us, finding us out. I would've much preferred the Eureka, the little Cypriot gaff up on Myrtle Parade. Friendly as fuck they are in there by the way, lovely little atmos they've got going. And it's not that cheap either. There's no end of professors and that from Millie's uni, fellas from LIPA and all kinds. But it's nice, end of the day. Down to earth. You can't deny that the grub's fucken gorgeous in here and that, but it's a phoney's paradise. I'm only doing this for her.

Can tell just by the way she's stood there that she's been caning it. Head lolled against her shoulder, hands clamped tight behind her back and her right foot jittering away. Pure keyed up body lingo that. Even before she comes bounding over, smiling brilliantly – which soon breaks into a scowl when she remembers how late I am, by the way. Even before I smell the whisky on her breath and wipe away a globule of beak-sodden snot from under her nose, I can tell you exactly what she's had and how much of it, too. Just by the way she's stood there. If the truth be known, I'm a tad disappointed that she's gotten in this state all by herself without waiting for us. There's nothing in the world like getting slowly, gloriously sozzled with your bezzy mate and your conversation flows seamlessly cos you're drinking at the same pace and you're on each other's wavelength. I was looking forward to that tonight, but I'll tell you exactly what'll happen now. We'll get past our starters and then she'll casually suggest that we skip the mains and head straight into town and if I say I don't fancy it, she'll start sulking and acting up and I'll give in cos I can't be doing with the hassle. And then she'll start *demanding* beak and note I says *demanding* cos that's what she does when she's done in like this and she's on a mission and if I don't deliver the goods she'll say something ridiculous like:

'Ah well, I guess I'll just have to get a taxi down Granby Street and go find my own then.'

Which'll leave us no option but to drag Sean into town who won't be too happy but'll do it anyway and then she'll start pleading with us to do a line:

'Oh please Jamie, just a tiny one? It'll perk you up.'

And I'll relent just to shut her up, but there's no such thing as 'just the one' with her is there? Which is why I do my best to avoid it these days cos next thing you know it's ten o'clock next morning and we're sat in Millie's kitchen talking pure shite and everytime I make hints at heading off, she'll go:

'Please, please, *please!* Just one more. One for the road.'

And then it's three in the afternoon and I'm walking to the bus stop cos the taxi that she swears blind she ordered never materialised and my heart's heavy with dread cos I know there'll be a hundred answerphone messages from an irate Anne Marie who's day/weekend/life I've ruined and I always swear down on our kid's life that I'm not doing beak again. Ever. And it's a fucken miracle that our Billy's still alive.

Millie

A skinny waitress guides us to our table. She has a pretty face and a delicate physique, but her arms and jawline are swathed in hazel down. A real friend would tell her – that's just ugly, that is. You don't want to be looking at something like that – not in a place like this. She places us at a window seat which looks right out onto Hope Street, the bleeding heart of the red light district. I make a clumsy attempt at steering us to a more central table but a sharp dig in my ribs summons me to silence.

'Best spec in the house this,' Jamie says when we are finally settled, 'What you playing at?'

I shrug my shoulders apologetically and stare into the faded felt black of the street, where headlights are prowling along in full throttle, breathing a plume of excitement and fear into the already frightened night. A demented silhouette stumbles past the window, pausing to look in on us. Just a shape without a face. It could be her. It could be anyone. I avert my gaze to Jamie who is eyeing me intensely and gulp down the icy dregs of my JD. I slam the glass on the table with more force than intended and Jamie's vision swooshes from left to right. He tosses a diffident smile to a couple who's attention it's caught.

'Chill out, for Christ sake – it's *Friday.*' I say.

He opens his mouth in instinctive protest but the waitress materialises and hands him a menu. I place mine flat on the table, fold my arms and lower my head. The words swim in front of me, meaning my eyes are drunker than my head. Not drunk enough to let that hairy wrist swoop down and scoop away the empty glass, though. I'm half tempted to take her to one side and ask her if she's aware of this fundamental defect. And how a simple course of lazer treatment would kill the problem forever and thus transform her from an unfuckable attractive lady to a fuckable stunner. I'd be doing her a favour. I hold her wrist while I double drain the glass. Maybe I will. Later.

The very idea of food causes my tummy to gripe. I forgo the starter and opt for a simple goat's cheese salad. Jamie orders two starters and steak with fries. He flounders self-consciously over the wine menu then decides upon a bottle of Pouilly Fume – my favourite. He can't afford this, but I don't have the heart to tell him I'm beyond caring what I drink. From now on everything will taste the same. I order another JD. The downy waitress minces off and Jamie throws me a disapproving look. I feel about four.

'What's that for?'

He thrusts a glass of water under my nose which I thrust right back.

'That,' he says through pursed lips.

I light a cigarette and pull a hopeless expression. The

21

sort worn by good men married to vile fishwives.

'Eh now, don't be looking at us like that. It was *your* idea to come out for a meal. And all you've ordered is a plate of rabbit food and enough whisky to sedate a gang of paraffins.'

I raise an eyebrow — my time-honoured taunt when Jamie tries to use words to impress me.

'Se-date!'

I roll my eyes dramatically and slip the jailbait sat opposite with her parents an impish wink. She drops her head and shifts uncomfortably in her seat. Jamie's now frowning — or maybe he's smiling. His face keeps shifting in and out of focus. I love his face. It's bold and elegiac. Steeped in history. It dances when he talks.

'Come on now Millie, mate. You're gonna get us kicked out if you're not careful.'

'She's gagging for it.'

'She's a *kid*. And she's with her Mam and Dad.'

'Still gagging for it though.'

'I'll remind you of that when you've got a daughter of your own and you catch some fat aul' perve leching her.'

'Somehow I don't see myself as a mother. A fat old perve perhaps but not a mother.'

'Aaaahhh, see! That's exactly what Anne Marie used to say! Not that she seen herself as an aul' perve mind you. Just, like, she never had no maternal instincts and that. Now look at her!'

Oh dear. Wrong move, Jamie darling. Just when you think you know someone they come up with some-thing so crass it can shock you. How can he even *think*

22

like that? How can he begin to try to put me in remotely the same box as that tanned tart!

'Wanna see her, babe! Can not even walk past a pram without blubbing, that one!'

His face slips into focus and it's all adoring. I feel sick.

'Yes, but I'm nothing like Anne Marie. We're worlds apart.'

'Aaaah, no – you're not *that* different,' he says, voice slashed with defensiveness.

'Oh yeah we are. The major difference being that when I see a mother and toddler in the street the first thought that flips through my head is how much easier my fist will slide in now that she's been stretched by child birth.'

'Aarrrr-ey! You've put us right off my food now.'

'Don't be getting all righteous on me, Jamie Keeley. You're the one who implanted those kind of thoughts in my head in the first place. I was a good catholic girl before I met you and your Billy. It's you guys that turned me into a *pervert!* You let me watch *Animal Farm* when I was how old, hey? Fourteen – that's how old! Which is tantamount to child abuse is it not?'

I'm having fun with him, now. He's biting on this one hook, line and sinker.

'I mean, did you not envisage how the exposition of such brutal filth would effect such a young and impressionable mind?'

'Now, stop right there. You *stole* that video from our kid's room. And if you remember rightly, I was extremely concerned when you told us you'd watched it. *Extremely* concerned.'

'I noticed. You started locking your dogs up when I came round.'

He twigs and laughs hard. I love making him laugh. I can't imagine *her* ever making him laugh the way I do.

Jamie

Here we go. Miracle she's lasted this long, in fairness.

'Jaaaay-meeeee,' she says with big molten eyes, 'Are *you* hungry?'

'Fucken starving as a matter of fact,' I goes, 'Wish they'd get a move on with my steak. Why?'

'Oh nothing.'

Her eyes wander sulkily around the room then fall south on the table. A short silence follows.

'Have you seen Sean recently?' she asks, dunking a piece of bread into her wine and making a little pyramid of the ash she's spilt on the table.

'No, honey. Ain't seen him. Not since training last week – which reminds us. How come I ain't seen *you* in there for over a month?'

'I start back at Uni next week don't I? And I've had to make a start on my dissertation.'

'What's that all about then?'

'*Duh!* It's like a very long e-*ssay*!'

' 'kinell Millie love, I know what a fucken dissertation is! Jesus! I'm asking you what it's *about*.'

'Oh ehhm, books. Queer theory, ehhm, deconstruction of stable identities in contemporary literature.'

'Liar.'

She grins cheekily.

'Sounds good though doesn't it?!'

24

'You haven't even started yet have you? Come 'ead Millie! This is your final year. The end of the road is in sight and all that. You don't know how fucken lucky you are, you!'

'Alright. Alright.'

'Serious, girl! You live with your aul' fella who pure fucken indulges you and gives you dough and I don't know what else . . . You do what the fuck you want . . . You don't even *have* to work by the way, it's all so fucken easy to you . . .'

'I said *alright!*'

Her eyes flash with that glazed chemical anger. I change the subject, pronto.

'Knocked him out in training, by the way. Sean. Caught him with a beauty! Left upper and that.'

'Is he coming into town d'you know?'

'Nah, doubt it, girl — I do, seriously doubt it. Goes down to Kellys of a Friday, done he? Him, our Billy and that — they're steering clear a town after that other thing. But you should've seen it Millie! Out fucken cold he were! Fucken O' Malley went fucken white, la! Was not happy about . . .'

'Do you fancy going up there after dinner?'

'Where?'

'Kellys?'

'You fucken wha'? Thought you fucken hated it in there. You said it were full of scum.'

'Respectable scum.'

'Still said they were scum . . .'

I'm having a laugh with her now. I've known the kid long enough. Course I know what her rap is, but anyway.

'. . . what's the sudden interest in Sean? Last time we all went out, the two of youse spent the night bickering like kids didn't youse? And you told our Billy that you'd pissed in his drink.'

'Did not.'

I stares into her long and hard, furrowing my brows and stroking my chin like I'm trying to solve some big fucken mystery. Then slowly, dramatically, I lets a knowing grin seep across my kite.

'Aaahhh, *I* see. *Now* I get it. You'll be wanting a bit of the other, will you? Now listen here Millie. This is the deal, yeah? We're gonna enjoy this lovely meal together right? And then we'll maybe have a few cocktails at the Platinum Lounge? And then I'll drop you wherever you want. Kellys, The Pod, Dreamers, wherever – but for me, it's bed. I've got to be up at eight to take Anne Marie to work and I'm on overtime myself. So there's no big mad beak bender going on tonight.'

I almost feel her heart hit the table. But that's how it is – I'm not giving in to her. Can pull as many pouts as she wants tonight. I'm not relenting.

'Arrr-ay, Millie! Be fucken reasonable, will you? You saw how much earache she gave us last time . . .'

I pause. There'll never be a better time. I go for it.

'. . . and I need to keep her sweet for next weekend, don't I?'

'Why? What's going on next weekend?'

I gulp. If I don't spit it out right now, I never will.

'*You* know! I'm taking her to the Lakes aren't I? The big one and that!'

'Er, hang on there, Jamie! The *big one?* What d'you mean the *big* one?'

'What we talked about, back at yours, after the Blue.'

'*What?* What did we talk about?'

All despondency leaks from her kite.

' 'kinell Millie! D'you not remember anything from that night?'

'Jesus Jamie. I don't even remember *getting* to the Blue that night, let alone being back at ours!'

'So? How could you forget something as important as that?'

'As *what* for fuck's sake?'

I pause. I'm shitting it, here. Here goes, anyway.

'Anne Marie. I'm gonna pop the question aren't I?'

Millie

My heart sinks way way down into the pits of my guts. I clutch my snatch involuntarily and swallow back a hot emotion threatening to erupt inside. His eyes are shiny, full of vim – and the olive hued skin of his face opens up like cracks in drying clay as he yields into one brilliant, terrified smile.

'Well? Say something will you!' he sparks.

I lean over and throw my arms around him and the warmth of his body radiates through me like a huge shot of Jamesons. I recoil a little, frightened that he might feel the thud of my heart which is pounding so fast that it's almost a flatliner. He pulls me towards him again and squeezes me and when he releases me and I'm staring right into him, I realise how stone cold sober I am. His face is in focus, smiling and dancing with stupid, stupid happiness and he's laughing his big hard laugh and I'm laughing too and swamping him with kisses and all the time I'm aware of this sickening sensation in my guts and throat and the painful hum of an organ threatening to shut down.

CHAPTER 2

Millie

The bronchial cough of next door's car drags me from a filthy dream – Angelina Jolie giving me a lapdance. It's the Jolie from *Gia*, a sultry womanchild – vulnerable and accessible and utterly fuckable. She's pulling that lewd expression she pulls for magazine covers and all the blokes in there are foaming at the mouth 'cos it's clear how much she's enjoying dancing for me. Three songs lapse and she's still slithering away, only just removed her bra, and the management's going berserk. She'll probably get the sack for this but she doesn't care. She's drop dead in love with me. I force a stubborn eye open and snap it shut again, willing her to carry on dancing or at least pull her panties to one side. But the car carries on spluttering and groaning and hurls me into the hub of an evil Monday morning. I fling myself upright, jerking my legs over the side of my bed and leap to the window.

Mrs Mason, the old boiler from next door, is stooped over the engine of her pristine Allegro. I prise open the window and shout down.

'Oi! Some of us are still sleeping.'

She bolts out from under the bonnet, knocking her head along the way.

'I beg your pardon, young lady?'

'I *said*, some of us are still sleeping! Keep the racket down, you selfish bitch!'

'I don't believe what I'm hearing Millie O'Reilley.'

'No, me neither. I mean, this isn't the first time you've woken me up is it? You should get rid of that heap. It's a fucking eyesore. Lowers the tone of the whole street.'

She looks crushed.

'I'm going to tell your father what you just said.'

'Well make sure you don't leave out the fucks and bitches!'

I slam the window shut and fumble my way to the toilet, chest tight and heavy, head pounding violently from the effects of cheap wine. And then it slaps me in the face – hard, wet and fast. I start back at Uni today.

I take a piss, which seems to go on forever, then haul myself downstairs.

Lying on the kitchen table is a timetable with all my classes and corresponding room numbers neatly filled in. There's also a couple of biros, a ruler, an A4 pad and a glass of freshly squeezed orange juice sitting next to a post-it which reads:

First day back!
   Don't be late Millie. If you want a lift home, meet me outside the Eleanor Rathbone building at 5.30.

Dad xxx

I feel lousy. About many things, but most of all about my absolute lack of enthusiasm for the year ahead. As it stands, time is still on my side. Although I got pretty crap grades last year, I have three clean terms ahead of me – terms in which I could hand in all my essays on time, go to all my lectures, participate in the tutorials and revise properly for my finals. But throughout the summer holidays, this final year has loomed over me like the inevitable death of a terminally ill relative.

I guzzle the juice in a few thirsty gulps, perch myself on the kitchen table and light up a cigarette. It tastes vulgar. My mouth feels like a chewed moth. I take another drag and kill it. I trudge back upstairs. I brush my teeth three times, tease my hair into a low pony, and slip into anonymous Uni kit – jeans, trainies and Dad's denim jacket.

Outside, my spirits lift slightly as the wind sweeps chip shop wrappers into the Masons' rose bush. A crumpled Coca-Cola can rattles over to my feet. I pick it up and gleefully stuff it next to the chip papers. As I lean over her garden wall I notice a few of the bricks have come unsteady. I attack them with my right heel, only letting up when I've smashed half the wall into her precious – and pathetic – bedding plants. 'There now,' I say, rubbing my hands and smiling triumphantly. I glance from left to right then scuttle away with the wind behind me, aiding my getaway.

I love the wind.

Always have done since I was a kid when Dad used to take us down to Cornwall to see Auntie Mo. To little me, she was the most amazing, exotic, glamorous woman I had ever seen. She lived on a cliff top. She painted and smoked cheroots and well-spoken men in polo necks would come and go. I'd comb her wild red hair and light her ciggies for her when no one was looking. It was our secret. No one else I knew ever called them that. Cheroots.

Winter was best. Our visits were always punctuated by wild, religious storms and as the skies presaged trouble, Dad would stop whatever he was doing and lug me down to the beach. We'd sit on the shore and watch from a dangerous proximity, the wind torment the ocean to a frenzy. The rain would lash down and burn our cheeks red raw and the silver scrolled waves would grow menacing and spit splinters of driftwood at us. And just as the storm threatened to swallow us, Dad would scoop me up and we'd tear back up the beach. Mum would watch with pursed lips from the back bedroom window and when we returned, saturated with rain and fearful excitement, she'd glare at Dad with bare-restrained fury. Had her big sister not been there to absorb the heat from her temper, Dad would have got a verbal thrashing to go with the sting of the windstorm. It was rare for Mum to give vent to her anger, and when she did I'd hurl myself into the crossfire, desperate for them to be friends again. She'd sit there, coiled and bitter, her porcelain cheeks stained pink with rage. Even at that age, I could see in her eyes that Mo was holding back. She didn't want to add to the tension. She'd look at her little sister and she'd wonder where all that anger could come from and she'd jolly us all up and open a bottle of wine.

Not even Mo could smoke cheroots all day, every day, and drink red wine and be so in love with living that she said yes to everything though. She died just before my twelfth birthday. They wouldn't let me go to her funeral.

I still love the wind.

I take a circuitous route to the bus stop to avoid walking down Bridge Road which is full of wannabe hoodlums. It and they depress the fuck out of me. Instead, I trot alongside two dogs with their snouts held high in the wind. You can always tell the quality of a barrio by its canine residents. Around this part of L18, for example, the streets are littered with distempered creatures of indiscernible breed. But over the railway and up towards the park, where we used to live and where Sean now resides, the dogs are good looking and obedient. That observation belongs to Jamie's Dad. It was one of the first things he ever said to me when Jamie took me round to meet him and Mrs Keeley. I'd asked him in all innocence why the dogs round their way, even the puppies, wore such ravaged faces. Lovely people, Jamie's folks. Just thinking of them sends my spirits slumping down again. I get this horrible feeling in the pits of my tummy that I'm not going to see them any more. That I'll no longer be able to just call round for my tea on my way home from Uni, or go drinking at The Dispensary with his Dad and his gang of old rascals. Since *that* night, I've avoided all contact with Jamie. He's been easy enough to dodge mind you, seeing as though he's spent the weekend in the Lakes with her. He'll be driving back this morning, hitting the M6 about now. Her hand on his lap and his myopic eyes shining with happiness. Or perhaps not. Maybe she's said no and she's staring bleary eyed out of the window with her arms folded and he's feeling as hollow and sad as I am. I don't know which would sting more – to see him sad or happy?

I push the thought away and make a sprint for the bus which is rammed with old people and teenage mothers with noisy babies. I hand my fare over and make my way to the back. Half way down the aisle, the driver calls me back and asks to see my pass. His voice is soft and squeaky and at odds with his appearance – badly shaven head, boxer's nose, and labourer's hands scarcely visible through fat chunks of sovereign.

'I don't have one,' I say.

He shrugs his shoulders.

'Full fare then isn't it?'

I pull a face which I've exhausted to perfection. It's my get what I want face. I exploit it shamelessly and apart from Dad and Jamie, most men fall for it. It seems to work. His face yields into a smile and I grin my way back up the aisle.

'Ehmm, not so fast Missus. I need to see a pass or you'll have to pay full fare.'

A few biddies start tutting and a fat girl in a tracksuit with two young boys lets out a long exasperated sigh. I turn and find his eyes smiling at me through the mirror. Smug little cunt. He's clearly enjoying the pathetic bit of authority that occasions like this lend his life 'cos outside that driver's cabin he's nobody. A sad little prick with a nondescript life. I slam the rest of the fare down and swagger back up the aisle. I park myself in the middle of the back seat between an old man who reeks of piss and two girls of my course, a blonde and a striking brunette, neither of whom acknowledges me. The blonde is wearing a tiny yellow jumper so tight it makes her breasts look deformed. She's talking in that loud self-conscious student way about her cold, uncaring mother and her absent father. I hate it when people *use* their parents in that self-analytical way. It's vain and unnecessary.

A group of schoolboys with glue sniffing complexions pile on at Toxteth. I recognise one of them as Dominic Myers from our gym. O'Malley's got him pinned down as the next Shea Nearey. He's definitely got Welter potential. You should see him dance. But the passion's not there. He loves the sport but he wouldn't hand his life over to it. Not like Liam Flynn's son, Tony. He's only ten, but boxing's all that drives him. It owns him. Like Christmas morning, last year – all the young ones were charging round the park on those micro scooters. Little Tony though, he was doing laps. And then in the afternoon, Liam went round to O'Malleys to get the keys for the gym so he could do some bag work. He's talented Tony, but only through sheer application and graft. It's not innate, not like it is with Dominic and a couple of O'Malley's other young hopefuls. I mean, Tony's footwork's pretty flawless and he's got combinations that disorientate me and he's definitely got the makings of a puncher's physique – the slim waist and the broad, sloping shoulders. But he doesn't have the rhythm of a fighter. There's no flow, no spontaneity to his

35

movements. It's like watching a white guy dancing to R & B. And O'Malley knows he'll never make it as a pro but keeps on urging him on just to keep his Daddy sweet, which is too cruel if you ask me. He's gonna break that little boy's heart.

' 'kinell la! Get on that!' The oldest and by far the mouthiest of the group points at blondie's assets. 'It's fucken Jordan's kid sister!'

'Come 'ead, Jordan junior – show us your tits!' chirps his sidekick.

'Dey falsies are dey, girl? Come 'ead, let's give 'em a little test!'

She's quite impressive. She eyeballs them one at a time.

'Oh fuck off will you, you stupid little *boys*. You wouldn't know how to handle a girl like me – none of you!'

' 'kinell girl, I didn't ask for ye hand in marriage or nothing!' he snaps back. 'Only wanted to see yer tits!'

His proteges guffaw on cue, all except Dominic who has spotted me and slunk low in his seat, pretending not to be a part of it all. She's quite a cutie this big-breasted blonde piece, but she bears all the hallmarks of someone who is incapable of finding a bloke who will offer her respect and commitment. She's mainstream. Universally attractive. Big blue eyes, large breasts, honey-hued skin, a cute button nose and a Colgate smile. But there's nothing to her. As Billy would say, a pure spunk deposit. Her mate though, the Pocahontas lookalike is a different story altogether. Her beauty inhabits a kind of aesthetic no man's land. And it either seduces you or alienates you. She's shockingly beautiful. Her cheekbones are dramatic, like she's permanently pulling on a badly made joint and her eyes are pure pupil. Her mouth is sullen and slightly lopsided. She's a skewed beauty. Pure Vogue material. And straight as fuck. Ah well, Millie.

I pull my timetable from my bag and the sight of Dad's handwriting brings on another flush of guilt. First lecture's at 12.00 – Classics with Dr Hallam in the Edward Naughton Lecture Theatre – followed by Postmodernism and Literature in the Politics block. Tuesdays and Wednesdays are fucking merciless but Thursday is pretty much empty and Fridays are blissfully and absolutely free.

I disembark at the bottom of Catherine Street to avoid the onslaught of students at the top of Myrtle Street. The very thought of facing them en masse is giving me palpitations. The bus pulls off and I flash Pocahontas a wink. I take a right onto Percy Street, then veer sharp left onto South Bedford Street where I pause at the nursery playground. I love just standing and staring at the kids in this place – they're stunning. Every race under the sun comes together here, sometimes the progeny of one common father, or mother, or several. For me, this little nursery is a showcase for all that's special about Liverpool 8.

I wish I could stay longer, but time's out. This is it.

I idle into the grounds opposite the Sydney Jones Library, which even in mid term, remains the most isolated part of the campus. I sit down on a bench and light a cigarette. I inhale deeply and empty my mind, savouring my last seconds of freedom for the next nine months.

★　★　★

37

Dad's lurking outside the Eleanor Rathbone building smoking a Marlboro, looking more like a broody post-graduate than a professor. I stand back and observe him, experiencing a sudden bolt of adoration. Two freshers walk past him. The more attractive of the two throws him an ambitious smile. He smiles back, professionally, neutrally. The girl walks away, glowing. I don't know if I'm proud or embarrassed. My Dad's a good looking fella – way too sexy to be a professor. He should have been a rock star or an actor or something equally glam-orous. His crow-black hair is flecked with grey now, but that only complements his chiselled, tanned face and his clever blue eyes. I love the way my Dad deals with being the campus fanny magnet. He's ice cool, almost blasé about it. I couldn't then and still do not reconcile the image Mum painted of him the night she walked out.

Grandad O'Reilley was devoted to my Mum. He thought she was just the best thing that could have happened to his boozy, vivacious son. She was a teacher, like him – and she had finesse. At Christmas when he and Granny would arrive with smiles and bottles of Jamesons and so much cheer and love, he'd stand back on the doorstep and just *glow* at Mum. He'd stare at her, like she was an apparition.

That day, he bolted all the way over from Ireland in the hope that he could talk her out of leaving his son and granddaughter. He sat with her holding her hand until way after dark, but it was futile. Her decision was immutable. Dad was a sleazy, sick old man who had wasted twenty years of her life. That's what she called my Daddy – sleazy and sick. Those two words cut like a knife. But in a way she did me a favour. It numbed the pain of her leaving. I just let her go, after that.

I spot Kennedy waddling her way over to Dad. She's a senior lecturer in my department and she'll be taking us for Postmodernism in Literature this year. She dresses as to discourage contemplation of her body, and yet somewhere underneath those baggy slacks and blanket blouses there must be tits and a cunt. I don't hate her. She just irritates the fuck out of me. She's one of those characters students neither like nor dislike. They just accept her as one of the many who neither inspire nor deter – a worthless piece of machinery that keeps the system ticking. She starts gabbing to Dad, cocking her head to one side and twiddling her ear, all over him like fucking eczema. It's a tragedy to behold. Dad's eyebrows are slightly raised, like the eyebrows of some-one politely listening to a joke he's already heard before. Her face lights up when she sees me.

'Millie! I didn't realise you'd chosen Postmodernism for your final year! Well done, you!'

I can't stop myself. I should have more restraint. More compassion at least, anyway.

'Yes, mad looking forward to it Mrs Kennedy. Postmodernism is something I feel very passionate about.'

She's actually a Miss, a title she wears with some discomfort. Dad glowers at me over the top of her head. He knows my slip of the tongue is anything but inno-cent.

'*Passionate*, Millie?'

I make eyes at him and return my attention to form-less Kennedy.

'Well let's just say that it's something that leaves itself vulnerable to discursive conflict, isn't it, Mrs Kennedy?'

'Indeed it is, Millie,' she says with an ebullient nod of the head.

'And, I suppose what I'm really looking forward to are the tutorials – the opportunity to discuss and challenge some of the fundamental principles that underpin orthodox postmodernist thinking.'

Dad rolls his eyes.

I gaze dreamily into the heavens.

'Postmodernism . . . It's disrupted all the truths and knowledge that have informed and shaped the very way we view our world. It's called into question the very foundations of our existence. Frightening it is. Something that students should not take lightly.'

'Absolutely,' she says, beaming. 'I can't wait to get stuck into this year. Looks like we have some very promising students.'

She raises her eyebrows and gives Dad a long slow nod.

'Right then. I best be off,' I say with a conclusive snort, 'I want to get to the library and do a few hours background reading before the lecture. See you then.'

I head off, and Kennedy throws me an urgent wave. Dad is scowling when I look back.

The Lecture theatre reeks. Like a London bus in a heat wave. Students are dawdling in, in clumps, fervently exchanging holiday anecdotes of sexual derring-do and mapping out their social calender for the year ahead. No one seems to notice me lurking at the back. Hopefully it'll stay that way for the rest of term. I don't hate students *because* they're students, it's just that the people I dislike most happen to *be* students. And I *have* had student mates in the past. I have. There was Louis and Tumbler, wasn't there?

Louis lived just round the corner from me on Rose Lane. He was another one who lived with his folks. We were virtually inseparable around campus during the first year but he was *so* difficult to talk to. Impenetrable he was, and not in a pretentious or a self-conscious way. He just didn't like talking. We probably spent more time in The Blackburne Arms than we did in lectures during our first year and I could still only tell you three things about him. That his favourite drink is Gin and Orange, that he's got a first edition Hemingway and that he had a twin brother who died at birth. We dropped an E together this one time but conversation was still muted. He just sat there with this gleeful idiotic grin emblazoned across his face, pointing at the ceiling and slapping his thighs like a madman. And then he just did one – offed to Goa with some hippie chick he met on the Internet. His folks were distraught.

Tumbler, my other mate, had one of those gormless faces that's easily forgotten. He was living in the Rathbone Halls of Residence, just at the top of Liam's road. I found him lumbering home one Friday night, sobbing. His nose was smeared across his face. Some scallies had hopped on him outside Chris' Chippy on Rose Lane and robbed his money – and his chips. I knew the lads who'd done it. Kids. They were no older than twelve or thirteen, but ruthless en masse. It wasn't the humiliation of the beating that had upset him, though – it was the fact that his own mates had stood back and laughed at the spectacle. Cunts. What sort of mates do that? So Mother Theresa here, overwhelmed with drink-sodden sadness for this big, daft lad and intent on bigging him up to his docile mates, asks him if he'd like to accompany me to the end of year ball. I figured this would do him more good than sending Junior Keeley and his mob round to chastise the diminutive robbers. It almost worked.

On arriving at the Student Guild, it became immediately and horribly clear that Tumbler was regarded as nothing more than gratuitous entertainment for his pals – a buffoon who was to be plied with drink and jeered at. So when I swanned into the room in a dirty red D&G number, with Tumbler traipsing behind reeking of Brut and polo mints, his mates were gobsmacked. I did my utmost to pull it off – laughing convulsively at his not funny jokes, applauding wildly at his karaoke efforts, even doing a slowy to *Careless Whisper* and I think I convinced everyone that by some inexplicable twist of fate, the oaf had hit jackpot. By midnight, sozzled and deluded by his newfound celebrity, he thought so, too. When I politely declined his clumsy advances he got nasty and shoved a chubby hand up my dress. I hit him with two devastating right hooks – one to the left eye and one to the chin – and a left jab to the kidneys. He produced himself at my door early next morning with a box of Dairy Milk and a swollen eye. Had I not been suffering a vicious hangover and had my ovaries not spewed muck all over my clean duvet in the night then I might have taken pity on the bloke, but the sight of his battered slab of a face on my doorstep at that unfeasible hour could only incite hatred and a feeble yet never the less productive left upper. I never saw him again. He didn't return after summer. Louis and Tumbler, my two student buddies.

The loud tapping of a ruler against the board slices through the chatter of students. The noise settles into a low murmur and the throb of bodies darting around the room slowly evolves into a class. Jacko, the head of Literature is standing at the front with his trademark furrowed brows, running a hand through his thick blonde hair. He waits until the murmur fades into a silence then starts.

'Welcome back everybody. Hope your summer was a little more colourful than mine. Now, those of you expecting to see Dr Hallam today should know that she's unwell. Sadly, we shan't be seeing Jean this semester, if at all this academic year. Those of you wishing to visit or send your good wishes just let me know, please. So this course will now be split between myself' – a huge sigh of relief floods the room – 'and Dr Kennedy.'

Groans and tuts all around. Everybody loves Jacko. He's not one of those that tries to befriend his students to gain their esteem. You can virtually guarantee that when he's taking a module, everyone will make a massive effort to hand in their assignments on time.

'So let's launch straight into it, shall we? As I've said

43

this course will be split up into two sections, if you'd all like to refer to the handouts that are going round. First three seminars are going to be taken by myself and the last four by Miss Kennedy. In terms of assessment, there are two options . . .'

I fancy Jacko. Whenever our eyes lock my cunt just melts. He's pushing fifty, but wears it well. His face has got that timeless edge to it like Steve McQueen or Robert Redford – terminally fuckable. He scribbles something on the board and the veins on his forearms swell with the movement. They're beautiful arms – slim and striated with sinewy muscle. I had a wank over them in the library toilets last year.

We're about half an hour into the lecture when my phone bleeps. One by one, their dull faces lurch towards me like a petroleum blaze and because I'm sat up here on my own, there's nobody to shift the blame onto. A prickly heat crawls across my face but I manage to force a look of manufactured nonchalance. I wait for the next set of handouts to go round, then slide the phone from my jacket pocket onto my lap.

One new message.

Jamie.

My head begins to spark and sputter. There's a disconnect here, an overload and it's all coming from the guts of my animus. I know it, I just know that this is going to be bad. I press Read and blink stupidly at the screen.

She said yes!xxx

Trickling into my subconscious, somewhere in the distance, is Jacko's soft Glaswegian voice, calling my name. I carry on blinking at the screen.

And then Jacko's voice is raised and he's vexed and it's aimed at me and I can't hear and I can't breathe. I'm leaden with fear and grief and the pure resin of a new emotion. Something big and dangerous. I edge my way along the empty row as quietly and as quickly as I can. I fly up the stairs and the door swings me out into a blast of white light. I pause for a moment, unsure what to do next but then my legs carry me over to a huge window. I press my face into the glass and stare out across the city's topography. Toxteth looks like an over-emotional oil painting – liquid and sinuous and shamelessly sentimental. I can see buses, just moving squares of light, running along the spinal cord that is Princess Avenue and behind them a stream of brake lights that linger long after the vehicles have moved on. I count six rooftops in from the top of the avenue – Jamie and Sean's old flat. My tummy hollows out.

'She said yes,' I whisper, 'She said yes.'

Jamie

She hasn't texted us back, yet – probably still in classes, isn't she? But I know she's going to be made up for us. She'll be well happy, Millie will. Aaaah – fucken boss day this is turning out to be. I just feel sound about everything, la. I've got everything to play for.

Millie

Walking out of these grounds always overwhelms me

45

with a sense of freedom – even more so when I'm doing a runner from a lecture or a tutorial. But today, the things I'm usually running to are the very things I'm running from. It's difficult to fathom, but Jamie, our friendship and the life I've built up around him and his family and friends – that's what's kept me going these last two years. *They*'re the ones who make it bearable. When I get home at night . . . I don't know. It's strange. Like, I'm *always* overjoyed to see Dad. Even that brief glimpse of him on the campus blitzed me with warm giddy feeling. But when I walk into the lounge at night and I find him sprawled across a pile of unmarked essays, I don't know. I feel trapped – like there's no escape from it. Jamie's a refuge from all of that. Neither him nor any of his mates have been to University. I mean, he's *mad* on books Jamie – people underestimate him but him and Billy and the gang, although they're all dead support-ive and inquisitive and made up with their swotty little pal, they don't give a fuck about academic life and all the highbrow bullshit that goes with it. That's why I like being with them. They all have ardently formed opin-ions relating to politics, society and religion but they carry those opinions with a graceful silence and when they do express them it is done with a lucid simplicity. Students, especially the middle-class ones, have none of that humility. And now it's gone, all that. Jamie, my rock, my big brother and fun buddy is fucking me off.

Jamie

Anne Marie looks fucken amazing today. She's always gorgeous even without the make-up – which she pure

46

does not need, if the truth be known – but today she is radiant. Her eyes are glinting, big blue blazers just dancing with happiness, and the sun has slashed her nose with a cute gang of freckles. Her blonde hair is dragged back in a simple pony giving her that fresh, supermodel just got out of bed look. Elle MacPherson but miles fitter.

We're stuck in the thick of a M6 tailback, both nursing vile hangovers from last night's celebrations and I'm gonna have her in late for her afternoon shift. She is a flapper where work's concerned, Anne Marie – dead conscientious and that, even if Sean is her boss. But today he can give her the sack for all she cares – not that he would and that. But nothing's gonna wipe that smile from her grid. I don't think I've *ever* seen her this happy. Proper makes my heart leap it does. It's funny like, I knew pretty much straight away she were the one for us – but I always thought Anne Marie deserved better. Don't get me wrong and that – no one can love her like I do and no one will look after her as good as I will. But, how can I put this? She *likes* nice things, Anne Marie. I always saw her shacking up with a footballer or a lawyer if you know what I mean – she's got the looks, no two ways about it. I'm not doing her down or nothing. No way. Why shouldn't the girl set her sights high after the life she's had? Spent most of it in and out of fucken foster homes she has, getting carted from pillar to post. Stayed in more different rooms than a fucken ambassador. What must that do to a kid's head, ay – all them beds, all them fucken bedrooms? Our bedroom was always my main source of security. There was four of us in there at one time, when our Kieron and Eddie still lived at home, but it was still my own little private world. Fuck knows what it must've been like for her. Pure burns my head out that, when I think on it. But she's a fighter Anne Marie. She's been fighting all her life and she's always said to us that all the things she never had as a kid, she'll double have em now. So I don't mind spunking two ton on a dress for her at that Karen Millen. And I was happy getting the loan out to get her the Tigra when she was starting work at Sean's. But the wedding, la – my folks are pure gonna go white when I tells em we're not having a proper church do and that. Not us two, la – not me and her. We're getting hitched in that Mexico, us. And she's right by the way. She's got no family, has she – just a handful of friends and that. I'm not being funny like, they're *good* mates, there's nothing they won't do for her, but at the end of the day how's she gonna feel walking into a church that's chocker with just *my* family and friends. Wouldn't be right, la. Would not be on, that.

Millie

The sight of the Blackburne Arms as I veer onto Falkner Street puts a big fat smile back on my face. I love this place. It's the only one in this neck of the woods that hasn't reinvented itself to appeal to the steady influx of students over the last few years. The Belvedere, The Caledonia, The Grapes and The Pilgrim, they've all been given facelifts for the worse. Me and Jamie used to drink in The Belvedere when I was still in school and I was utterly smitten with that place back then – that pub and its night owls and their tales. It was full of mad characters which were as much a part of the place as the nicotine-hued walls. There was a seamy element to the pubs round here, and there was no shortage of brass — good looking brass, too. These girls were a class apart from the emaciated urchins that litter Hope Street now. These were well-groomed women who could talk as eloquently as they could fuck.

But The Blackburne Arms is immune to evolution. Mr Keeley says it's exactly the same as it was when he was a kid. The only thing that's changed are the songs on the jukebox, and even there the classics have prevailed.

No one notices me when I walk in. Heads don't even flinch. I like that. It means I can sit in here for hours, uninterrupted, with neither threat nor hassle from men other than the random smile here and there.

There's half a dozen bodies scattered around the room, all stooped low over pints of dark heavy liquid — solitarily drinkers with faces as timeworn as the furniture. The television is on, its iridescent drone the same as ever, the usual crap. No one is paying any attention to it, but no one seems bothered by it either. It stays on all through the day and all through the night. I order a pint of Stella and put two songs on the jukebox — Aretha Franklin, *I say a Little Prayer* and Van Morrison, *Moondance* — perfect lazy afternoon drinking material. I settle down at a table near the backdoor and an old man sitting opposite raises a welcoming hand while his bald brown skull stays slumped to his chest.

'Afternoon Sir,' I say.

He replies with the merest nod of his head. I might go and sit with him after this one, maybe buy him a pint or two. I could reinvent myself as a runaway – a Romany gypsy from Prague. I swirl the cold, crisp liquid around my mouth and let it slide down into my gut. Pure magic.

Time passes. The music's drowned out the television now and I'm starting to feel nice. All my troubles slowly slithering away. Jamie. I'm going to call him as soon as I get out of here. What we've got is too powerful, too beautiful to let slip away. And even if they *do* get married, it doesn't mean I'll lose him. Jamie doesn't strike me as the type of lad who'll abandon his mates for a woman, even Anne Marie. He would have done it already. Fuck, I'm family! I'm like a daughter to Mr and Mrs Keeley and nothing is going to change that. I won't let it. I'll call him as soon as I leave here, tell him how pleased I am for him, tell him *how* much I love him. I will, I will. I'll even tell him I'll take the bitch for a celebration night out. Aaaah, it's giving me the best feeling this – the best! I can see his face now, all crumpled with joy and relief that the two women in his life are going to be fine with each other. And then there'll be anxiety, immediately, 'cos he'll worry that Anne Marie will try to get out of it, make excuses, won't want to come. He's so *desperate* for her and me to get on. Fuck it, though – I'll do that for him. I'll take the amber tart out on the town. But for now I'm just going to sit back and enjoy the soothing drawl of Van.

Jamie

When we breaks the news to Sean he does his usual, acts half like I'm telling him I've won a deuce on a

50

scratch card. But then he gives Anne Marie the rest of the day off and he gets on the blower and books us into that French one on Lark Lane. He tells whoever it is on the other end, who we gather is some friend of their Liams, that they're gonna serve us their finest champagne and he'll be in sometime in the week to pick up the damage. He also tells us he'll be flying us First fucken Class to fucken Mexico. At first I'm having none of it. Don't get me wrong la, it's lovely what he's trying to do and that but, end of the day, a lad's got his pride to consider, hasn't he? But then I cops the look that Anne Marie is trying to hide, which is disappointment but ultimately shame. Shame at herself for feeling that way. And then it's myself feeling a cunt, isn't it? I feel like a twat for nearly letting my own stupid pride prevent her from getting something what she really, really wants. I accept with a heavy heart.

The French gaff on Lark Lane *is* fucken sound. So lovely, in fact, that I half allows myself to get excited about being here at Sean's expense. It's intimate and warm and the staff make you feel dead welcome and the whole thing is just that much nicer than the other night in 60 Hope Street. I mean, fair do's like and that, Millie was pure done in and by the end of the night, I weren't exactly Joe Sober myself. But that's the thing with lil' Millie – you can't *have* a nice time with her. Everything has to be so fucken confrontational with the girl. Ah, feel last now, saying that about her. End of the day though this, now, with Anne Marie – it's nice.

★   ★   ★

She orders a mixed salad for starters – no dressing or nothing, *dead* conscious about her figure, she is – and stuffed aubergine for her mains. I goes for the French onion soup and the veal but the waitress tells us that they've had to take the veal off the menu cos animal rights activists kept putting the windows through. I tries to act that little bit disappointed but inside I'm grinning from ear to ear. This now gives us a legitimate excuse to order the fillet steak! Anne Marie looks skyward and shakes her head. She's always on at us to try something different when we goes out. She sees my unwavering loyalty to good aul' steak and chips as a huge embarrassment, a tell-all about my background. Well, one, I got no thingio about my background – it is what it is end of the day. And, two, I'm always telling her what Millie says, that it ain't like that no more, these days. Fish and chips, bangers and mash, jam roly-poly, you name it – it's all the rage at the best gaffs. I'm half expecting her to make some little quip about Millie, but instead she looks down, fingers her engagement ring and gives us this adoring look.

'What d'you think about me and the girls going that London for a Hen night?' she says with half a nervy look in her eye. She's got that from her last fella, by the way. Never let her go nowhere, that cunt. Proper fucken jealous-head he were – one of them. Used to tell her what to wear and who she could and couldn't see and all of that shite, and I suppose she still ain't got used to the fact that I'm not like that. Way I sees it is, that if you love someone, you should want them to be happy whether that means they goes on big mad benders with their mates or goes snake hunting in the Rain Forest. I've got no time for fucken jealous arses, me. Fellas that lock their birds up and that.

'Fucken right girl, you'll have a riot,' I goes. And I mean it and all, too. 'I'll get Liam to sort you a guezzie for that Met Bar if you want?'

'Ah sound, yeah – the girls'd buzz off that! That's where Robbie Williams and that goes, isn't it, that Met Bar?

'Fuck! When he's not in L.A. trying to act like he ain't a quegg!'

'I could learn to live with that, mind you – money that cunt's on!'

Then she gives us a dead affectionate little look to show she's just having a laugh and a joke with us, and she takes my hand in hers, dead sincere and that and goes:

'What about you though, babes? I want you to go somewhere boss and all, too.'

The sympathy lasts all of five seconds.

'But don't think you're going nowhere mad, by the way! You can forget that Amsterdam, for starters!'

'Nah, babes – bit too mental for us, that Dam. Had somewhere more serene in mind . . . like Thailand.'

'You wha'! You being serious, James?'

'Fucken right I am, girl! Liam's already offered to fly us all over, hasn't he? We're gonna spend a couple of nights in Bangkok then do a week in one of them islands. Punyani I think it's called.'

'*Thailand*. You can forget that one straight away! You can go back to that Liam and tell him he's got another think coming. Thailand!'

'What's so bad about Thailand, babe? Liam's paying for it. Thought you'd be made up for us.'

'I'm sorry James, no – you're not on. We're getting *married* in six months. We'll be spending three weeks in fucken Mexico! How you gonna get time off work to go Thailand, hey? Cos if you think we're cutting our honeymoon short so that . . .'

Her North End accent comes raging through. Her face starts to tense and burn as she remembers and flinches and I realise I've taken the joke too far. I make a big winding gesture with my hand. She stares at us, bolly-eyed.

'Anne Marie. I'm having you on.'

Her face melts with relief.

'You hard-faced . . .' She drops her voice right down and leans into us. 'You hard-faced bastard. I believed you and all.'

'So. Where *are* you gonna go, then?'

'Haven't give it that much thingio, if the truth be known. Couldn't take it for granted you was gonna say yes, could I? I can start thinking about all that now, can't I? Probably just have a quiet meal in town and that, go round the bars and what have you.'

'Oh you're makin' us feel last, now! Couldn't you at least go that Society or something?'

'Oh aye, yeah – can really see my aul' fella throwing his hands in the air for Dave fucken Graham. Nah babe – just gonna keep it low key. Me Dad, our Billy, Sean, their Liam, Millie and one or two of the lads from work.'

'*Millie?*'

'Yeah?'

'Er, 'scuse me, James. You havin' a laugh?'

Her face tenses up again. How do I tell her that this *isn't* a joke?

'Why? What's up?'

'You can't invite Millie to a stag do!'

'Why not?'

'You just can't. She's a girl.'

'So?'

'So? Don't be so fucken stupid, James! How the fuck d'you think that makes me look, hey?'

The accents back again now, thick and flagrant and tight with contempt.

'Hadn't really thought about it that way, to be fair. She's just another one of my mates and that, Millie. Maybe she could go down to London with the girls then.'

'I don't think so. I've got no problem with the girl James, you know that, but it'd be a little bit awkward having her there. She doesn't know no one, does she?'

'You mean your pals wouldn't like her?'

'I mean, she wouldn't get on with my pals.'

'Why not?'

'Ah, come 'ead, Jamie – don't make us spell it out to you.'

She raises her eyebrows and a thick silence wedges us. She cracks first.

'She's a lovely girl and that, I'm not saying notten about her, but . . . she's, well you know, she's . . .'

Another long pause.

'She wouldn't fit in,' she says, letting go, 'Not to the places where we want to go anyway. She's *embarrassing*

James. She's a fucking oddball – and she half thinks she's a lad. Have you seen the way she looks at girls? Girls, James. Not women. Kids if you like. It's fucken. It's fucken *sick*.'

I'm burning with hurt. It's like it's myself she's slagging.

Minutes pass. The waitress comes back with a basket of hot bread. I plunge straight in, avoiding Anne Marie's eyeline. She's having none of it, mind you – pure will not have none of it. She gives us this half flirty, half 'grow up' sort of a look and she kicks off her shoe and she finds us under the table and she does us with the ball of her foot, and her heel, and her toes. Does us through my kecks, she does, just like that. I'm easy. I'm hers again. Two bottles of champagne later, and Millie ain't even coming the fucken wedding. Like Anne Marie points out – who's the only one that hasn't had the goodness of ear to send their congratulations and that? I know she's been busy with classes and that, new start of term and what have you – but if I was texting her to meet us in town she'd have well been back to us by now.

It's only when we're back at hers, lying in bed and she politely shrugs off my advances, tells us she's just that little bit done in from all the excitement of the day that I can lie back and watch her dozing and take it all in though. Lil' Millie ain't replied – and I can cover it up any which way, make all kinds of excuses for her but, end of day, she pure has not got back to us. Fucken hurts, that does.

Millie

The door swings open and a woman walks in. Skinny, savage face and a dark wiry shock of hair. Brass. She stands in the doorway, her eyes flitting around the room 'til they fasten on the back of a young Kurdish bloke. He's sat at the bar, hunched over The Racing Post. The barmaid nudges him and he pivots his head round, slowly, like an owl and acknowledges her with a sideways jerk of the head. She mouths something to him, shrugs her shoulders then she's gone. He returns to his paper. The image of her legs, white and skinny – whore's legs – linger in my mind. I'm horny but not quite drunk enough to go after her.

I've had a time-lapse. I don't remember this Kurdish guy coming in, or the old ladies to my left or the lads in trackies playing backgammon at the end of the bar. And my old boy from opposite has lifted his bald brown skull off his chest and slunk away into the night unnoticed. When did it get dark, anyway? It's not so long ago that it'd still be mellow sunlight at this time of day – but out there, the darkness has enshrouded the windows. I spark up a fag, strangely frightened and detached from everything. The three empty pint glasses on the table, the ashtray heaped with ciggie butts, the drone of the TV and the assembly of dilapidated bodies slumped under a thick fog of spiralling smoke, all seem at a distance now.

I order another pint and buy more fags. I sit at a different table, opposite a drunk with a sloppy face and stunted fingers. I'm thinking that this new vantage point might reassure me, remind me why I love this smoky old room. It doesn't. The lager just makes me numb and I can no longer remember what it is I'm drinking myself away from. It's all a blur of faces, fears, misgivings – just a mess. It's Jamie. University. Loneliness. A remote and gnawing sense that this is the start of the end. Jamie. Mum. Dad. Jamie. Anne Marie. Mum. All dislocated thoughts and snapshots, all running at the same time, in the same direction. But then I blank out again and abandon myself to the numbness.

I think I'm the last to leave the pub. I'm drunk and heavy on my feet but the autumn night is crisp and sharp and sobers me a little. The sky is alive with stars, just there, just an arm's reach away. The city is stretched out before me in brilliant shades of red and blue and yellow, dancing and flickering like a Chinese lantern. I start walking in no particular direction. My stomach feels queasy. I haven't eaten a thing all day. I head back down Falkner Street, thinking of the Kebab House on Leece Street but knowing there's another pull back this way, too. I check my watch. Nearly midnight. I should go home. The Monday streets are silent and empty of business apart from the occasional taxi rumbling past and the odd lone figure slouching home, head stooped low and hands in pockets. All the girls will be stepping out of their veneer now – stripping off their makeup, taking a bath, washing away the filth and ruthlessness of the streets, reinventing themselves as mothers, as wives, girlfriends, daughters, somebody's neighbour. They'll flop out and watch the telly, make a cup of tea, slice of toast, maybe. They won't be whores any more. The thought of them going about their everyday lives, in their own warm places submerges me with a sense of helplessness. The promise of a warm bed in my own house offers no consolation. I keep on walking.

I'm slouched in a doorway on Hope Street, sparking a ciggie. My mind is flitting hopelessly between home and booze and just staying out, seeing what may happen next. I think of Jacko. He's fuck all to me, but I wish I were with him now. The cigarette end is burning my thumb before I've even had a drag. I light another one.

A skinny silhouette totters unsteadily across the road. This one's actually dressed like brass – heels, skirt, grinding arse. As drunk as I am I know it's her – the girl from The Blackburne before. She's walking towards the Cathedral. I drag myself up and follow. The glare of a headlight jolts her into a bouncy, hard-assed swagger. The driver slows and takes a good long look but either he doesn't like what he's seeing or he loses his nerve. He lurches off, the screech of his tyres piercing the queer stillness of the night.

I stay on my side of the road and try to catch up with her. When there's nothing but a width of tarmac separating us, I slow right down again. I can see her clearly, now. She pauses outside the newsagents, hitches up her skirt and thrusts her hips out casually, classic hooker stance, like she's just taking a rest.

My cunt is throbbing. I suck in a deep breath, ready to cross the road. I'm shitting it, perched on the top ready and waiting for the plunge, but paralysed with fear. I do it. I jump. I cross over and walk up to her, as casual as my thumping heart and tense fanny will allow.

Close up she's harder, and troubled. She's not quite with it. Behind the narcotic glaze her eyes throb with some dark desperation. She's marked up badly and her make-up is worn like a mask – layer upon layer upon layer, as if to hide her from those that gaze upon her. The only thing sexy about her is that she's a whore.

Her mouth jumps when she sees me but recovers quickly and contorts into a scowl.

'Yeah?' she growls. 'Worrisit, girl?'

Her top lip recoils to show stumpy grits of teeth. Somehow, I'm no longer scared of her.

'Have you got somewhere we could go?'

'Yer wha'?'

'Is there somewhere we could like be together?'

She stares right into me. I glance from left to right and all around. There is nothing but the night, velvet and stock-still.

'Yer trying to be funny, girl?'

The scowl intensifies.

'No, I'm being serious. Have you got a pad we could go to?'

'If I was yew girl, I'd fuck off quick-quick.'

I stand there. I'm thinking that if I stand there she'll change her mind.

'Are you with me, girl? Fucken do one!'

Still I can't give up on it.

'Are you sure?'

I try to drop my voice to a seductive croon.

'It's all the same money, you know – and it can be really nice, girl on girl. Who's gonna know, hey?'

Her eyes flash with hatred and she pushes past me, onto the road where the beam of a police van's head-lamps sweep the back of her neck. It drives on oblivious but the incident unnerves her. She lunges back towards me. My body tenses in fear, but she barges right past and breaks into a fearful trot. Only at the top of Percy Street does she swing round in anger. Her voice is hurt and confused – and pathetically girlish.

'Yer fucken perv!' she spits. And then she's gone, swallowed up by the night.

Chapter 3

Millie

Since Mum left, a protocol of silence has been established between Dad and I. At first he tried to sit me down, to talk it through, to help me see – all those things that parents feel they need to do. To me, it wasn't like that. It was something else. It was a pure and instant shutdown. It was the shock of my life. It happened, it flattened me – and I just did not want to know anything else. I think that suits him fine, now. He still wears his wedding ring like an old thick scar, but to a stranger walking in the house, it's as though she never existed.

In my heart and mind though, she lives on.

Winter nights.

Me and Dad playing cards in the living room. Dad sneaking me nips of Jamesons. Mum in the kitchen, preparing supper – humming a different tune to the one on the radio. The three of us laughing and talking late into the night.

She left one Thursday evening, late in August. I was still high from my A-level results and all the beckoning promise of the days and months ahead. It was a gorgeous evening. The sun had hammered down all day. It was the hottest day of the year, and as it sank into the skyline, it drenched the streets in a hundred shades of crimson. I sat on the garage roof, puffing a joint, watching the smoke drift off in nostalgic layers. I gazed out over to the Welsh mountains and beyond, the beauty of it radiating through me like a glass of red wine. I should have been in Manchester, fixing up accommodation, books, this, that – but the heat of the day took the heat out of me. I could always go tomorrow. So I stayed up there until dusk had drained all colour from the sky, until it was just a dome of molten lead. No stars. No moon. Just acres and acres of felt blackness. And that's where I heard it.

I wasn't supposed to be there.

I stayed up there til I heard the horn of the taxi, the front door open, the slam of the door, the click of her heels on the path, the taxi pulling away and the low rumble of its engine fading into the night, gone, gone, gone. Along with my mother. I waited some more for the taxi to come back and when it didn't, I finished my smoke and went inside.

Grandad was sat at the kitchen table, eyes wide and unfocused, clutching a glass of brandy. He was shocked to see me. I wasn't supposed to be there. Dad was stooped over the sink, filling the kettle with water. From the back, he looked as old as Grandad. I loitered in the doorway that separated the kitchen from the conservatory. Grandad pulled a chair out, signalled for me to sit down. There was an envelope on the table. He passed it to me. I tore it in four and tossed it into the bin. There could be no reason. Dad's eyes burnt wearily, pleadingly, from a face that had suddenly acquired a lifetime of crevices. I couldn't look at him, could not go to him. I slunk upstairs, packed an overnight bag and biked it over to the Keeley's.

Mrs Keeley put me in the boys' room and the three of us drank bottled Makeson and stayed up for the Naseem fight. Naseem was up against a young Mexican, agile as hell, his punches quick and sure – but stripped of all confidence. He simply did not believe he should be in that ring with Prince Naseem. Naseem stood him up with a left hook thirty seconds into the second round and that was that. He tried to cling on, right through the count of ten – but his body was beat and finished. His face at the final bell reminded me so much of my stooped old Dad's in the kitchen. Sad yet dignified. Soaked with loss.

I crawled into bed around four but although my body was heavy from grief and shock and sheer exhaustion, I slept not a wink. The night was punctured by alien noises – a party from the house next door, water gurgling in the plumbing, a dog howling, the raw cry of help from a woman in the distance and the constant churn of Hackney cabs picking up and dropping off. I felt safe there, though. I felt happy in that room. The air throbbed with the soothing smells and sounds of the Keeley boys, and when the first shafts of daylight pierced the paper-thin curtains, I pulled the blanket over my head and clung to the night like a dying joint.

When I eventually went back home, Dad had put the house up for sale. It was a big, airy Victorian. Five bedrooms, Belfast sinks, deep, old, cast-iron baths and beautifully manicured gardens. It sold quickly. Half the money from the sale went to Mum. She'd called a hundred times while I was at Jamie's, but I didn't phone her back. I couldn't. Three or four times I saw her waiting for me — at the bus stop, at the end of the road, just waiting, waiting, waiting. I turned and walked away.

We moved into our new house two weeks before Christmas, the day before my eighteenth. It was a box house, really — a Glovedale Road terrace on the other side of the railway line. It was a neat enough street, neat and nonedescript — the sort of street where the Masons' live. It was fine. I hated it.

When we moved in, we both, silently, independently, moved Mum out. At least I thought we had. Into the boxes and crates went all the feminine, the womanly, the motherly trappings. The touch and the soul that had capered through the old house was packed and sealed and taken away.

The house now resembles a bachelor's pad. The walls are dusty and unadorned. Our previous garden, a tumbling miasma of brilliant colours and sensations has now waned into a small ugly yard, brimming with empty whisky and wine bottles that never quite make it to the bottle bank. The fridge that was permanently stacked with organic produce and litres and litres of freshly squeezed juice is now filled with last night's takeaway and curdled milk. In our stealthy endeavour to get over her, we have only carved her memory even deeper into our existence.

Today, walking up Myrtle Street towards campus, she drifts through me again. It's a patch of her favourite

66

perfume, Gucci, lingering in the air. Gorgeous smelling Mum with her mahogany locks and her alabaster skin. She is out there. She is everywhere.

Jamie

I'm usually upbeat of a morning me. Work rarely gets us on a downer and that but every now and again I'll admit it, I do – I get handicapped by the sheer fucken fruitlessness of it all. Get up, go to work, slog your guts out and come home too spent to enjoy the things that make it all worth the George. Life is shite at times. It is. But like I say, I'm not usually one that gets down in the mouth about it. I'll just get on with it, me – what will be will be and that.

On a bit of a downer right now though, to be fair. I had a pint with our Billy last night, didn't I? He said a few things that got us thinking. About lil' Millie. He's been working on the houses up near Knight Street this past month and he's said, she's *always* out – daytimes and all, too. And my aul' fella saw her staggering up Hope Street last week – on a school night too.

Fair do's and that, I know it's thingio for them students to get fucken hammered every night of the week, and I know most of em come out with half-decent grades end of the day but I can't help myself – it still burns my head out, all that. Makes us boil if the truth be known. I feel like going over to the hoards of em that congregate in Kinsellas of a morning, all terifically hungover and too done in to go to their lectures, and just laying into em. Fucken made up with emselves, they are. So fucken proud and smug to have gotten emselves in that state – think that's what it's all about, they do. Cunts.

And that's the one thing that's always been iffy between Millie and myself, truth be known – she's fucken blasé. She is, la. I'm not arsed where she's from or what fucken privileges she's had from her aul' folks and that – none of that means fuck all to me. What does my head in is the way she don't *use* it. It's all so fucken *easy* for the girl. And fuck la, I don't like saying none of this, I truly do not like having to even *think* this shite, but there's times when I know she's just slumming it. She is. Pissing her days away in them slimy hovels up behind the Uni – fuck's she trying to prove end of the day?

I take a slash and peer over my shoulder, into the mirror. My reflection flinches back, guilty as fuck.

Fuck are you kidding, anyway? It's not even *that* that's bringing you down this morning – not if you're honest with yourself. It's all to do with the other thing what Billy's told you isn't it? He's meeting Millie for a couple after he knocks off this avvy. Said he whistled down to her from his ladder. Said she was made up. Never mentioned you. Couldn't exactly push the lad could you, but he never said nothing. Never said she'd mentioned you.

Millie

None of the course books are in the library. And the ones which should be in the 'Do Not Remove' section have of course been removed, which means I'll have to buy them. I begrudge blowing fifteen quid on a book I'll only plagiarise and chuck to the back of a cupboard. My stomach puckers when I think about the selfish cunt who's done that – someone who was sitting in the same lecture room less than twenty minutes ago. Looks like I'll be piloting my new shoplifting system at Waterstones, then.

I discovered last week on entering the shop, that our University library books activate their alarm system. I was asked by a Security schmo with a sloppy face and lazy eyes to empty my bag. When his search yielded nothing more than two dishevelled library books, he simpered his apologies. And that got me thinking. As long as I make a point of showing my library books on the way in, I can exit with whatever I want – can't I?

In the library I get my own back by removing a couple of third year key texts and placing them on a shelf devoted to urban regeneration in Korea. It'll take weeks for the library staff to locate them. See how someone else likes it. Then feeling a little more cheerful I go to the obese and elaborate section that is Sociology and find row P. And then the book with code number P 654 1769 AB which is as familiar as a best friend's number. *Crime and Deviance in Contemporary Britain* by Jerry O'Reilley. I pull the book down and flick to the fourth page in. 'To Andrea and Millie' it reads – 'For all your love and support.' I read it again and again and I am filled with such a deep gush of happiness that it hurts. I stand on my tiptoes and slide it back on the top shelf, where it belongs. Alongside Marx and Engels and the other founding fathers of Sociology.

By the time I reach Waterstones, I'm radiant as hell. The

sun is shining – a gorgeous late October sun. Warm, but not oppressive. And Billy has left a message on my mobile confirming our drink for three o'clock at The Grapes. Fantastic! That'll give me time to plough through some work and steal a few Stellas at The Blackburne beforehand. (All bottled beers half price between 12 and 2.)

I swipe the necessary course books, *Deconstructing Shakespeare* and *Postfeminism and Literature* and march out, head held high. On leaving the shop, I am struck with a childish sense of getting away with it and celebrate by handing over a couple of quid to a Big Issue vendor and insist that he keeps the mag. I light us each a cigarette, flash him a devastating smile then caper back uptown towards The Number Seven where I aim to drink obscene amounts of coffee and write an essay that amounts to genius.

Walking past Slater Street I notice that the area is gradually becoming pedestrianised. There are new bars, coffee shops and restaurants cropping up all over the place. I don't like it. The city is starting to take on the guise of a salesman who lacks faith in what he is selling. Artificial. Insincere. A barrage of plush eateries bought by drug money and run by pseudo gangsters who lack the erudition to pull it off. Menu's that try too hard and waitresses with ugly vernaculars and kindergarten understanding of wines. I love this city, I do. I love these streets and all the hunger and resoluteness that throbs through them. I'll miss them. I'll miss them like fuck, but once I've finished Uni, I'm off.

As I'm crossing Falkner street, I catch sight of a man in

a maroon Rover, parked up outside The Number Seven. I half recognise the registration but the sun has cast a blinding shield across the window so the man is nothing more than a silhouette. I draw closer and the sun dips behind a cloud. It takes a while for my eyes to recover from the dramatic experience of light but when they do, I see that the silhouette has a face.

It belongs to Terry Matthews.

He's staring right into me.

My legs turn to liquid. I stare into the nowhere of the cobbled street and scud headlong past his car, past The Seven and across Catherine Street. I swerve hard right onto Little Percy Street and when I'm sure I'm out of sight, I break into a run. I sprint through a maze of side streets and alleyways, this way and that, doubling back on myself lest he snare me. Everything around me is hyper-real. Intense and slow. I drift past a hooker and her john, past a gaggle of tramps glugging greedily on bottles of raw liquor, laughing raucously. I cross a decrepit housing estate that spews me back out onto Parliament Street, where the freshly laid tar of the street sucks at my trainies and slows my pace. When I reach Princess Avenue I pick up my pace again and run faster and faster down the grassy central reservation where people and trees recede on either side like the dark sides of a tunnel, finally collapsing at the side of a duck pond in Sefton Park.

I met Terry Matthews in Shenanigans – another solitary drinking haunt, the Christmas we moved into Glovedale. I was savouring a pint of Stella before heading off to the Mandarin for Mr Keeley's 50th. Terry walked in and my heart vaulted. His face was spellbinding – nefariously chiselled with thick lips and steely blue eyes. He looked like a thug. As I was leaving, I downed a couple of stiffs and handed him a box of matches with my name and number scribbled on. He called within seconds of me walking out of the door and we arranged to meet the next day.

He picked me up outside Moorfields and took me to a café on the Dock Road, where the smell of rancid fat clung like a skin to your clothes and your hair. He was telling me something, Terry. By bringing me here, he was telling me how it would be. He was warning me. My cunt was almost sick with anticipation.

He drove me to an industrial estate and he fucked me. It was shattering, draining – I rode him in the seat of his car, but it was him fucking me. I'd never, never been fucked that way before. His eyes never left me throughout. As he drove deep inside me, his steely eyes never left my face – and they told me nothing.

I was dizzy with him. Madly in love. And when he dropped me off later I willed him to die on his way home, so I could preserve the last forty-eight hours forever. So that nothing we could do or say would taint that chink of history.

He didn't call the next day.

I texted him.

He didn't reply.

I felt anxious for days. Empty. Debilitated. Despondent. It hurt. Hurt like fuck. I made love to him in my head one last time then purged him from my memory for good.

Five months later, I saw him at the Mayday fair in

Sefton Park. He was carrying a little girl on his shoulders with golden locks and a button-cute face sticky with candyfloss. I couldn't help smiling at her. They ran to meet a woman with a severe red bob and a face so perfect and symmetrical it looked airbrushed. I followed them for a while, my thudding heart lurching over empty beer cans, weaving through bodies, bruised and nearly broken. And when he slipped an arm around her tiny nipped in waist, and planted a kiss on top of her head, something inside me curled up and died. What I lost right there and then were the last remnants of my girlhood – lost in one simple and crushing moment. The invincibility of adolescence was gone. And as I sobbed and fought my way beyond the screaming crowds and blurred mechanical beats, I swore I would never allow myself to fall so helplessly, pathetically in love again.

But by the time I reach the Grapes, I'm tipsy and content and that gnawing knot in my chest has begun to loosen. Terry Matthews – who can blame him? Not me. Not any more. After I'd mooched around the duck pond like a crestfallen tramp I sat back and watched the skies grow grey and broody. As I made my way back into town, a burst of rain had plunged me into The Belvedere. It was like walking into the front parlour – like coming home. A belligerent throng of original denizens was holding court in there – Horris, Miss Mary, Vinnie and Kenny, all chattering effusively, nonsensically, about days long gone. I sat with them for a while, a one woman audience, drinking in their madness, storing their conversations and before I knew it I was late. I bribed Kenny into sneaking me a fingernail's worth of Miss Mary's beak and skeddadled.

Billy Keeley is sat in a corner with two lads of similar age, both sporting skins and hard faces. He introduces us all to each other but I don't digest their names. The better looking of the two has a lively intelligent face, with a deep scar that tracks from the side of his mouth to his chin. He's in workwear – navy kecks and a ribbed Army and Navy store pullover, rolled up at the arms. Glowering from under his left sleeve are a gang of indecipherable prison tattoos that look as though they've been scribbled on with a fading biro. His eyes are brilliantly astute, flickering with questions, slashed with deep, dark thoughts. He catches me studying him and holds my gaze.

My tummy dips and I look away.

I sit down opposite the three of them and divert my attention to *The Sport* on the table. Kelly Brook's on the front cover in a lime bikini. I pick up the paper. She's looking straight into the lens but her body is turned away slightly. The result is unflattering. She looks wide. Not fat – just wide. I chuck the paper back and stand to get the round in. Billy can't decide between a Stella and a JD and the expression he's wearing tells me he wants both. But his mates have other plans. They decline with phoney pride and gulp down the remains of their pints conclusively. When I return from the bar they've gone. I throw my eyebrows together and feel the corners of my mouth slide down my face.

'Something I said?'

'Nah babe – official clocking off time innit? Stay out any longer and their wives'll come a looking.'

My heart sinks for a moment.

'*Wives*? How old are they?'

'Twenty-one, twenty-two.'

Billy's eyes match what I'm thinking.

'Bin lids?'

'Don't think so.'

'Then . . . *why*?'

'Dunno, kidder.'

'Like – how can anyone – *especially* a young bloke – entertain a life sentence of monogamy at that age?'

He shrugs his shoulders.

'I mean could you, Billy? Even if you thought you'd met the love of your life. Could you confine yourself to one pair of tits and one hole forever?'

'No. Yeah. Maybe. I don't know. But for most fellas, marriage ain't *about* that, is it?'

'So you're saying they put it about.'

'What do *you* think?'

A feeling of relief seeps through me. Confirmation of the impossibility of monogamy – and the impossibility of true love.

Billy stares beyond me philosophically, then without warning thrusts his eyes into mine.

'So tell us then, Mill – and you're not allowed time to think on this, I just want you to give us an honest answer, okay?'

'Okay,' I say, feeling a wave of panic rise in my throat.

'What did you think of our kid's announcement – him and her?'

The bluntness of the question shocks me a little. I scour his face to see if it's some kind of trick question but all I see is a mildly tipsy Billy.

'Fantastic,' I say, 'I think they're really good for each other.'

And I say it with such a seamless sincerity that I almost convince myself of it.

'Aaah, suppose you're right. He could do worse than that Anne Marie, end of the day. Thinks the fucken world of her, he does.'

I immediately regret answering so disingenuously. I could've given him a lead-in, there. If I'd have presented him with the opportunity to say how he really felt, it might've offered *me* some fucking insight to why I so badly resent Jamie's happiness. I've exhausted every possibility, even the most painful and unlikely explanation, I've dragged to the surface and analysed to fuck and still I come no closer to understanding why I feel the way I do. All I know is that there's suddenly a rift between me and Jamie that is gently but immutably nudging us off in our own different directions. I take a sup of my pint and try raising the subject again, but the expression on Billy's face has already moved on.

We're half way through our third pint when a girl and boy plonk themselves at our table. I immediately recognise them as two of Dad's third years. The lad is fat with a bursting red chin. The girl is fatter, her badly reconstructed harelip dominating her face. Both are drunk. I raise an eyebrow at Billy and he rolls his eyes.

We could have done without an audience tonight — especially such a visually offensive one.

The evening slips away and the onslaught of darkness entices a new clientele. A jam of could have beens and should have beens pack the room, self-appointed musicians, poets and actors all smoking badly made roll ups and wearing identical expressions of disaffection. The music slips up a few notches and Nick Drake's *Fruit Tree* swirls over. Fucking glorious song, that. I bet he was ensconced in exactly the same whisky bliss as I am now when he wrote those lyrics.

Safe in the womb
Of an everlasting night
You find the darkness can
Give the brightest light.

That's too beautiful. I love being in here with Nick Drake singing to Billy and me. I tell him and we celebrate with a couple more Jamesons. I decide that I adore the Me that a few sharp whiskies can conjure. She's bold, happy and depraved. The sober version is a fraud.

Feeling more and more happy about myself and the loveliness of this whole evening, I half begin to feel sorry for Fatboy and Harelip. Especially Fatboy. He strikes me as being utterly sex starved. I empathise with him — him and all the ugly men of the world. I know too well, the abject frustration of unrequited lust. I know what it's like to be smitten with a hundred images every day, all served up in Fuck Me poses. In the street, on TV, in the papers, everywhere you look there is fanny. Knowing that the closest you'll ever get to it is a clinical encounter with a whore is enough to break your heart, some days. I'm about to share this revelation with Billy when he bolts upright.

'Fuck!'

'What?'

'Jeez! Bin talking about the cunt all night – he'll be fucken chocker!'

He pulls me up out of my seat with one hand – the other tips his glass to his lips, draining off the last of his Jamies.

'Come 'ead!'

We grab our coats and make for the door. Outside the streets are grey and fuming with rain. A bevy of girls gallop past, all mascara smeared faces and naked arms wrapped tightly around their bodies. We tear down the street, jumping over puddles and giggling like kids. When we reach the taxi rank, Billy checks his watch again. The rain and the reality check have sobered him up. As he speaks, he won't look at me.

''kinell!' he says, hunched over, his breath smoking in front of him. 'I'm well late. Fuck! Sorry, girl . . .'

I'm not letting him off that easy. I ignore the statement and light us both a ciggy – Billy's not going *anywhere*. I'm high on the mood and the whisky and I want to carry on and on and on.

'I'm gonna have to do one, kidder' he says, lurching towards the approaching taxi. 'Mum's doing a big mad celebration dinner, isn't she? Taxi! Anne Marie an' that, innit? TAXI!'

Anne Marie.

'Come 'ead – I'll drop you off, hey?'

The taxi pulls up. He opens the door.

'Nah,' I say, throwing my hands into my pockets and stepping back from him, 'I'm gonna have a mooch around town.'

'But you're fucken soaking. You'll die of pneumonia if you don't go and dry off.'

I shrug my shoulders.

'Ah, come 'ead, Millie! Just jump in, will you? I feel a right cunt just leaving you here like this. I'd ask you back an' that, you know I would, but I think it's one of them, innit? Celebrate their engagement an' that.'

'I'm fine, honest. You know I don't go in for all that family stuff, anyway.'

'Arr-ay, Millie! Don't go like that on us. Look, just get in will you. You're as good as family. Come 'ead – they'll be made up to see you.'

'Shhh. Forget it, okay? I'm fine. I'll call you tomorrow.'

I force a smile and turn on my heels. I get three steps down Hardman Street.

'Billy? Look. Don't go. Please? Don't leave me here. '

'Ah, babes! Don't do this, yeah? Come with us.'

'*Why* do you have to go?'

'*Millie?*'

His shoulders fall with his face.

'Fuck you, Billy.'

I turn and walk away. He calls my name a couple of times and in the reflection of a window I see the cab swing round and I feel as miserable as the night.

When I'm out of sight, I fling my arms around myself,

79

throw my head to the floor and with my shoulders hunched into the wind, stride into town. The cold immobilises my thoughts. I can't whip up any coherent plan for the rest of the evening, though my animus is screaming for drink, food and more drink – and in that exact order.

At the bottom of Bold Street the germ of an idea forms and I flag down a cab. I instruct the cabby to take me to the financial district, an area teeming with suits, B-grade celebs and the vacuous self-made rich but an area, for all of that, devoid of students. I ream him a story that I'm the House Mother at Dreamers. The tale is transparent nonsense, told more for me than him – but I keep it going right to the drop.

I alight at the very top of Old Hall Street and the sky lets out a low guttural cry. I light a cigarette and stare in awe at a Mersey that's flinching from storm light. I smoke it right down to the filter and toss the sparking butt into the night. A couple of young girls scurry past with naked torsos and wind whipped legs. I laugh out loud. The rain has petered out now, but the bloated sky hangs heavy as it drags the storm cross-river to the city. For a moment the night is still. Apart from the gentle lapping of the wind against shop windows and the distant click of heels on pavement, everything is calm.

And then it bursts.

The sky surrenders and collapses on the city, stampeding its revellers into random venues. I throw back my head and let the slanting silver deluge drench my face till I can take no more, and then I sprint across the road and scamper into Sam's. Like most bars in bad weather, it's warm and noisy and packed. Tonight it's seething with pink faces in wet suits. There's not much to look at in terms of fanny, either – a party of busty middle-aged women, a couple of bottle blonde stripper types and a clutch of nine-to-fivers seeking refuge from the rain. I shake myself like a wet dog, take a sleeve to my rain-slicked face and advance to the bar. I prise myself between the lapdancers. Our bodies make contact, jolting my cunt to life.

I order a bottle of Stella and settle in a booth in a dark secluded corner. The big breast brigade start swaying in unison to a Madonna track, singing along theatrically and dissolving into la la las where they don't know the words. The most restrained of them, easily a 36E, is leaning forward slightly. Her magnificent bust, scantily framed in a low-cut blouse is directly in my eyeline. Christ, they are *huge*! Even the girl serving her cannot prise her eyes away from them. I stare at her long and hard and commit them to memory.

I finish my drink, fire up another cigarette and try to attract the attention of a waitress. An unsmiling face trudges over and plonks a menu on the table. Even as she's walking off I can see the light bulbs popping in her head. She swings round and does a double take. Her face is strangely familiar. I shiver – she's exquisite. Soot black hair, big pellucid eyes, fat lips and Slavic cheekbones. Her waist and hips are tiny. As she turns her slender back on me once more I drag my eyes down her entire and absurdly beautiful frame, from her collar-bone, to her arse to her lithe calves. My eyes fuck her and feel her, everywhere. Her long, slim legs; her tight little bum; her sharp and jutting tits – she's fucking gorgeous. She returns seconds later with a pen and pad. She rolls her eyes apologetically when she sees I haven't even opened the menu.

'Sorry,' she sighs, 'I'll come back.'

Her voice is deep and confident. Everything about her says accessible.

'That's okay'. I smile and hand back the menu. 'Just bring us a bottle of house red and a plate of fries.'

'Mayo with your fries?'

'Nope.'

She scribbles urgently on the pad then throws her eyebrows together.

'What was it you asked for – red or white?'

'Red.'

'Sorry. Been manic in here today. The rain. Drags 'em all in.'

She slides her eyes in the direction of a table of fat leering suits. I snort sympathetically.

'Clock off in ten, and I tell you – it can't come soon enough.'

She's telling me she's finishing her shift any minute. Unnecessary information. Fuck! She wants to fuck me. I rack my memory to place her, but she takes the lead.

'You're *Millie* right? You're on my course.'

My heart lurches to the dizzy pit of my tummy. It's her. Pocahontas. Voguey from the bus – protagonist of a dozen masturbatory fantasies.

'I'm Paula.'

She holds out a hand. Slim and soft, but with a firm shake.

'We had Classics and Shakespeare together last year. And we were in the same tutorial in the first year.'

Fuck, this girl knows my entire life history. I tighten my eyes to quizzical slits.

'Introduction to Classics? Spittle face? Come on you must remember *him*.' She says.

'Christ yeah. Didn't he have a nervous breakdown or something?'

'I sincerely hope so.'

A flicker of mischief plays on her eyes. I drop mine low and innocent. I pick at the Stella label.

'Look – why don't you join us for one when you clock off?'

She looks at her watch, feigns a look of indecisiveness then responds with a diffident smile.

'Okay. Thanks, I'd love that. Back at you!'

I trace her narrow arse all the way back across the floor, and the rudderless night suddenly acquires a narrative. I, Millie O'Reilley am going to have sex tonight. Mad horny sex with an exotic beauty. I neck the dregs of my lager and slink to the toilets to dry my hair and slap on some lipstick.

I return to a table strewn with undercooked fries, every sauce and dip imaginable and a bottle of tepid red wine. The promise of sex has deadened my appetite and the very smell of heated fat causes my stomach to turn. I push the food and the platter of dips to the far corner of the table and pour myself a large glass of wine. I work my way through three consecutive cigarettes, chug another glass and then sit back and assume an air of indifference. Minutes collect and accumulate into an empty bottle and I start to feel faintly ridiculous sat here alone. Before it was just me with a clearcut purpose. A solitary drinker, minding her own business. Now I look pronounced and transparent. A girl hanging on for sex. I toy with the idea of doing one but the sight of two paraffins outside on the street being rocked and tossed about like wrecked broken puppets persuades me to stay. I attract the attention of a waiter and order another bottle of wine which he delivers with a cussed faced. He asks me if I'll be ordering anything to eat and flicks his eyes in the direction of the bar where a queue of rain-soaked diners has collected. I offer him a simpering smile and point towards the plate of untouched fries.

I'm well into my second bottle when she appears at the other end of the room and takes my breath away. She's wearing a simple white t-shirt with a pair of skintight jeans that cup her supermodel's arse. The t-shirt emphasises the jut and thrust of her tits, and the elegant longeur of her arms – pipe-cleaner thin yet slashed with definition. An epidemic of stunned head-turning accompanies her as she glides across, leaving me weak.

With a self-conscious rake of her hand through her hair, she settles down and splays her beautiful arms out across the table. Our flesh is almost touching. We exchange big grins. My cunt somersaults. I sip at the wine and soak her up over the rim of the glass.

I love this part. These next few minutes – I wish I could live them in slow play. This bit is almost as good as the shock of fresh cunt when you peel down their panties for the first time. The shape and the smell. The nudity of their wetness, soft liquid explosions on the senses. And this, right now, is just as intense. Flirting. Slightly hazy from the booze. The inevitability of sex, of cunt, hanging over us both like a spell.

'So, did you take the dissertation op?' she says, breaking the tension.

'Yeah. With deep regret.'

'I haven't so much as thought of a theme. How about you?'

'Sex,' I lie, trying to coax her onto the subject, 'I'm doing it on the construction and subversion of sexual identities in modern literature.'

'Wow!' she says, genuinely impressed. 'That's brilliant.'

A short but benign silence follows. She takes a packet of cigarettes from her handbag. Marlboros. She offers me one. Her fingers are so slim and womanly, yet her nails are bitten and bare.

'So, who's your dissertation tutor?'

'Kennedy. I think. Which I suppose is a good thing. It means she can't mark it.'

'Kennedy hey?' she says and sucks in a breath of air like a backwards whistle, 'Don't know if I could handle her. D'you remember that berserker she threw in the first year, when Paddy nodded off?'

'Don't think I was there, mate.'

'Yeah, you were! You were sat a couple of rows behind me, sandwiched between Ben and Carla.'

'Ben and Carla?'

'You must know *Carla*. Everyone knows Carla. Big lips. Stupidly pretty.'

85

Couldn't be that pretty. Trust me, I'd have frigged off over her.

'Christ, I can hardly remember what classes I took in the first year let alone who I sat next to.'

'Well I wouldn't normally,' she says with a sudden defensiveness, 'Know who was in my lectures like. But most of the girls made a mental note when you were around.'

'Oh?' I say, trying hard to ignore the warm glow spreading through me.

'Well – yeah. I mean, no disrespect and that, but you must have wondered why every female tried to befriend you in the first year?'

'They didn't!' I say with real surprise. They didn't.

'Maybe that's a bit of an exaggeration. But you were living at home right?'

'Yeah. Still am.'

'Well there was definitely a race for the first girl to know you well enough to be able to pop round for coffee?'

I look intently at her face for some kind of explanation but all I see is ineffable beauty. Is she saying that every girl on campus wanted to fuck me, her included? Surely not. No. She is. She must be. That's what she's saying. She's handing it over on a plate, and now that it's there, staring me in the face, wide eyed and lucid, I don't know what the fuck to do with it.

'Are you saying what I think you're saying?'

'Come on. You must have been aware of it.'

She puts a hand lightly on my wrist and I almost involuntarily flinch away. A huge hole opens up in my chest, slurping in every inch of her.

'Well no. Yeah. NO. I mean, it was always at the back of my mind. I saw the way other girls looked at me, but I just thought it was, well you know. Just girls looking.'

'Hardly surprising though. You're the mirror image of him. Uncanny.'

She withdraws her hand leaving within me a sudden yearning to pull it back again.

'Of who?'

'Has he always been that good looking? I could never get involved with someone like that. I'd be like *terminally* paranoid. I mean, it must be bad enough being you. How do you cope with the knowledge that every girl in Uni wants to fuck your Dad?'

Suddenly I'm back in real time. The hole in my chest tightens, spitting every inch of her back into the busy hum of the bar. My eyes go lazy, lazy and glazed, blurring her face into the backdrop of a neon-tinged window. I place my hands on the table and push myself up, my legs prickly and uncooperative, threatening to collapse underneath me. I'm hardly aware of her being there, Paula. Pocahontas. I gulp down the remains of my glass, and stagger my way out through the throng of bodies, out into the cold blast of air which slaps my face and sobers me.

I walk quickly down rain-black streets, eager to put distance between us. Once I'm back weaving through the smouldering core of clubland, dodging bodies and fun and laughter, the anxious spacey pang in my head starts to lift. In its place, I feel foolish and embarrassed at reacting like that – for seeming so brutally stung. For having misread her so badly. And for feeling so intensely jealous of my father. Dad. My lovely old man. So, utterly, adoringly oblivious to the starving adulation he so innocently accrues.

My next port of call is The Living Room. A few ropy blondes sprawl the length of the bar, eyeing up a noisy cluster of doormen types skulking in a booth. I pick up a cocktail menu. The words swim in front of my eyes. I flick a wet slab of fringe from my forehead and order a vodka cranberry.

'One Theebreathe coming up,' the bartender goes in a super affected lisp. I grab him by his wrist.

'I don't want one of *those*,' I tell him, 'I want a *vodka* and *cranberry.*'

A flutter of injury streams his forehead. He snatches the fiver from my hand.

'Keep the change ' I say sincerely, and turn my back on him.

It's shite, this place – but footballers and gangsters flock en masse and that, in turn, rakes in the fanny. It's that much easier copping a bird when there's eligible guys around cos they love playing up to that whole girl on girl thing. They use it as a pulling mechanism. Of course most of them bottle it when you get them someplace on their own.

'*What the fuck you doing, girl? I was only winding the lads up!*'

The climbdown is usually accompanied by a look that's a fifty-fifty compromise between disbelief and disgust.

I order another 'Theebreathe' and perch at the far

end of the bar. I light a cigarette and make eyes at the fanny.

Time passes.

A hand squeezes my shoulder and the shock of a human touch yanks me from a group orgy with the blonde bits at the bar. I turn and find Liam Flynn, Sean's big brother, his huge smile almost touching his eyebrows. I haven't seen him in ages. He looks great – tight black polo neck worn under an expensive-looking suit. The spotlights strike the planes of his face, accentuating his high cheekbones and the broad boxers nose, putting a pinpoint of light into his dark liquid eyes.

'I *thought* it was the lovely Millie!'

He plants a kiss on my cheek. His breath is boozy and sexy.

'Hot date?' he asks, wiping a stray droplet of rain from my nose with paternal delicacy.

'Nah, I've come to try my luck with one of them old boilers.'

I point to the blonde tarts who are all looking over at Liam, a look of needing-to-be-fucked stranded on their faces.

His smile expands a couple more inches.

'Don't waste your time,' he says in a low whisper as though he's implicating me in some dark secret. He looks around subversively before bending his head into me again. 'They're Mids.'

'What?'

'You know Middies, Midsters.'

'Don't get you' I say, adopting the whisper.

'Men in Drag.'

I laugh loudly and one of the tarts throws me a filthy look. Her mate has a sexy face – big lips, cheekbones, hungry eyes, but Liam's right. Her calves are that bit too pronounced. She may not be a fella, but she's not far off.

I go and sit in a booth with Liam and his mates who turn out to be the bouncers I spotted when I first walked in. Two of them used to work the door at Cream. Nice guys. The other, I take an instant dislike to – a big daft steroid head with a bad beak twitch and a burst capillary face.

Liam raises his hand and a waitress with a black matt bob and a menstrual gut springs over.

'Same again my love – and a glass for the lady,' he says pointing to a gang of empty champagne bottles.

'Thanks Liam,' I say. 'But could I have a bottle of Stella instead?'

'Whatever you want, little'un.'

He nods the waitress away and lights a cigarette.

'Can't half tell she's a student, ay?'

'Is that why you called her 'love', you wind-up merchant?'

'Not her! You!'

'Piss off!' I snort. 'You should know I'm allergic to cheap champagne, Liam. Burns my delicate princess' guts red raw.'

'Ay you, Lady Penelope! What d'you mean cheap? That's fucken Moet, that is!'

'I rest my case, darling.'

'Fucking good swill, that!'

'Yeah, but it's not exactly Cristal is it?'

Liam grins and feigns a slap to my face. The roid-head

gives me a nasty sideways look that makes me shudder.

I like Liam. It's hard to believe he's Sean's brother. And not just in terms of physical constitution – Liam's half-caste, short and wide, Sean's white, tall and slim – but just in terms of who they are, too.

Liam's a gentleman and, in his way, he has morals. He's a great Daddy to little Tony and you rarely see him flaunting his money or power. In fact, most people don't even know what Liam Flynn looks like. It's just a name with it's own mythology that's as deeply ingrained in local folk-lore as Kevin Keegan or Paul McCartney. Sean, on the other hand, is a self-created B-grade scouse celeb who goes to more bar/club/restaurant openings then Tara Palmer fucking Tomkinson. And it's not as though his lifestyle is something he's earned through his own graft and flair. It was *handed* to him. When Liam went down for a five-stretch, he only had Sean to oversee the businesses – an impressive raft of tanning salons, cafés and tenancies – a tidy little earner for an eighteen-year-old.

Poor Liam didn't have a choice. His henchmen went down with him, and he had a Missus and a baby to feed. Sean may have kept the empire ticking over, but his wideboy antics did immeasurable damage. The family name, once revered by the city's underworld, is little more than a celluloid How To Be A Gangster cartoon these days – and Liam knows it.

Steroid cunt asks a couple of the blonde tarts over and offers them a glass of champagne. Both of them have identical crinkled brown breasts and hands that look as though they've been dipped in a chippy's deep fryer. They're pathetically pleased at being called to the table. Close up, they're horrors. The skin around their eyes is cracked and thin and scummy with cheap blue mascara. When I walked in before with my sodden denims and blurry face they looked at me like I was a tramp. Now that I'm sitting here, as a guest of Liam's, they're all Colgate smiles and 'In't she pretty. Are yer a model, girl – yer pretty enough, well!'

Slags.

My mind meanders over to the streets of Liverpool 8. Skinny whores with bad complexions, girls who reek of cheap perfume and rubber and the street. I can't help myself. The very notion stirs something so deep in my groin that I should be shocked – troubled, at least, that I should itch so greedily for such a wretched thrill. But instead I feel alive – drunk and fearless and wonderfully, fervently alive. I contemplate what sort of girls will be braving the weather tonight. Crackheads, old women with cancer breath, girls with cruel pimps and other nightcrawlers driven by sheer desperation. Desperate enough to fuck me, maybe?

I say my goodbyes, plant a suggestive kiss on Liam's lips and flick my tongue at steroid head. I decide to walk it, some innate safety-mech stalling me, trying to change my mind.

On Bold Street I withdraw £80 from a cash machine and march briskly in the direction of Hope Street. Storm light flickers across the sky and the cold whips me like a cane. I pull my jacket high above my head, but the wind only savages the chink of bare tummy that exposes.

The skein of the sky rips open whetting the sting of the wind.

Taxis flare past with drunken faces pressed up against steamy windows. Windscreen wipers flurry and skew, headlights burn through the rain and all along Leece Street, bodies duck and dive in and out of bars. It's a horrific night for anybody to be out. There'll be no one out on Hope Street.

By the time I get up there, my clothes are saturated and my ears wind-burnt. My hankering for brass has slithered into the fomenting gutters, frothing vehemently with a wild and coffee-coloured spume. I curse myself for being like this, for being so unable just to shake it off. Forget about it. Other people do.

I walk to the nearest bus stop on Catherine Street, but I spot another one with a shelter a little further down. I sprint over, leaping and dodging great gaping puddles. An old Somali gadgie with a long, grave face is huddled inside. He's locked in thought, but looks warm and content enough. I delve into my jacket and my spirits soar at the discovery that I still have ciggies left. As I cower from the wind to light one, I spy a wraith-like figure sliding into a silver Mercedes at the top of Canning Street. A feeling of envy flares up inside but is quickly strangled and replaced by a feeling of folly. That I should feel jealous of him is absurd! A big fat suit, for fuck's sake – somebody's husband! And he's picking up a *whore*, the wretch. He's shopping for a crackhead. Where's the challenge in that? There is none. Still, as a man, and a man with a car, he has privileges that I can only dream of. Even if he's obese and miserable, even if she's the lowliest, most rancid wraith, I still wish I were him.

The rain relents a little but the wind howls and screams around the shelter, flinging debris into the road. Cars swerve this way and that, and a woman beeps her horn as an empty can launches itself at her windscreen. I ask the old guy how much longer for the next bus and he shrugs, lifts his arm up to consult his watch and shrugs his shoulders again. His hand is thick and knotted like a vine. He hunches himself up again and pulls a forlorn expression. His eyes loom large in his old head. I try a smile on him, but he's back inside his thought chamber. I take out my last, crushed cigarette and straighten it out with my fingers. As I'm striking a match a sudden movement catches my eye. Over the road a woman is opening her curtains and lingering at the window. A naked light bulb hammers down on her. I narrow my eyes and squint through the slats of rain. She's wearing a negligee – and she's tidy from this distance, toned and lustrous. Too tidy for brass. She flicks her hair from her face, folds her arms and throws out her hips.

I watch her a while longer and the miserable night explodes. There's no doubting it – the girl is on the game. I'm still in the hinterlands of red light central, but women in windows? It just doesn't happen round here. I know there are girls who bring punters back to their pads – I've ogled in silent envy enough times – but they use the streets to ensnare them. This is sheer audacity. It isn't happening. Abandon the idea.

★ ★ ★

A blue Saab pulls up outside and a skinny bloke with a pony gets out. He hovers at her door for a while, then disappears inside. She draws the curtains.

I let two buses roll past.

Eventually he emerges and as his car pulls away, she opens the curtains and stations herself again at the window. I sidle closer to get a better look at her. She is thirtyish with brown shoulder length hair and a gaunt but striking face. The rain has stopped now and the streets are empty of life and activity. The air is damp and big in its stillness. I gulp hard and deep on it and cross the road.

A length of rusty railing separates her house from the pavement. Condoms have been crucified on the railing spikes and the word SLAG is emblazoned across her door in green paint. I step towards it. There are three buzzers. Only one of them has a name. *Sabrina*. I press it.

'Yeah?'

'Are you the woman in the window?'

A broad Salford accent booms back, putting me on the back foot.

'Oo *are* yoh?'

'My name's Sarah. Can I come in?'

'What d'yoh want?'

'I'm gay,' I say, despising the sound of the word. 'One of the girls on Hope Street told me you'd sort me out.'

'Fuck off, will yoh! Oo told you that?'

'I can't remember her name. She had a bad scar on her face and . . .'

'What d'yoh *mean*, sort yorrowt?'

'Look, it's teeming down, here. I'm not going to stand

here making a cunt of myself. I made a mistake. Sorry. Goodnight.'

I linger for a while, staring at the buzzer, the silence punctuated by the chattering of my teeth.

'Yoh better not be wasting me time.'

Another silence follows broken this time by a tentative sigh. Then the buzzer clicks me in.

I shut the front door behind me, and am plunged into a dense black fog. The sheer thickness and intensity of the dark panics me but a chink of light soon appears at the end of the corridor. The same voice, softer now, calls out.

'Down ee-yoh.'

The door throws me straight into a kitchen that's tiny, dank and depressing. There are bowls of cat food strewn across a dirty lino floor but no sign of a cat. A badly constructed archway separates the kitchen from a cramped lounge where I find her sitting on a small couch, her bare legs crossed and arms folded. She's hard but fuck, she's sexy. The room smells the same as the kitchen – cigarettes and cat food. I can't help staring at her face. She has an ochre complexion and deep sunken misty blue eyes. She blinks a lot. When she first sets eyes on me, her surprise – her *pleasant* surprise – is plain to see. She was expecting a Diesel.

'Av o seat' she says, eventually. 'Me name's Sabrina.'
Sss-ebb-rrrr-eee-noh.

I sit down on a rocking chair opposite her. 'Sarah,' I tell her.

'I thought yoh were Filth.'

The quip's sitting up pointing at its chin, but I let it pass.

96

'First time?'

'What – with a woman or with a . . . where I've had to pay for sex?'

'Either, I s'pose.'

'No. On both fronts. But it's not something I make a habit of you know? I was just . . .'

'Look, yoh don't have to explain nothing to me, it's not in me profession to make judgements is it?'

She flicks her burn-blue over me, calmly appraising the goods.

'I'll tell yoh though, *Sair-oh*. I was a bit shocked when yoh walked through that door.'

'Half expecting Pat Butcher were you?'

She grins.

'So? Am I *your* first woman, then?'

'No. Don't talk daft.'

Somehow I'm not convinced.

She unfolds her arms and folds them back again.

'How old are yoh?'

'Twenty one,' I lie. 'Do you have a cigarette?'

She unfolds her arms, reaches down the side of the couch and lobs a packet of Lambert and Butler at me. The lighter's inside the pack. I take a cigarette out and shake the lighter to life. I inhale deeply, holding the smoke in my lungs like it's a joint. I feel oddly at ease, now. I feel in charge.

'You can't quite get your head around this, can you?'

She shakes her wiry head. I exhale a thick plume of smoke up to the ceiling, nicotine-stained and strewn with cobwebs.

'Like I say, it's not in me profession to make judgements – but yoh could have any girl yoh wanted, you.'

She throws me a nervous, vacillating look.

I shrug my shoulders.

'How d'you know I haven't got a girlfriend?'

I raise an eyebrow playfully.

'Fifteen years on the streets, love. Bet yov got a fella, though?'

I raise the other eyebrow and shake my head.

'I was watching you from across the street.' My voice drops to a whisper. 'You've got an extraordinary face. Stunning. What's your – you know? What's your background?'

She folds and unfolds her arms again, and runs a shaky hand through her hair. She's blushing!

'Me mam's Icelandic. I was born in Reykjavik. My father, he's from Manchester. I grew up in Salford.'

'You're beautiful.'

'Thanks.' She gulps and looks away.

I'm deadly horny. My cunt is throbbing so hard it hurts and my limbs are starting to feel warm and floppy. And it's not just the idea of being here that's turning me on – that I'm about to have dangerous sex with a stranger who'll do anything, *anything* I want her to. It's more than that. There's chemistry between us. The room is charged with it. I want her badly and she knows it and she wants me, too. She tries to regain the balance of power.

'If yoh go through to the bedroom and take the door on yoh left, yol find a bathroom.' She switches into business mode. 'Take a shower. There's clean towels in the cupboard above the sink. Put them in the linen basket when yov finished. There's a clean dressing down hanging behind the bathroom door. Put it on and I'll meet yoh in the bedroom.'

She holds my gaze for a while, contemplating some thought and then continues.

'And I'll be needing payment first. D'yoh know what you want?'

I open my mouth. Words form but she continues.

'I'll do yoh a massage for fifteen, oral and masturbation for thirty and I'll do the full Monty for forty.'

She stands and with a coquettish flick of the hair walks into the kitchen and squats down at the fridge.

'I've also got a selection of vibrators and dildos in the bedroom but that'll cost extra. Water sports, scat, I don't do.'

Rather than estrange me, the clinical tone of her voice excites me badly. Partly because it implies that my identity as a punter has superseded my identity as a female but mainly because it alerts me to the fact that this is a whore. A woman prepared to hand over her body and allow me to indulge myself in any which selfish way I choose. It's filth – sheer filth and I can't get my head around *that*, that you can *buy* sex, like fags, books or beer. The most potent and precious of human interaction reduced to the price of a new top from Morgan. I saunter over to the kitchen. She looks dirty squatting down there like that. Like a reader's wife.

'How much to stay the night?'

'Fifty,' she says, peering into the fridge, 'But yol have to be gone by 7.30.'

She looks up at me and the nervous, vacillating look returns.

'Can I get yoh a drink. Av got coffee, tea or yoh can av a bottle of lager but yol have to pay for the booze.'

She pulls a bottle from the fridge and eyes the label with squinted eyes.

'Scorpion?'

'That'll do. Are you going to have one too?' I ask, beseechingly.

'Yeah. Why not.'

She smiles coyly and sets about opening them.

I go through to the bathroom. I peel my wet clothes off and hang them on a radiator. I wonder how many other bodies have stood naked in this room. I shower but don't wash my hair, put my panties back on, remove them and put them back on again. I slip into the dressing gown and go through to the bedroom. It is chaste and harsh and the naked light bulb gives the room a jaundiced glow. There is a box of tissues and a never watered plant clinging on to life on a bedside cabinet. An imitation Monet hangs lopsided on the wall. It's like a consulting room of a backstreet abortion clinic. It dawns on me that apart from the bowls of cat food I saw in the kitchen, there are no trappings of her life in this flat. I know absolutely nothing about this woman I am about to fuck. For a few fleeting moments I feel absurd stranded here on the bed in this silly silk dressing gown. But then she appears with a candle and our bottles, and the sight of her skinny legs gives me gooseflesh. She flicks off the switch with her tongue, hands me a bottle and slides alongside me. On the walls, our candlelit shadows are big and deformed and have already made contact.

I take a few swigs and tell her I want full sex but without the massage. She kisses me softly on the cheek. She smells of cheap body spray. She runs a hand up and down the inside of my thigh and my legs spread instinctively. Then, removing the bottle from my hand she rolls it between my legs and shocks me by pushing the ice-cold length of it into my panties. I gasp. My cunt somersaults and pulses against the numbing cold. She misinterprets my arousal as apprehension and slackens the pressure, rubbing me gently with the tip of the bottle.

'It's okay,' I say, slipping a hand round her neck and pulling her towards me, 'I like it.'

She sinks her fingertips into my hair, twisting and pulling and a madness enters her eyes. We pause momentarily, then kiss deep and urgently and when she withdraws, I am breathless and limp, pleasure rippling through me, overwhelming my senses.

She lifts the bottle to my lips and tilts it so that the liquid froths and trickles in parallel streams from the corners of my mouth and spills onto my tits. She shadows the liquid with her tongue, over my chin and neck, lingering to gnaw at my tense nipples, flicking them hard with her scaly tongue. I watch her mouth against my tits, breathing life into them, altering their shape and texture. Strange and beautiful sensations skid up and outwards from some gorgeous inner coil that I never knew existed.

We kiss some more, then she puts the bottle to rest on the bedside table. I feel a stab of disappointment. I liked having it down there between my legs, within such dangerous proximity of my most sacred part. And I know it – it's implanted a hankering in my mind that can only leave a bitter aftertaste of frustration, no matter how skilful her tongue and fingers. She pulls my wet knickers down over my knees and I flick them off with my feet. I lie there, supine and waiting. Her hand snakes around my belly which churns at her touch. The gliding, guileful hand lingers over my hips and thighs. When I can stand it no longer, I thrust her back down to my cunt and beg to be fingered. She dips two fingers inside, and opens them up like scissors, then, kissing me deeply and holding my gaze, she slips in another finger and fucks me softly, her pupils dilated with lust and power. I close my eyes and abandon myself to her touch and I let her, I just lie there and let her finger me.

I come powerfully and my cunt contracts around her like a glove. When I open my eyes she is staring right into me, her face betraying a flicker of smugness. A self-congratulatory smile seeps across her. I always come like that, I want to tell her – but instead I remove her hand, which is glistening in my juices, and instruct her to her knees. Momentarily, she looks humbled and naive, but she removes her negligée, quickly and skilfully, revealing a cunt that's been shaven with a cheap razor. The evidence of childbirth is there in her tits and her lower abdomen. She kneels on the bed, legs spread slightly, exposed, subservient. Now who's smiling?

'I want you on the floor,' I say.

Her eyes flick round, shining with insolence. Reluctantly, she hoists herself off the bed and drops to the floor like a cat. I kneel down behind her. The carpet is coarse and claws at my knees. I part the cheeks of her arse. I run a flat tongue over her cunt and lap her like a dog. She tastes vulgar – rubber and cunt juice and stale, stale sweat. I love it. As the lust in me swells, I have to refrain from asking about the bloke with the ponytail. Is this his spunk I can taste? What did you do? Did he fuck you up the arse? Did you suck his cock? Did he lick you like I am doing now? The images run amok in my head. Him forcing his cock into her tiny arse and fucking her hard and wild. Her cunt soaking, belying the face that feigns such apathy. I bet you love getting fucked don't you? I bet you lie in bed at night, wanking over your punters. You love being a whore don't you? You don't do it for the money. You do it cos you *love* it! I feel a tension mounting in my limbs as a new desire swarms over me, the yearning for absolute depravity, to degrade and myself be denigrated. I bury my tongue deep inside her arse and this time she slumps like succumbing to anaesthetic. She drops down to her elbows and rests her limp head on the floor, and slowly her legs spread wider and wider til her clit is just inches from the floor. Dirty images crash through my head, clashing with my hidden most disgusting fantasies. And she too seems gripped by the same depraved sense of desire that drives me. Billy once told me that it's a whore's code of practice to switch off when she's getting fucked. Pleasure is not a perk of the job. That being the case, she has violated that code of conduct over and over again – moaning unashamedly, allowing her cunt to slurp and drench my face, loving the fuck as much as I am. I rim her a little longer and when I feel her stiffen towards orgasm I pull back and reach for the bottle. She throws me a look that's both dread and excitement. I kneel down behind her and run the tip of the bottle up and down her slot, feeding a few centimetres into her arse.

'Other way,' she whispers, thrusting it out with her muscles. 'Can do damage like that.'

The bottle's too wide to put in her arse, so slowly, carefully, I feed her cunt. She gasps hard.

'Would you like me to stop?' I ask, slipping her a little more length.

She throws me an ambivalent expression. I ease the bottle out a little.

'If you don't like this I can stop. Just say.'

I remove my hands, but the bottle remains stationary so her cunt is just gripping the bottle.

'I'll stop then, shall I?'

A rainbow of emotions slides across her face. She shakes her head in wordless intensity.

I grab her hair and yank her head back and make her look at me as I thrust in the whole of the bottle. I do her fast and rough. The muscles in her back arch and subside, glistening in sweat. I bottle-fuck her harder, syncopating from the wrist. Her cunt sucks greedily on the bottle, dictating the speed and force of the ride. I stick the forefinger of my free hand inside her arse which seems to dilate and contract with each lunge and surge of the bottle and I'm shocked by how silken the skin is that separates cunt from arse. I fuck her without skill or compassion. I've lost it, now. I'm just slamming the bottle in and out as fast as possible. Her groans turn into screams and her whole body shudders and spasms til suddenly she buckles and falls to the floor and the bottle shoots from her like a bullet.

She pulls away and lies there spent, shimmering in sweat. I slide down beside her, all senses slowly return-ing, and I am enraptured by the moment. Whore and punter united, as intimate as newlyweds.

We lie there in the hazy aftermath, our shadows accen-tuating the rise and fall of our chests. We are strangers once again, silent and awkward and coming down. I'm taken over by that old familiar impulse to abscond. I don't want to be in this room, with this woman. I can smell her cunt on my lips and I feel nauseous and dirty and damaged. I should put on my clothes and go. That's what I'll do.

In a minute.

I'll go.

I awaken. I don't know where I am. It's unfathomably dark. Loud music seeps down through the ceiling, slews of beats and bass. No voice. No melody. It's just stripped sound tearing up and down the scale, defying all tonic logic. My cunt feels damp and uneasy. Slowly, I become aware of her lying next to me. Sabrina.

The night flashes before me. Pocohontas. Liam. The old gadgie at the bus stop. Her.

She has thrown a duvet over us that smells of cats

and men's bodies. She's lying on her back with her head turned away from me, whimpering softly, trapped in some distant dream.

The disorientation and fear fade and a feeling of lust swells in its wake. My hand crawls over to her body and finds her naked. I reach down to her cunt. She's soaking. I dip a finger in her cunt and massage her clit with a wet fingertip. She stirs a little and lets out a low moan. I rub her some more and she opens her legs involuntary. This is wrong. Gently, I slide a couple of fingers in. Her juices are thick and stale. I leave my fingers sleeping inside and with my other hand masturbate. I come hard and violently and it rouses her from slumber. She sighs angrily and turns over, releasing herself from my fingers. I tut back and collapse into the nowhere of my pillow.

When I come round it's morning – a vile and gradual realisation that burrows into my consciousness. A blinding shaft of light stabs through a tear in the curtains, forcing me back down under the covers. It stinks down there. *I* fucking stink. Outside, the city is still dosing. The streets are empty of traffic and noise. My throat hurts and I feel hostile to the body lying next to me. The musky smell of her knocks me sick. I pull back the covers and snatch a quick look at her. Her hair is damp against her forehead, her face paint smeared across the pillow. She's a decade older than she looked last night. The light from the curtains picks out a starving cold sore on her chaffed bottom lip. I recoil – how the fuck did I miss that last night? I slide gingerly out of bed and creep through to the bathroom. This is how married men must feel when they wake from a boozy one-night stand with some slapper, this acrid stew of horror, guilt and disgust. My jeans on have been stiffened to cardboard by the radiator. I slip on the vest I find underneath them, washed of all colour, but warm and dry. My trainers squelch, and my jumper and denim jacket smell like a wet dog. I swig orange juice from a ragged carton, spilling it down my chin. I spot a pack of L&B among the bills in the fruit bowl, and slot them.

On the street the light makes my head hammer behind my eyes. It's that period of beautiful nothingness between dawn and sunrise where yesterday and tomorrow are both within equal grasp.

Yesterday sucks.

I blew a week's living expenses on an experience that's left me feeling spent and unloved. I drove Billy away and made myself look foolish. I have two unconsummated essays that are now two days late, and I didn't bother ringing Dad to tell him I was staying out. I dip in my pocket and find I've plenty left for a cab, but I decide to walk yesterday out of my system instead.

Princess Avenue is staggering this time of year. The leaves have begun to harden and fall and the autumn air has sharpened and cleansed everything. My breath smokes in front of me and I have to keep blowing on my hands to stop them stinging. I walk on the grassed central reservation which will soon be littered with elderly Jamaican gentlemen cogitating serenely, all with twinkling eyes and benevolent smiles snuggled beneath grizzly silver beards. The scene fills me with a wave of nostalgia and I'm suddenly remembering again what I love about Toxteth. It's a law unto itself. Whatever schemes and innovations are foist upon L8, its citizens will take no notice and carry on doing their thing. They're hard, the people round here – no doubt about it. Jamie, Billy, Sean, Liam – even Mr and Mrs Keeley, they all wear the countenance of the barrio, and they're all of the best people I know. Even fucking Sean is worth ten of Jacko in charisma.

I find myself wondering what last night might have been like for her. Sabrina! Mandy, more like, or Michelle. I feel for her. I feel badly about my own part in keeping a foot on her head as she wriggles and gasps for breath. A rare tear dribbles from my eye and grows cold on my cheek.

I walk down Devonshire Road, but instead of turning left towards home I peel right into Admiral Street, down towards Keeleyville. I skulk on the pavement opposite their house. His car is in the drive, all the windows frosted over. I pick a stone that's light enough, yet still heavy enough. His bedroom window is right there. Another tear slides down my face. This is bad. This is as low as I've known. I let the stone fall to the floor, throw my hands into my pockets and turn on my heels.

Slowly, the city is beginning to uncoil. The light is bleary-eyed, unsure which face to show at first. Then as I turn back on to Princess Avenue, the sun bleeds over the Cathedral and the new day comes rushing on. An Echo van pulls up at the side of the street and out fly a bundle of morning papers. Life goes on. The detour to Jamie's sinks back into yesterday. Another tear slips from my eye and suddenly I've gone under. I'm walking and crying and crying in thick, violent sobs. Not about last night. Not about Jamie. I'm crying for something else. I'm crying for me.

CHAPTER 4

Millie

I'm hovering outside Kennedy's office with a sore throat and a swollen cunt. My mind's oscillating madly between the wild excuses I'm about to hit her with and my humbling encounter with Doctor Ali, this morning.

'The good news' he said, peering over his spectacles, 'Is that we've got to this in good time. That's good – we've eliminated a lot of potential damage. You see, often, when gonorrhoea infects the throat or rectum, there are no symptoms . . .'

'Gonorrhoea?' I murmur. He holds a hand up.

'The bad news is that the other problem looks more serious. The sores and swelling on your vagina seem to be related to genital herpes. This can be controlled with the correct creams and treatment, but this *is* an STD that is with you for life. You need to think carefully about informing your partner – or any one else you choose to have sexual relations with.'

'*Life?*'

'Well – yes and no. Think of it like an oral cold sore. Although some people carry the virus all their life, they may only suffer one or two outbreaks.'

'Yeah, but even when the sores have cleared up, are you saying that I can still infect people?'

'People you have sexual relations with, yes.'

I don't know what to say to him. I don't know what I think.

'It's unfortunate Miss Reilley . . .'

'Miss O'Reilley . . .'

'It's unfortunate Miss O Reilley, you've caught these diseases – but they're not life threatening. They *can* be controlled with the correct care and treatment. I'm going to give you a course of penicillin to treat the gonorrhoea and some creams and bath soaks for the other.

But what we really should be concentrating on now is perhaps the type of contraception you've been using or perhaps *not* been using.'

Head down, he writes out the prescription. He can't even look at me. Being branded a sexual leper is bad enough, but to have the messenger wallow in my embarrassment is too much. I stare at the family portrait on his desk. Dr Ali and his blowsy-faced wife and five bloated children, all wearing the frozen smiles of middle-class beatitude. I put my *life* on it that behind the virtuous veneer was a sick and depraved man. I knew his type all right. The Jags and Mercs of Hope Street. Doctors, lawyers and bankers. Dirty, sick men. Proud husbands and proud fathers. The fucking hypocrisy of it all.

'Your partner? Is he aware of the situation?'

He's looking at me all right, now. I meet his gaze full on.

'*She,*' I say. I get up and walk across to his desk with

as much attitude as I can muster. I take the prescription from him and exit.

After that, I don't know if I can take any of Kennedy's shit. I don't know if I can even be bothered lying to her. She's sprawled across her desk with a stern face and a pencil stabbed into her hair. I loiter in the doorway for an instant then step into the room. A fug of crude spinster's perfume cloys in my throat.

'Have a seat, Millie,' she says, settling back in her chair and removing her glasses. I sit down and my jeans rip into my swollen cunt. I still can't believe it − a lifelong punishment for one lousy, drunken encounter.

'Now, you know why I've sent for you, don't you Millie?'

I sigh affirmatively. She evades my gaze, and fixes her eyes to a piece of paper that has my name printed at the top. My surname's been misspelt. I contemplate pointing this out.

'We're now on week six of semester and according to your quarterly report card, you've got an attendance of 47% and you've handed *all* your essays in late. And Mr Jackson is still awaiting a piece of work as am I . . .'

I switch off and slide my vision over to the window where a slate sky is raging above the concrete sprawl of the city. It's staggering, the view from up here. It's religious. I wonder just how much of that vista is lost on Kennedy or any of them gobshites down there on the grass. Jamie though, Jamie would look at that sky and well up. He'd feel the same fearful downpour of emotion as me.

'I can't emphasise just how serious this is Millie. The drop in the standard of your work is cause enough for concern, but your attendance . . .'

She pauses and sighs. A muscle tenses below the wad of fat on her jaw.

'All students are required to achieve eighty percent attendance unless there is a legitimate and valid reason to exempt them.'

'*But* have you seen that sky though?'

'What?' Her voice tightens. 'Millie, you *do* realise that you may have to repeat the year again and that being the case, you are only eligible for a pass. And this is very sad . . . I mean looking at last year's marks. You were a high 2:2 weren't you? A 2:1 was certainly within your grasp but now, it looks like . . .'

Another theatrical sigh.

'. . . I didn't want to have to do this, but unless you can produce a Doctor's note or provide a sound explanation for your absence then I *will* have to escalate this matter.'

I lug my eyes from the window and stare right at her. She looks like one of those silhouettes on Crime Watch.

'Look,' I say, squinting hard. 'There is. There's a reason.' I pause and sink my teeth into my bottom lip. 'Something bad happened.' I take a deep hard breath and throw her a helpless face. I can't. Not Kennedy.

'I, erm – I was assaulted. Sexually.'

'Millie?'

She's up and out of her seat, shuddering over to me, this heaving mass of fear and concern.

'Oh my God! Millie, darling – have you, I mean . . . ?'

'I've reported it. My Doctor, Doctor Ali, has examined me. Whatever documentation you need . . .'

She's stunned. She does not know what to say.

'Please don't tell anyone else, Miss Kennedy,' I plead, addressing her with the correct title. 'Please! Not Mr Jackson and especially not Dad . . .'

I drop my eyes into my lap.

'Oh Millie, darling – of *course* I shan't say a thing. Please. Just be sure that you can tell me as much or as little as you wish, you poor dear. My God this is . . . If there's anything at all I can do . . .'

'Thank you. I knew I'd be able to confide in you . . .'

I tilt my head slightly, meet her gaze then sink back into my lap.

'Oh, Millie – how foolish of me not to have suspected! I should have *known* there was something . . . Now don't you worry, don't worry about a thing. It's all going to be OK.'

She reaches out to me and the flesh on her naked arms sways and knocks me sick.

'Thank you, Miss. Kennedy. Thank you.'

I can't say I feel fantastic about what's happened, but what can you do? You have to play the hand you're given.

I tear down the stairs, repressing a grin, upsetting a couple of studes along the way and as I'm exiting the building I pass that blonde girl with the falsies who I sat next to on the bus last month. Pocahontas' mate. I don't recognise her at first. Her face is drawn and full of fading bruises and her hair is greasy and has been clumsily scraped back into a pony. She's wearing no make-up and has an ugly splatter of spots on her forehead. The magnificence of her breasts is lost in a useless Rugby sweatshirt. I smile at her, a nice one, not a lewd one and she smiles back, gingerly. I turn back and watch her disappear into the building, all fragile and sapped of life.

I sprint across the slab of lawn that separates Literature from Sociology and a gardener with a browbeaten face and a cigarette hanging from his mouth shouts over at me to use the path. I flick my tongue at him and plunge into a jam of students walking in the same direction. A few of them I recognise as second year students of Dad's — Marxists and Socialist workers. I hate their type with a passion. You see them marching through town on a Saturday afternoon accosting innocent shoppers, preaching the evils of globalisation and exploitation of labour in third world countries. It's not that I disagree with what they're saying it's just the hypocrisy of it all. You just know that ten years down the line, most of them will be carting their GAP kids around in their Renault space mobiles, all munching away on McDonalds Happy Meals. And they'll be throwing dinner parties for their pals, who have all ended up working for big fuck off global corporations. Dad says I get unnecessarily wound up about it all. And just because a lot of them abandon their beliefs in the aftermath of Uni, it doesn't detract from the fact that they're very real at the time. All part of the identity process.

Bollocks.

Fucking hypocrites and that's the end of it.

Dad is in his study looking debonair and gorgeous. He's wearing that blue Paisley DKNY shirt I bought him last Christmas. The top two buttons have been left undone. My eyes settle in the milky hollow of his clavicle and I feel a twinge of something in my loins. Pocahontas, who can blame her hey?

'Something happened?' he says, eyes pinned to his computer screen.

'Why do you always suspect the worst? Can I not drop in because I love you?'

A smirk tiptoes across his face. He consults some papers to the left of him and drums furiously into the keyboard.

'Grant dried up already, has it?'

'Nope.'

'Come on Millie, hit me with it. How much d'you need?'

'A couple of grand would be nice but that's not why I've come to see you.'

'Oh?'

He puts his pen down and swivels round. Dwarfed in his black leather chair, he looks donnish and important. I feel proud and protective of him.

'I was wondering if you wanted to grab some lunch or something?'

'What – today?'

'Yes, in a bit. I've just got my . . .'

'And everything's fine, you're not in any trouble?'

'NO DAD! I've just got my loan money through and I thought I might treat you to a bowl of soup at the Number Seven?'

His face softens into a warm smile. Into Dad.

'That'd be swell. Shall we say 2.00 then?'

He swings back round, throws his eyebrows together and observes the writing on his screen with suspicion. My eyes zig zag around his study. It's so Dad. Methodical yet careless. His books – and there are shelves and shelves of them – are arranged by theme. There is not a trace of dust on his desk, yet there is a platoon of empty cups strewn around the room, with week old tide marks. And the air hums with exhaled tobacco. Marlboro Reds.

'Haven't you got a Classics lecture to go to?' he says, glancing at my timetable which is pinned to the wall, above his computer.

'I s'pose.' I sigh and pull myself up reluctantly.

'Toddle along then.'

'You should tell her you know. She'd get far more out of us if she got that handlebar muzzy whipped off. It's outrageous, inflicting *that* on her students.'

'Excuse me?' He turns round and removes his glasses. 'Don't you dare speak about my colleague like that.'

A grin snakes my face. I feel about four.

'My deepest apologies, Dr O'Reilley.'

'Out!' he smirks. 'I'll see you at two.'

I sigh dramatically and slot a book lying on the table. 'Sexual Deviance in Post-war Britain.'

'I *saw* that Millie. Don't you be losing that – it doesn't belong to me!'

'I won't,' I say, closing the door behind me, both of us knowing full well that I will.

Jamie

I'm sat here in the window of the canteen staring up at the sky. It's fucken beautiful, la. Big and moody and sombre as fuck. It's a manic depressive's sky that. I pull her name up on the screen of my mobie. I've got to sort this. One of us has to. It's getting silly. My forefinger hovers over the green button but then strays over to the red. I can't do it. Haven't got the arse for any more of her shite. I takes a big mouthful of pie which is all pastry and no meat, slump back in my seat and abandon myself to the sepulchral pull of the sky. Fucken Millie. Doing my head in, she is.

I picks up the phone and scrolls down to her number again.

It's three weeks since that morning she was lobbing stones at my window. I should've gone to her and that, but what could I do? I've got Anne Marie there, the house is upside down from the do – just weren't on, asking lil' Millie inside. I watched her go. Felt last, I did. Seen her walking off down the street with her head hung low and her hands clamped in her pockets and I did, I felt a cunt. I went back to bed and I just lay there, thinking about me and Millie and how it's all gone wrong. There's been periods when the pattern and rhythm of our friendship has altered. Like when she was going through the trauma of her Mum and Dad splitting up, but there was always that sense of constancy between us which guaranteed we could take off from the exact last moment of departure. Our friendship was inviolate. Suddenly, it feels almost as though she's fallen out of love with us. Like, she's grown up and realised that what we had was nothing more than a big mad teenage love affair. Just like I did with Sean five years ago. And instead of severing it, you just keep it at a safe distance and hope that destiny or geography will widen the chasm and the demise of the friendship won't be attributed to anything unpleasant. It'll just be logged as one of those harmless, *we just drifted apart* type things.

I don't want to drift apart just yet. Not now, not ever if the truth be known. There's too much behind us and too much in front. I fucken miss the little waif, I do. Got to fucken sort it.

I pulls her name up on the screen again. I squash the green button with my forefinger and lift it to my ear with a big mad lump in my throat.

It rings and rings. I can picture her staring at the screen, hoping that the next ring'll be the last, hoping that I'll just kill the call. One more ring and that's what I'll do. Kill the fucken call.

'He-llo?'

Sounds like a kid, she does – all small and frail and what have you. Makes me feel like going right round there and hugging her. I swallows hard.

'Hiya babes – it's your big pal here. I'm just about to go into a meeting and that so I'll keep it short. I was wondering like – well, I haven't seen you in ages. D'you fancy a bevvy tonight or something?'

'With you?'

'No babes, with our fucken Billy! Seems like he's the new fella in your life . . .'

A short silence follows. I've blown it. What a soft fucken jealous-arse thing to say!

'I'd love that, Jamie. You don't know how much . . .'

Thank fuck. My heart practically lurches with relief.

'Right then – I'll pick you up at six bells.'

'And thanks for remembering, Jamie.'

Remembering what? I'm grappling for clues, but she goes right on.

'Six whole years hey? Mad isn't it? Seems like a whole lifetime away – that morning I turned up at yours.'

Fuck! Is *right*!

'I know babes. Does done it? I've been racking my brains, thinking of how we should celebrate. I was think-ing we should go down to the docks, and just sit off. Me, you, a six pack and some ciggies. River'll be moody as fuck tonight, la. Or we could do what we did last year – just fuck off into Wales and . . .'

'Yeah! Let's do that. Don't think I could face the city tonight.'

'Ok then, let's see. What time you got to be in Uni tomorrow?'

'I haven't.'

I don't believe her, not one bit, but there's no way I'm pulling her up over it. Not today.

'Right, that's that sorted then kidder. We'll go pop a pill on top of Snowdon shall we?'

'Ah, Jamie! I'm *so* excited!'

'I know. See you six bells?'

'Can't wait. Oh and Jamie, you seen that Joy Division sky?'

'Thought you'd never mention it. It's fucken breath-taking, la. Almost got half a lob on looking up at that you know.'

I put the phone down, heart still doing flips. Job's a good 'un.

Millie

I snub the bus and walk home, happier than I have been at any moment this year and by the time I reach Seffie Park, I feel dead excited about the future and at ease with the past. I've even mapped out a structure in my head for the overdue essays and am actually looking forward to writing them. Well, the one for Jacko anyway. It involves re-writing any passage from Romeo and Juliet in the style of a contemporary author. I haven't yet decided which chunk of Shakespeare brilliance to pervert, but I'm definitely going to take the guise of Kelman. Early Kelman too. Around about the time he wrote *The Burn*, a collection of shorts which is one of Jamie's favourites. He gave me a copy for my fifteenth birthday. I hurled it to the back of a cupboard at page nineteen. Having been reared on a diet of Bronte and Austin, I found Kelman dull and pointless. Dot to dot Dostoevsky. Then, a year later Jamie introduced me to Selby. I was dazzled. He urged me to dig out Kelman and give him a second chance. I started reading on the bus to school and stayed on right past the school gates and all the way to Bootle shopping centre. Each and every page was cardinal and ripe with meaning. Kelman became a genius.

The park is gorgeous. It smells of autumn – air scraped raw over damp grass and leaf mould and a savage wind which tastes of winter. Up by the lake, I spot Reg, who owns the video shop at the bottom of our road. He's yanking conkers from a tree, splitting them open with a penknife and collecting them in a plastic bag. I yell over to him but the wind snatches the breath from my mouth and flings my words back and behind me. The lake and gardens have been badly neglected over the summer. Everything is wild and unkempt. If Mum were here she would purse her lips in disapproval and mutter to herself. Dad would give an acquiescing nod, but silently he'd love the overgrown grass and the tousled hedges and the paths that lure you west then throw you east. He'd adore the chaotic glamour of it all.

Patches of voices swim through the wind. A man shouting, a noisy altercation between two dogs and the hollers of school girls, playing football or rounders perhaps. I light a cigarette and walk with a spring in my step, past the decrepit coffee shop, past the duck pond and up towards the Palm House. I stare at its shimmering perfect wholeness. It's too intact, too pristine. I pick a big shiny conker from the floor and hurl it at a big flat pane. It misses by ages.

I take an offbeat path that runs parallel with a fast-flowing stream up as far as the playing fields to the north of the park, where it vaults off at right angles towards the main lake. I have been walking with my head hung low, deliberating my essays, gently snug and content. When I look up again I see a field seething with the lunge and surge of adolescent limbs. Girl's limbs, naked and delightful. I sidle closer. Fourteen to sixteen year olds in airtex t-shirts and navy gym slips, about to start a game of hockey. I find a safe spot from which to observe – a bench which is damp and encrusted with pigeon shit. The bulk of them are undeniably average looking girls, who will grow up to be average looking women, but all of them, even the fairly hefty red head, carry that hypnotic sexual potency that belongs exclusively and exquisitely to the genre of teenage girls. Two of them are loitering at the side of the pitch. Reserves. The smaller of the two is standing akimbo, swaying her hips from side to side. Her face is plain and pretty. An open canvas, no history. The other has her back to me. Her legs are long, bronzed and sculpted and her arse is full yet narrow. The t-shirt she is wearing is two sizes too small for her, accentuating the dramatic dip of a wasp waist and a strong powerful back. The way she holds herself – it's effortless, it's dangerous, it's salacious. It's cruel. She knows she's got it, and with that she holds the potential to rip your heart out and shred it to pieces. I sit and gape and hope for a glimpse of her face.

An unexpected blast of white winter sun leaks out from the sky and she twists her head round to meet its glare. She shadows her face with a hand. The sky snatches the sun back again and she drops her hand, but now a drift of wind trails her hair across her face. She fingers it back into place and turns away. Fuck. I sit there for a further twenty minutes, willing her to turn round, feigning interest in the game, my eyes like caterpillars, eating two holes in her arse. Increasingly, I hope that her face is not as spectacular as her body and poise imply.

The temperature drops a little and the sky sags and bloats and suddenly I feel foolish sitting here, but the need to see her face has consumed me. Fuck it. I'm going right over. I scrape my hair back in a messy bun, light a cigarette and swagger round to the opposite side of the field. A blur of eddying bodies separates us. I was good at hockey when I was in school. It was one of the few sports I would willingly participate in. Everything else I hated and managed to avoid through a combination of injuries, brutal periods and making myself so unpopular that no captain would pick me.

A throb of high-pitched screams presage the violent clang of hockey sticks and the ball is freed. A small Asian girl grabs it and hares towards the goal post, dragging the mirage of bodies with her. My girl holds back though, and suddenly, I am looking straight into a face that is too perfect for words. I smile and she smiles right back at me. I stand there smitten, overwhelmed by weird, clumsy emotion. But her side scores and the moment is shattered.

She runs over to her team-mates, punching the air wildly and lunging into a clumsy cartwheel. The temptress becomes a normal teenager. I am both relieved and distraught.

I turn on my heels and head towards home with a clear image of that moment instilled in my mind. When the temptress caught my stare. Before she became a normal fourteen-year-old again.

Rain clouds tear and split as I approach the bottom of Rose Lane, and the glow of Jamie's phone call fades along with my spirits. The episode with the schoolgirl has dragged me to a place I've never been before and by the time I reach the house, that grim and queasy foreboding has locked into the dead grip of tristesse. As soon as I get in, I go out into the yard and roll myself a joint. I sit cross-legged on the concrete floor and inhale hungrily, chasing streams of smoke into the lugubrious vault. And it's then that it pricks me. This cold weight in my tummy. I know what it's about now. It's the realisation that I was once fourteen and carefree. That I was once a kid.

I run a bath, deep and hot, and pour myself a glass of JD. I put PJ Harvey's *One Line* on at full volume, slide into the bath and watch the world grow dark. With Dad's classy razor, I shave my legs and pits of my arms but avoid the groin area. Since those sores materialised last week, I've fallen out of love with my cunt. I've refrained from trimming, shaving and moisturising her and I've started wearing knickers. Period knickers. As from last Wednesday, my cunt functions only to dispose of piss. Sex and masturbation have been put in abeyance and in a strange way the abstinence has brought about a sense of self-satisfaction. For each night I go to bed without masturbating about whores, I feel richer and better for it in the morning. I know though, that once prostrated by the evils of alcohol I will crave them like a drug.

Dad has moved the shampoo and conditioner from the side of the bath to a shelf above the sink. I make steps towards retrieving them, but my legs are heavy and uncooperative, so I wash my hair with soap instead. I loaf in the bath 'til darkness seizes the room and the cold evening pours in through the window and after the music dies, there is a long stretch of silence scarred only by the distant wail of an ambulance. Only the gradual sensation of too-cold bathwater brings me out of my trance.

As I haul myself out of the bath the realisation that I've stood Dad up sinks me. Shite! His little face when I suggested lunch, as well – he just lit up. I leg it down-stairs and punch his number into the phone. The answer machine kicks in. His voice sounds gentle yet serious, then two bleeps and it's over to me.

'Hi Dad, I was just ringing to . . .'

Unable to say whatever I think might make it better, I kill the call. I stand in the hallway, shivering, and wait for the right lie to enter my head. Formulating untruths has not always been a forte. I was a hopeless liar as a kid, but I was happy and well behaved, so there was never any *need* to lie. I had no deviant pathways to pursue. I start drying my hair, trying to visualise the young Me. I laugh out loud for an instant, cocking my head back as I picture myself – all attitude and braces. But then something sinister fingers the back of my neck and silences me. She has the same hair and the same face but it is someone else that inhabits this skin now. Time has poisoned out all the goodness. If you put all my school and Uni photos in chronological order you can see the savage and gradual build-up of filth and deceit. I swear, I look in the mirror sometimes and I'm terrified of the girl lowering back at me. I don't know her and I don't like her.

From next door the sound of plates clicking together

as they're stacked into a dishwasher cuts through the silence. It gives the hallway an empty, gutted feeling and the absence of Mum crashes in on me, transporting me back to our old house. I'm up in my room, reading. I hear the crash of crockery on the kitchen floor so I go downstairs and sling my head over the banister. I see Mum crouching over a mountain of broken plates and cups, clutching her skull, fragile female tears heaving from her chest. Dad's face appears at the door of the cellar. His face is white and alarmed. I see his gaze fall upon Mum and I wait for his familiar raucous laughter. But his face remains frozen. He kneels down beside her, slips an arm around her and hangs his head. There's a tightening in my guts, a lurid foreboding, and then the roar of blood to the eardrums as Mum's coiled fist leaps from nowhere and slams full force into his face. He's never raised so much as his voice to her, Dad, but I'm expecting him to hit her right back. He doesn't even restrain her. He just lets her lunge out at him again and again and when she's limp and exhausted and flecked in his blood he cradles her whole and rocks her. I can forgive her for that though. And I did. The death of her sister trampled her. What I can't forgive her for though, is not letting me say goodbye. I fucking loved Aunt Mo as much as she did.

The hockey girl slips into my thoughts again and I try to shake her from my hair with a scrag of the towel. I dip into the drawer and pull out a notepad and pen.

Dad,

Sorry I let you down today. I'll make it up.
love,
Millie.

It reads thoughtless and selfish. Superficial. Careless.

But it reads true. At least it reads true.

Jamie

The first thing that flips through my mind when I pull up is that she's stood us up. On purpose like. The house is devoid of any sign of light or life. I sound the horn a couple of times and next door's curtain spasms slightly exposing for a few seconds a vested torso. Then the room falls dark. A few seconds later, a couple of faces materialise at the window. One significantly larger than the other. That's classic curtain twitching that la! Haven't seen that sort of thing since I was a kid. Nosy fucken cunts. Wait 'til I tell lil' Millie.

I call her mobie. It just rings out.

The next thing to enter my head is that she's fallen asleep, which if the truth be known, would not be the first time. I call the house. No answer. The clock on the dashboard reads 5.54. I'll give her 'til 6.10, then I'm off.

6.05 and still no sign of the little newt. I try both numbers again. No avail. I go knock on the door. No joy. I gets back in the car and skims through the sports pages of the Echo. The Shite are still three points above us. More rumours that we're selling Heskey.

6.07. I start the engine. If the truth be told, I was a tad relieved when I pulled up and found the house in darkness, but only in a spineless sense. My stomach's pure been in knots all afternoon about seeing Millie, but now I s'pose, I'm more fucken frustrated than anything. I just want to get to the bottom of it all, you know. Want things back the way they were.

I wait a further two minutes then check the screen of my mobie for any sign of a missed call. Blank. With the tiniest tremors of anger spilling into my throat, I slam the car into first and glance into my mirror with the intention of doing one. But a couple of hundred yards behind us, I see a red dot bobbing up and down. I fix my eyes to it and I can tell by the period of delay between its rise and fall, that it is Millie. Smoking urgently. At 6.08, her face is pressed against the condensation of the glass. A wide-mouthed pout and slightly sheepish eyes. And fuck, I've missed the little waif. She slides into the car, dragging the thick odour of beer and fags with her.

'You started already?'

'No!' she splutters, kite writhing into a scowl, 'You're early. I thought you were coming at 6.00.'

I tap my finger against the clock on the dashboard.

'That'll be that clock in the Rose of Mossley,' I say, 'It's a good fifteen minutes slow that.'

She lobs us another scowl which quickly melts into an expansive grin when she realises she's been well and truly sussed.

'Only had a half, you know.'

I give her cheek an affectionate squeeze. She looks striking in a cream mohair jumper, skin-tight jeans and no make-up. She's lost a few inches of her hair too, a neat bob that falls level with her chin. It's softened the kite up a little, taken away that gaunt constitution.

At first, we're just speaking in snatches of desultory conversation, second or third date material with someone you've clicked with but are not yet at ease with – How's Billy? How's your Dad? Have you seen Sean recently? Did you hear about the lads who done over the bookies on Aigburth Road? And other mundane shite that doesn't really lead anywhere but gives us an insight nevertheless into what's going on in her head. For example, while she is mad for gossip pertaining to Sean, Liam and our kid, she completely shuns any conversatory inlet that might lead to the subject of Anne Marie or the wedding. She pure does not want to hear about it. Like when she asks us what I done over the weekend and I say I've been looking for a pad for the Missus and that, she fucks off on some mad tangent. 'Did you know there's been a twenty per cent increase in diagnosed cases of gornorrhoea and syphilis on Merseyside?' And by the time we reach the last set of traffic lights on Speke Boulevard, we've exhausted the possibilities of airbrushed conversation and a thick silence creeps over us. She sits there, gazing out of the window, swooshing air from one cheek to another, trying to appear all nonchalant and that. Her knee's a dead give-away though. Rattling like fuck. Pure nervous body lingo that. And I'm not feeling that different myself if the truth be known. My head's whirring madly and my throats choked with a thousand and one words, all refusing to organise themselves into sentences. Eventually, she spots the Echo on the floor, flicks on the dashboard light and plunges herself into the front page, and for a while the silence acquires a purpose.

Thing I still can't get my head round is where the fuck this has all come from and more to the point, what the fuck it *is*? There's no trace of animosity in her kite like there was a few weeks back. That's for deffo. Quite the opposite if the truth be known. There's almost a hint of vulnerability. A sadness about her. And para as it may seem, I get the feeling that I am in someway deemed the cause of that sadness. I s'pose the key to any kind of revelation lies in the tinfoil parcel in the dashboard. Should just stop fannying around and drop the bastards now. It's fucken aaaayges since we done a tablet together and that's clearly what's needed. A few hours of pure drug-fucked divulgence. Still, can't help thinking that this is a tiny waste of the most pleasurable drug known to man. Like I say, I only limit myself to one or two a year and my philosophy has always been that you should use a tablet to make a good time *better* not a bad time bearable.

It's just gone 6.45 and we're still trapped in the thick of rush hour. Traffic flow across Runcorn Bridge has almost come to a standstill. And I'm in the wrong lane for the M56, and no cunt'll let us in. A mini bus is crawling along side to our left. Auld'ns on a night out somewhere. All sour twisted mouths. Miserable as fuck. I try and grab the attention of the driver, but he's goosing about with the wing mirror. I fucken hate being stuck in traffic by the way. It pure burns my head out. I would rather've taken a fifteen-mile deviation then be stuck in this bollocks. I sigh heavily. Millie throws us an empathetic look, then snaps the light off and hurls the paper onto the back seat.

'Have you seen that over there?' she says suddenly, pointing beyond the opposite side of the bridge.

'What?'

'*That*? Look! My God, what the fuck is it?'

I twist my neck round and narrow my eyes to slits.

'What? In the Mersey d'you mean?'

'Yeah, a few metres from the left bank.'

'Can't see a thing. It's pitch fucken black. What am I s'posed to be looking for by the way?'

'This,' she says, in a low blunt whisper.

Millie has removed her top and is flicking her tongue at the aul' gadgies on the bus. A woman with a blue rinse and a mouth stretched into a perfectly formed O clamps her hand over her husband's eyes. The pair of them are pure mortified.

'JESUS CHRIST Millie? What the bleeding hell are you playing at? You'll give em both a heart attack!'

She sucks hard on a finger and commences rubbing her left nipple.

'There's cameras all down here. Get it back on now.'

I reach round and grab the paper from the back seat and lob it over her tits. She shrugs it off and there is a bit of a struggle as I try to snatch her jumper from the floor. My elbow hits the horn. The bus crawls forward.

Everyone is staring. A blur of horrified kites and waggling fingers. And as if this isn't enough, she frees

133

herself from the seatbelt and manoeuvres her body, so her breasts are pressed right up against the window.

I look away, twisting my neck right over my shoulder so it is nearly snapped from its socket and shield my kite with a forearm. The traffic in our lane inches forward. I linger back amidst an onslaught of blasting horns and wait for an opening in the next lane. No cunt'll let us in. I have two options. Equally harrowing. Stay put for a while, let the bus move out of sight and deal with the road rage from the drivers behind, or carry on moving forward alongside the bus and risk headlining tomorrows Echo. You can just see it now. *Pensioner dies in Indecent Exposure Shock.* Anne Marie would fucken murder us. I stay put.

'Show's fucken over now. Stop fannying about and *get your* top back on. Or I'm coming off at the next exit.'

She just sits there defiant, pure wallowing in the aggro she's causing. The driver behind starts doing big mad wanker signs at a hundred miles an hour. I'm losing my patience. Quickly. With Millie, but more with the cunt behind. Finally, a gap opens up in the next lane, between a truck and a red Corsa. I nudge my way in and the woman in the Corsa pulls a spastic face. I ignore her. I am just pure relieved that the truck in front has dwarfed us from sight. Those faces la. Those poor aul' dears.

By the time I recover from the ordeal, Millie has slipped her top back on and has returned to swooshing air between her cheeks.

'What the fuck's all that about then?'

She shrugs her shoulders, snorts, then goes:

'I smiled at that old couple and they just fucking blanked me.'

'Probably blind *as*, for Christ's sake!'

'Then they wouldn't have seen nothing would they?'

Takes us a while to see the funny side of it but once we're over the bridge and picking up speed on the slip way which feeds into the M56, I can't help but laugh to myself. Fucken face on that blue rinse la!

By the time we're deep in the heart of hillbilly land, Millie has tired of larking about and I've taken control of the conversation, steering it towards more serious stuff.

'So, how's your course going and all that?' I ask, conscious that I'm stumbling into another discursive no man's land. She responds with another teenage shrug of the shoulders. I glance sideways at her and try to read her thought processes from the tilt of her head and jut of her lips.

'How's that lil' noggin of yours coping with all the stress of your final year?'

'Okay, I s'pose.'

'You were a fucken nightmare when you were doing your A-levels you know. I can trace the origins of this receding hairline all the way back to that spring.'

'I know,' she smiles, 'But I was a nightmare cos I actually wanted to make the grades. I wanted to get into Uni.'

'And now the novelty's worn off?'

She frowns and shakes her head.

'Oh Jamie, come on hon, don't let's go down that road again.'

I try to let the subject drift but I can't help myself.

'I'm not, I won't. It's just that it's so fucken gutless Millie, to be giving up when you're this close to the end. You just don't know how easy you've got it, you...'

'*Jamie,* you just said you wouldn't? Why are you trying to ruin tonight?'

There's anger in her voice now. and I'm wishing I kept my big daft trap shut.

'Soz babes.'

I squeeze her shoulder – all slim and fragile. She sighs, crosses her legs and uncrosses them.

'You're not even wide of the beam though Jamie. You're way way way off course. I mean, I shouldn't *have* to justify myself – not to my best mate, but if you *must* know I shouldn't *be* on this course. What I wanted to do . . .what I *should* be doing . . .'

She hesitates, snorts.

'What I should be doing is sociology.'

'Study of the mind and that?'

'*No!*' She tuts. 'That's psychology.'

I raise an eyebrow and grin, let her know I'm just winding her up and that.

'I mean most of it's theory tripe taught by conceited old cunts who can't be arsed doing their research. Just lock themselves up in their fusty chambers, gobbling up huge sums of grant money and regurgitating other people's work. Gets to me that. But there's some, you know, who are so fucking passionate, so fucking brilliant at what they do. There's this one fella, right, who's spent sixteen years studying the habits of doggers. You should see his thesis. It's staggering.'

'Sounds like a weird cunt to us.'

She elbows us affectionately.

'So why didn't you do that then?' I go.

'Dad.'

'What, he wanted you to pick somet more academic?'

'No! It's dad's subject at Liverpool isn't it? That's what he lectures in, criminology.'

'Well then. Sounds perfect to me. A blueprint for success – help with your homework, sneak previews of exams and that.'

'Yeah and Dad keeping tracks on every thing I do. He's bad enough as it is now. Anyway, it's not called homework anymore, it's called assignments.'

I flick the top of her thigh.

'Well, there must be somewhere else you could've done it?'

'Manchester has a good criminology department.'

'So why didn't you go there? There'd be no shortage of scum to study.'

'Dad.'

'Yeah, well, can half understand where he's coming from. He's a true Red you know, aul' Jerry. Right down to the . . .'

'It's just, I couldn't leave him could I?' she interjects, 'Not after Mum . . .'

She trails off and turns away into the silhouetted land-scape racing past the window. I'm lost for words. Should've seen that coming a mile off.

A silence ensues, separating us again.

We drop the eckies, half an hour before we reach

Llangollen. There's fuck all to do up there by the way
– a decrepit town full of crap boutiques, stuffy tea-rooms
and a couple of arcades jammed with libidinous town-
ies but if you take the A524 and follow it right up into
the Snowdonia mountain range there's this pub over-
looking a lake – all leather couches and log fires and
badgers' heads strewn around the walls, *tons* of draft beers
and a juke box full of aul' classics from the likes of New
Order and Numan.

Passing through the geographic depression of
Llangollen and nothing has changed. It's fucken aayyges
since I last come up here. Going back a good eight or
nine years I reckon, and the only embellishments are an
Indian restaurant, a couple of five-a-side soccer courts,
a Yates' Wine Lodge and the Spa has matured into a
mini Somerfields. Me, Sean and a few of the lads used
to come up here of a Friday for the pure and simple
reason of getting laid. As with most hillbilly towns, the
crumpet have all done the rounds with the locals three
times over by the time they hit fifteen and are just
gagging for a bit of the exotic. Scousers, Mancs, Wools.
Anything but fucken hillbillies. Proper goers as well if
the truth be told, the local skirt. Like fucken battery
hens let loose on a hillside. Aye, there were that bit too
much for us, in fairness. Unnerved us they did. Sixteen-
year-olds with glaring white faces and tight perms flecked
with the cheap gold of bottled peroxide, demanding anal
and gangbangs. Too much la, too fucken much.

We snake higher and higher towards the Snowdonia
mountain range, which lunges towards us at the turn

of a bend, then shrinks back into the sky at the turn of another. Like someone's waving a magnifying glass in front of my eyes. Suddenly a cobalt blue light dazzles out of nowhere. Filth. I pull over. A sweat breaks my forehead. A Volvo estate blares past at ferocious speed, knowing every curve and jut of the road. My heart bangs dementedly. I've never been in any serious trouble with the law and that but I always get a sweat on at the sight of filth. Even when I spot them at the match or walking through the city of a night, I always feel like there's gonna be aggro and that. You hear about it all the time though don't you? About ordinary innocent folk like myself, just walking along, minding us own business and then next minute we're slammed up in a cell being accused of all sorts. Drug dealing, necrophilia, armed robbery . . . I pull off again and I see that Millie is sniggering out of the window, reading us like a book.

Just as the road threatens to fade into a footpath, a badly lit sign for 'Good food, good ale and a warm welcome' swings us sharply into a long winding drive which slices right through the thick of the forest and delivers us straight to The King's Head. It's not changed one bit – right from the cast-iron boot scraper outside the door to the smell of pine leaves and carbon that hangs in the air. It's pure mind blowing, the view from up here. You can see right into the crux of the valley, right down to the lake which is pure glowing in the electric blue hue of the night. You can tell by the colour on that sky that's it's gonna be a fuck of a full moon as well. Wish I'd brought my camera. Pure National Geographic material that is. I tell you, if someone blindfolded you and brought you up here, there's no way you'd know you was in Britain. Canada or Russia or somet. In fact, I'm half expecting to see a bear lumbering towards us. We stand in the car park for a while, in silence, just gazing, soaking it all in, sharing a cigarette and in the midst of all this natural euphoria, it dawns on us that the tablets have shown no signs of life. Not even a glimmer. In all honesty, I'd've been just as made up to've gotten slowly soaked on a few pints of local ale, followed by some tasty pub nosh – gammon and egg or scampi and chips and that, but if it turns out we've been ripped off, it will pure destroy my evening. It's unlikely that Sean would've been handling duff gear though. He picks up in bulk, and no one's stupid enough to try and fuck the Flynns over. Mind you, with the war and that tightening up security . . .

When we walk in, or should I say when Millie walks in it's like a scene from a Western. She brings the whole pub, which is mainly full of aul' men, to a lull. Pints are suspended in mid air, smoke collects in layers above the bar and then slowly the talk starts up again. The Millie effect. Millie takes a pew in a dishevelled leather couch in a secluded corner. Above her a badger's eyes are flickering orange from a roaring fire. I sling my coat over the couch and get the drinks in. The barman who I remember from the last time I was here has not changed one bit. Like everything else in this joint – impervious to time. I order a pint of Stella and a pint of Theakstons for myself and with the change I put a couple of songs on the jukebox – that *Jamming* by Bob Marley and *Crystal* by New Order.

When I return, Millie is singing away, clicking her fingers and sucking hungrily on a cigarette. The pair of us are in a fantastic mood. We take a sup on our pints.

'It's great doing this, just the two of us. Like aul' times innit?'

'Old times? Don't start all that memory lane gadgie stuff on me.'

'You know that's somet I were thinking on before. How I always use the past as a reference point for the present and you use the future.'

'*Reference point!*'

'Well, yeah, you always talk about the things we're going to do or we should be doing and I always talk about the things we've done. I'm just like my aul' man you know. A hopeless nostalgic.'

'I'd say you're finding it difficult to come to terms with the fact that you're about to wave goodbye to your twenties. You're about to wave goodbye to a life.'

'Eh you you fucken ageist. You're not long off twenty yourself and in bird years that's ancient.'

'I'm not arsed though. I'm actually looking forward to growing myself a big wild mot and having a legitimate excuse to watch Frost.'

'I think you're right though, la. I probably *am* going through some kind of premature mid-life crisis. All joking aside, I look in the mirror some days, and fuck, there's no point deluding myself. I look fucking *old* Millie. I do.'

I must admit. I'm half expecting her to challenge us but she don't. So I fucken do look ancient then.

'Did you know that mid-life crisis is just a euphemism for sexual misery?'

She sparks a fag and runs an eye over us and I feel my neck ignite. I can hardly spit a vindication out fast enough.

'Well, there's *no* problem in that department, la.'

And there isn't. It's just what with me doing all that overtime at the mo, and Anne Marie doing earlies, I've, *we've* just not got that burn what we had last year. That's all. But there deffo is no problem.

'Bastard. For all I don't envy being resigned to one pair of tits, and she has got great tits your Missus, I'll give her that, it must be ace having all that sex on tap.'

'It's not just about that though is it Millie hey?'

'Nah. It's about possession. Property. That's what it's about. Fucking ownership.'

'You come up on that tablet yet?'

She lifts her pint to her mouth and stares intently into its mattress of foam.

'It's a great analogy for the nature of relationships, sinking a pint you know?'

'Oh aye, let's have it.'

'Well, you buy it, take it to your table and for a while you enjoy it. The first few sips are fresh and exciting, the next few are comforting and the ones that follow lose their spark and fizz. Your tastebuds gets sluggish. You sling away the dregs and trade the empty glass in for a fresh pint. '

I lean right into her and grin. She pushes me away. She always goes into a big mad one when she's coming up Millie. Fucken things that lil' head's spewed out la!

'I'm more like a yard of meths though me. I'd fucken kill you before you got chance to trade me in.'

She trails off, face stumbling into a reverie. Her

brows knit together and a look of confusion spreads over her.

'What was I saying?'

'Meths. Ownership.'

'Where are we?'

'I don't know where *you* are girl, but I'm in the Kings Head in Wales.'

She sinks back into the couch and her face smashes wide open into a brilliant smile.

'I'm going to write an essay on that. Get me a pen and pad *now*. I can explain the metaphysics of monogamy through the politics of methylated spirit.'

Her eyes do one into the back of her skull and then lunge back demented and pure black.

'Run that by us again,' I say, creasing up.

Her face expands and her jaw begins to tremble.

'Jeeeez! I'm up. I'm fucking up there Jamie'

It takes a bit longer for us to come up, and I just sit back and laugh at her. I'd forgotten that it always hits her three times as hard as anyone else, little waif that she is. Should've just given her the half to begin with. When it does kick in, I'm hovering over a urinal, shaking the dregs of piss from my dick. It doesn't crawl up on us, no warning signs or nothing. Just pure batters fuck out of us. Swipes all thoughts and memory from my head so I don't even know who I am. Just a blank being with two tons of pure lead euphoria charging through my legs and up towards my groin and my guts and my chest – exploding in a kalei-doscope of unbelievable sensations in my head.

Ecstasy, la.

Fucken love it!

Seems like ages before I'm able to make sense of where I am and what's happening. My body's paralysed. That's what's happening. Can't move. I'm standing here with my dick in my hand, which feels fucken lovely if the truth be known, unable to do up my kecks. On top of the world I am.

A man comes in, has a piss and leaves.

Just a blur.

And another one.

Absolutely on top of the fucken world.

My surroundings veer into focus and my limbs begin to feel lighter and lighter 'til they are suddenly springing me over to the sink where I do my trousers up and splash cold water on my face. I gaze into the mirror and my reflection vaults across it and right back again.

I can't remember whether I've pissed or not. I try and piss in the sink but my dick is hard and can't make it's mind up.

I stay in the toilets for a while longer and get my head together. I wait for the euphoria to abate. I'm always like this me, coming up on an eckie. It just knocks us clean out for the first twenty minutes or so and then I'm fine. And I've figured that the best thing to do is just sit back and hand yourself over. Don't try and fight it, or control it or it'll mash your head to pieces. Sit back and enjoy it. It'll tune into your body's natural rhythm when it's good and ready and when it does there's fucken nothing like it in the world.

Ecstaseeeeeey!

I need to be with Millie. I'm so looking forward to

walking out of those doors and seeing Millie's face. I love her I do. I fucken love that girl to bits.

There's no one I'd rather be with, if the truth be known. Even Anne Marie. Nar, would not be right her seeing us like this – all loved-up and with my emotions running amok and that. Thinking of it almost sends us on a downer.

I forget where I am.

I remember.

The toilets are situated at the other end of the pub and I find the journey back a task and a half. I have to walk past the bar which is mad busy with ruddy-faced chaps in flat caps, and concentrate on being straight and not knocking into people like a prick, but everyone seems happy enough. Maybe they're all eckied up too. Millie is sat there with a stupid lockjaw face, tearing a gutted cigarette packet to bits.

'Jesus Jamie! Thought you'd done one. You been spiel-ing your whole life story to some farmer.'

'Had a bit of a mad one in the toilets, but I'm fucken sound now.' I sit down opposite her. 'Are you on to that by the way?'

'What?'

'Just slide your head round there and tell us if I'm seeing things. But it looks like the whole pub is eckied up.'

Millie cranes her neck round and surveys the bar through shuddering eyes.

'I can't see Jamie. Everything's just liquid. Everything's just perfect.'

We sit there for a while, indulging each other, smiling,

smoking, barely lifting our glasses and I'm floored by a big swell of love.

'I fucken love you you know Millie and I'm not just saying it cos I'm on one and that, you're my soul mate you. D'you know that?'

She smiles harder and raises a thumb likes she's too made up to speak or somet and then *Crystal* floats out the speakers and a terrific rush thrashes through us, overwhelming us, disorientating us.

'I fucken told you la, the whole fucken pub is on one! I mean, why the fuck would they have put this on? This is a State tune? D'you remember it?'

The sensations get stronger and stronger, and my head goes all fuzzy and when I look round I see that the whole pub is sliding to and fro. People jutting in and out of their tailbacks wearing crazy clown faces.

Whoah!

Everything snaps back into focus.

I take a sup of my drink and stub my fag out which I've sucked all the way down to the filter. I light another, take a bang on it, and sit back. The sensations abate a little or maybe they don't, maybe my body's just acclimatising to the eckie and that, but whatever it is, I feel more in control. But only for a few seconds, cos then the chorus kicks in and scrapes the skin from the back of my neck and I have to clutch my ears to stop my skull splitting in three. It's too strong this time. I don't like it. Doesn't feel right. It's poisoning my brain, solidifying my blood. Mashed I am. Pure fucken mashed.

★　★　★

I've got to get out of here, get my head together. Get out of here before I lose it completely.

My kite must be exhibiting the full extent of this nightmare cos Millie's suddenly on her feet isn't she? Still grinning but looking right into us analytically. I can't summon the words to tell her how I'm feeling. Mashed, is what I want to say, but I can't. The word is buried deep down in the pit of my throat and will not come out. She squats down in front of us, face blurring over and she asks us if I'm all right.

'I'm fine,' I say but immediately regret saying it. Like it was my last fucken chance of coming clean before I completely lose it. Ah, but this has gone too far now. There's something serious going down with my wiring and my ticker, la. Fuck, I can't die. Not like this. What would our Anne Marie say? And my lovely Mum? Ah fuck James, lad – you soft fucken cunt. You hear about it all the time though don't you? On the news and that – about people who've done tabs for years, think they're immune to everything and then one day their body throws a big mad paddy and just shuts down.

Serial Killer
Club drug claims yet another young life.
Jamie Keeley, 28, of Admiral Street lost his struggle for life, four days after slipping into a coma caused by cerebral haemorrhage. His death is believed to have been caused by the drug ecstasy . . . . . .

I can see it now, front page of the Echo. My Dad coming in from work and finding his son's face sticking out of the letterbox. It'd kill him that. His firstborn. A druggie. And my Mam bawling her eyes out as she goes through my stuff in my room looking for that will I made when I was eighteen and my donor card and then finding all my mags and vids and the dildo I bought Anne Marie for Valentine's Day but were too embarrassed to give her and then she shows my aul' fella and they think it belongs to us. Their first born. A druggie and a fag.

I try to pick my head up from my lap. Millie's hands are suddenly upon us, massaging my thighs, easing my fears and giving us a brilliant lob on but then the music stops and the panic thrashes right back.

I need to get out.

'Just sit down, don't panic Jamie' she says, pushing me back down.

'No, I need to get the fuck out of here, Millie. Done in girl.'

'You'll be fine in a few seconds. You're going through exactly the same as what I was going through before. Just sit back and enjoy it. Don't repress it.'

'Honestly? Were you really feeling like this back there or are you just saying this to stop us going into one?'

'Yes! And you'd fucked off to the toilets. I thought I was going to have to climb out of that window up there cos I couldn't handle walking past the bar! These are really pure tablets, that's all. They're how tablets should be. Just enjoy it baby.'

The panic thaws a little but as soon as I sit down and start concentrating on how to get my head together, I go to bits again. Right, that's fucken it.

'I've got to get out of here Millie. Please. Get us out of here.'

'Jamie? You'll be fine. Here, I'll get you a brandy, that'll sort you out.'

'IF YOU'RE A FRIEND, YOU'LL GET US THE FUCK OUT OF HERE!'

The air is cold and sobering and snaps me from the eckie stupor. We get in the car and recline the seats to their full extent and sledge for a while. Millie's eyes have started to roll a little as though she's about to slip off on one again, but it doesn't seem to bother her when she loses control. I remember in The State, always having to pick her up from the floor and drag her to the dancefloor to stop her from sledging. She would've quite happily've spent the whole night slumped under some table, having her neck massaged by some sweaty hopeful.

She squeezes my hand and mumbles something. I squeeze it back and close my eyes, abandoning myself to the gorgeousness of it all.

She squeezes again, harder.

'Put some music on,' she pleads.

I haul my hand from my lap which is like a slab of lead and flick the radio on. The car is suddenly filled with a rabble of angry Welsh voices. Millie bolts up and shrieks.

'What the fuck?'

She clutches her chest and I roar with laughter.

'Dick head. You've brought us right down. Put some fucking music on before I have a heart attack.'

I laugh even harder.

'Jamie, put the fucking music on. I'm having a heart attack.'

I pull an aul' Ministry album from the dashboard and feed it into the stereo and watch with awe as her body responds to the onslaught of beats. Her kite swoons in dizzy appreciation. The beats acquire a melody and all of a sudden I have a big mad yearning to drive. Into the night. No particular destination. Just snaking through the landscape with this music lunging though us.

My hand's on Millie's lap. I'm rushing madly. The moon's a blue-tinged smudge in the nocturnal pastures of the sky. To the left, Wales speeds past the window. Sheep-strewn fields leak into the silver-blue gulf of the horizon. Turn a bend. Tummy swoops. To the right, ploughed corduroy fields bunch together and hare towards the huge mountains whose asbestos tips are shimmering, melting, sliding beneath the diluted moonlight.

Limbs like liquid.

Eckie love roaring through me. Euphoria sliding this way and that way. No direction. Rudderless desire.

Face suspended in hardened glee. Thoughts enter my head and erupt into fragments of colour. Piano breaks thump the car. The beat kicks in. Pleasure finds a rhythm. Euphoria abates a little. Turn the music up. Massage the melody into Millie's thigh and the throb from her heart slides down to meet it. Beautiful sensations thud through us, pounding our bodies as though we are one.

A main road with cars throbbing in and out of focus. The pleasure is less intense now. The music has detached itself from me so the melody pounds from the speakers and not from my chest. I can't feel my tongue. I pull down the mirror to see if I've bitten it off. It's still there. Millie is awake, her eyes dilated and completely black.

'Welcome back.'

'I'm back,' she says, 'From where though?'

The music becomes a part of me once more, layer upon layer of melodic pleasure mounting in my groin, exploding and solidifying, liquefying and snapping.

Millie is proper out of it now. Her eyes are closed. Eckie dreams flicker her eyelids. She grinds her teeth and clutches my hand, dips in and out of her dream world. A different beat or direction of melody and she'll leap out of her seat, wide eyed, confused. She'll remember and her face will rip into a big lucid grin. She'll enjoy the way music sounds with her eyes open, she'll enjoy the way colour and melody interact in the throes of their altered states. And when the feelings get too intense, her jaw will start to rattle. She'll fight to keep her eyes open but the weight of the euphoria will force them shut once more.

Millie is touching herself. Down there. No two ways about it. She's got her hand in her jeans. Doesn't know she's doing it in all honesty. I try to ignore her which is a task and a half cos this eckie has given us a massive lob on which materialised miles before she started messing with herself by the way but her sitting next to us, doing that, does not help. Not one bit. It's pure agony in fact. I've been dying for a wank ever since we left

The King's Head. I might have to pull over under the pretext of taking a slash in a minute. This is agony. I'm about to explode down there.

I slacken my seatbelt and undo a couple of buttons and I hear my little fella almost sigh with relief. I slip the music up a notch and try and just lose myself to the eckie but I can't stop myself from stealing little looks at her. Ahh, this is fucken sick la. It's incestuous almost. That's as good as my sister sat there. It's YOUR SISTER FOR FUCKS SAKE. The realisation sobers us, brings us right down and I forget why I'm feeling so last with myself but then next thing I'm back up again, falling deeper and deeper into a lagoon of deep blue eckie love where everything feels pure and honest and next thing I'm staring at the jut of her collar bone and the soft milky dip beneath her throat and her tiny pianist's fingers working their magic underneath her kecks which kisses my dick back to life. I badly want to reach across and touch her leg so she can feel as beautiful and perfect as I do but then the music ends suddenly. Millie has propped herself up and is staring right at us with a frightened face. My dick sinks shamefully into my lap.

'Where are we?' she says, clutching my arm, but before I've got time to answer her face yields into a terrific, terrified smile and she's pointing out of her window towards the sea which is black and immense and shimmering under the moon.

Millie

We park up along the sea front. The beach is empty. The clouds have dissolved into the blackness allowing the moon to cast a thick silver scar across the water.

We walk along the beach in silence, oblivious to the cold which causes our breath to spume like car exhausts. We remove our shoes, abandoning our feet to the lovely cold shock of the night sea which is elegiac and docile, just like the moon.

The strong powerful rushes that overwhelmed my body for the last few hours have subsided now, leaving in its wake a smouldering happiness. Things are suddenly lucid and simple. I feel open to long meandering conversations. I want to speak, endlessly, fearlessly about life, about us, about Mum and Uni and Anne Marie and all the things that have for so long loomed so big and frightening but are now so small and penetrable. There's so much I need to say to him right now, but somehow the silence, it says everything and more.

The descending tide forces us back up the beach and we sit against a stray boulder and share a cigarette.

I huddle close to him, hugging his arm and resting my head on his shoulder and I'm hit with such a staggering bolt of completeness that I almost cry.

'Jamie?'

'Yeah baby?'

'That distance between us. I don't know how it happened. But it's gone now hasn't it?'

He doesn't answer and my heart stills for a moment and I feel myself being sucked into the loneliness of the big black night but then he speaks and it starts up again, loud and hard.

'It felt like you'd fell out of love with us?'

'I think I fell out of love with myself. You and Dad. I'd die for you both.'

His grip tightens and I point towards the big old moon which is massive and perfect, and in the distance a harbour glitters like jewels and the sea bounces its iridescent droplets of light towards us and he turns to me with molten black eyes and kisses my forehead, a gentle kiss that seeps through my skin and into my skull and explodes in its crux, a wonderful blast of energy and colour that spills down my throat and into my guts and down to my cunt and limbs till I'm just a huge ball of pleasure and then he turns my head back towards the glittery harbour and the big old moon and says,

'If I could paint our friendship then that's what it would look like.'

The pleasure balloons and balloons, sucking the breath from my lungs and blinding me so all I can see is a brilliant light, drawing me, guiding me to something so powerful and beautiful that I never want to return to anything before it and go to anything beyond. I just want to stay in this light. Stay here forever. Never, ever going back.

Chapter 5

Millie

Bonnie night! My favourite night of the year. Not least because of its magical location on the seasonal landscape – that brief inimitable period where autumn yields to winter, and with the promise of Christmas twinkling on the horizon. But also, for the last five years, Jamie, Billy and their pals have congregated on Sefton Park for the firework display then headed into town for The Big Mad One. The year before last was my favourite year. Jamie and Sean were still living on Parlie. They threw a Pimps and Hookers' theme party after the bonfire and Billy and I came as hookers. His outfit was a lazy collaboration of mine and his mother's wardrobes – white wonderbra, kilt, bedroom slippers and a Crystal Carrington style fur coat. I opted for classic Hope Street garb – Lacoste tracksuit worn two sizes too small with the legs rolled up at the knees, hair scraped back in a vicious high pony, and my face, slubbered in orange foundation. My entrance was one of the most chagrined moments of my adolescence. No one got it except Sean – the rest of them just assumed that a) I had forgotten it was a theme party and b) I had crap dress sense. My embarrassment was shot to bits, however, when moments later Billy lumbered through the door looking like the Tralala from *Last Exit to Brooklyn*.

As with all Sean's parties, there was an abundance of champagne and beak. And Billy and I gorged so much, we spent the bulk of the night marching up and down Percy Street looking for johns. There was nothing particularly momentous about that party, but with hindsight, it was one of the happiest nights of my life. We were all so close back then, such brilliant friends. Even by that Christmas, the gang had shed some of its unity and our Boxing Day lap-dancing bender for which two dozen hand written invitations had been sent out amounted to me, Jamie, Billy and Sean. Jamie was relieved. He doesn't buy into that stag night mentality. He likes to keep things as intimate and low-key as possible. I was gutted.

Since the ecstasy odyssey to Wales, I've led a fairly abstemious life. I've cut back on the booze – a decision that was more or less made for me by the antibiotics (which have slapped all evidence of deviant pursuits from my body) – and I've reinvented myself as the model daughter. I've cooked Dad some amazingly scrummy nosh, sent him off to Uni in ironed shirts and pressed trousers, fixed a leak in the bathroom, cleaned the yard and done the shopping. *And* I've made a huge effort with Jamie – negotiating myself around *his* life, rather than expecting him to fit around my timetable and nuances as and when it suits me. I've adopted a more congenial attitude to his Missus too. Alright, we'll never be lunch buddies, but at least I don't clam up whenever he mentions the M word. If Jamie wants to talk about the gold digging tip rat, I'm not going to pull a face.

My only real shortcoming is a failure to knuckle down to any meaningful work. I've managed to hand in all my overdue assignments but have not as yet made a start on my dissertation. I can't even muster up a proposal. The far-flung ideas I've suggested to Jacko have been rejected for one reason or another. Fifteen thousand words is a fuck of a lot to write about something you don't feel passionate about.

By the time I settle down to some work, it's a quarter past midday. I kick my noggin into gear with a mug of sugary builders' tea then sit cross-legged on the living room floor with my books spread out in front of me. I open a book and try to read but my eyes are drawn towards the window. A late autumn sky hangs raw and blue. I swivel round and away from the vista and try to concentrate on concentrating, but the depth and lustre of the sky is anchored in my mind, triggering an unshakeable restlessness. I fling the book across the floor and pick up another with a more beguiling cover. I flick to a random page. The sentences are long and complex and resist absorption.

Time passes. I lie on my back and slide a hand into my trackie bottoms. I don't *feel* horny. I haven't done for a while but a brisk wank might purge some of this restlessness from my system.

I slump through to the kitchen, make another inky mug of tea, then relocate to Dad's study (a room I am forbidden to enter), on the premise that a studious environment will be conducive to study.

I pick up a pen and try to write something.

Time passes.

I stare at the paper. The paper stares back.

I spin round on Dad's leather chair, pausing at 180 degrees to admire his ravishing collection of books. The room assumes the same methodical carelessness as his University study. His desk is littered with empty cups, unpaid bills, a dirty ashtray and a slew of change strewn haphazardly over unmarked papers, yet his books have been nurtured with a paternal tenderness. I swing back round to the desk and will myself to write. *Anything!* An introduction, a conclusion or a few good sentences. I settle for a smiley face with a speech bubble stemming from its ear. 'Hullo!' it says. 'Hello,' I say back. I designate it a gender by sketching in a stupendous pair of tits.

I go upstairs and sling myself across my bed. I lie there for a while, watching a lone cloud scud across the sky. Dusk sloughs off the last patches of daylight and a drowsy calm swims over me. I close my eyes and fade into slumber.

I wake in a blind panic. My pillow is wet with saliva. The darkness is thicker and it feels like I've slept for hours. I prop myself up and blink my surroundings into focus. I crane my neck round to my bedside table and fumble about for my mobile. I switch it on, anxiously willing the blank screen to light up with text. 5.30. My heart drums with relief. I get up, stretch and play back my answer-phone messages. There are three from Jamie, each a little more urgent than the last, all reminding me that we're meeting at Sean's at 7.00 and to bring a change of clothes for later.

I take a new pack of ciggies from my top drawer, open the window and perch myself on the ledge. The air is clean and cold and the sky aches with stars. A scimitar moon hangs high and aloof. All over the city, the pop and crack of early fireworks puncture the night.

As I'm sitting there, Mum's voice swirls into my conscience. It's the time of year. She's always there in my mind, but things seem so much sorer in autumn. This is the time I associate most with her, with family life. She'd pick me up from school and we'd walk home through Seffie park with the wind and the leaves flickering down from the weathered black trees and a big rusty sun blazing on the edge of the world and when we got home we'd light a fire and set the table and Mum would conjure a big, bubbling casserole. Dad would smile through the door, bringing in the dusk and everything was safe and happy and forever. I wallow in the thought for a while then fling it far, far away. I light a cigarette. I love smoking at this time of the year. Sometimes, it's just a matter of habit, but on nights like this, I want to savour every bite of every pull. There's something about the winter's air that makes them sharper and fuller but they die quicker too, and leave you yearning for more. I toss the stub into Mrs Mason's garden. My lungs are still hungry for the dirty deep buzz and I contemplate lighting another, but the phone rings aggressively downstairs. That'll be Jamie, panicking. I race downstairs, skidding slightly on the last two steps but managing to grab the banister in time to save myself from a serious injury.

'Thank you for calling Millie's Massage Parlour,' I purr. 'Please select one of the following options. Press one to remove my bra. Press two to remove my knickers. Press three to caress my nipples . . .'

'Press four to speak to my daughter?'

'DAD!'

Jamie's familiar laugh cackles down the line.

'Aaaah! Had you for a second there eh, kidder!'

'That's sick that is, Jamie Keeley! That's just – what sort of a man even *thinks* like that!'

He sounds sheepish.

'Arrr, ay! Don't be like that, Mill – not tonight! Just like, I seen your aul' fella this morning, passed him on Prinnie. That's how the idea come to us.'

'I see. Well now you put it like that, I can appreciate all the delicate prior planning that must've gone into it . . .'

He quits while he still can.

I'm half way back up the stairs and the 'phone goes again. It's Dad. My tummy just caves. I know exactly what he's ringing about.

'What are your plans for tonight poppet?'

'Why?' I ask, trying to muffle my despondency.

'I thought we could go down to the Docks. Just you and your old fella?'

'Could do,' I say, 'But didn't they have their display at the weekend?'

'Nope. Checked in the Echo. It's tonight. How about we do that and then I'll treat you to a spoilt supper at L'Alouette.'

'Ah that's just lovely.' I say.

'So I'll pick you up around sevenish?'

'Yeah, seven's fine.'

'Then why do I suddenly feel like I'm trying to sell you on the idea? Have you made other arrangements?'

'No, don't be silly.'

'What's with the hard-done-to tone of voice then?'

'Time of the month.'

'Hmmm. Not convinced but I'm not going to deny that I'm made up to be going out with my little girl tonight. We'll have fun. We always do. I'll see you at seven. Wrap up. It's freezing.'

I sink down to the floor and sit there in the darkness, listening to the tick tock of the clock from the lounge and the crack and snap of the radiators as the boiler begrudgingly rises from slumber. A damp draft staggers listlessly through the hall finding every recess and creaky hollow. I sit there a while longer, long enough to feel the blackness soften and swell with the rising heat and long enough to hear the clock ding six times and then I vault up and pick up the receiver. I punch in his number but kill the call just before the ringing tone kicks in. I do this three more times but then on the fourth, take a deep swig of air and let it ring out.

'Dad?'

'Yep?'

'What time did you say you were picking me up?'

'Seven, but it's looking more like half past now.'

'Ok.'

'That all?'

'Yep.'

'See you later then.'

'No, wait,' I splutter. 'Da-ad?'

'Ye-es?'

'You know tonight.'

'Ye-es.'

'Would you be disappointed if I gave it a miss?'

'Ahhh. Now we're getting somewhere. I kind of guessed you'd made arrangements with your pals. I was just being selfish.'

'No it's not *that*,' I say, suddenly mowed down by guilt, 'It's just that I've been a bit of a slattern where my works concerned and I've got a bit behind with one of my essays, so I was . . .'

'Say no more. If I don't see you later this evening, come meet me for lunch tomorrow yeah?'

'I will, but Dad you're wheezing you know.'

'I know.'

'You smoke too much.'

'You drink too much.'

'Love you!'

'Absolutely, adore you!'

I shower, slip into my favourite Diesel jeans, throw on one of Dad's jumpers, brush my hair, put on Dad's LFC bobble hat, moisturise my face, add a lick of make up and douse myself in one of the many Unisex perfumes we share. I select my glad rags for later – a black strapless dress, some MiuMiu kitten heels and a fake fur jacket I slotted from Oxfam. I bung them in an M&S freezer bag and set off with a spring in my step. I pull my hat down over my ears and throw my hands in my pockets. Everything is just tickety boo.

★   ★   ★

All around Mossley Hill the streets are dotted with small bonfires, some fresh and furious, others smouldering with a lazy amber flush. It's too early to go to Sean's, so I divert to the bonfire at the back of The Allerton Arms. It's a strange little barrio this, a tiny council estate full of North and South enders, regarded by the wealth that girdles it as the burst appendix of L18. You're forever hearing urban myths from freshers in the nearby halls of residence about little urchins sat round injecting heroin, ferocious girl gangs and a Rag and Bone man that sells Bang and Olufsen TVs. The reality is a placid if run-down estate comprised mainly of single mothers and old fellas.

The bonfire is roaring wildly, flames whooshing up, clinging onto air currents and dancing dangerously with surrounding trees. Fireworks hiss and spit aloft. Catherine wheels spin and spew forth lurid sprays and rockets tear the night vault with their blazing egress. Just as you can judge a neighbourhood by its canine residents, you can also judge one by its bonfire. There are prams, tyres, an ironing board, magazines, clothes and everything imaginable, stuffed into the bonfire, emanating from the shell of a burnt-out Ford Capri. The air is baked with the toxic bite of burning plastic. Everyone is drinking and laughing and dancing to chart music booming from a couple of speakers placed within dangerous proximity of the roaring fireball. Three young scals check me with lascivious eyes. I flash them a smile and they shuffle nervously, grinning among themselves.

All at once hundreds of fireworks riot across the night sky and the revellers recoil in a gasp of awed applause.

I sidle up to a shell-suited family, wanting to be part of it all.

Suddenly, I feel a flick against my ear and my hat's gone. I spin round to see a tight knot of diminutive tracksuits weaving through the crowd. They vault in and out of sight for a moment before disappearing from view. The shell suits exchange amused glances. I skulk off, deflated and in need of a large shot of something.

I tailgate an old man into the main reception of Sean's block of flats then take a lift to the top floor. There are three doors and I cannot for the life of me remember which is Sean's. I take a lucky guess. Sean answers the door, bare chested and rubbing a towel through his hair. He seems a little startled.

'How did you get up?'

'Sorry! I should have buzzed. I sneaked in with one of your neighbours. Am I too early?'

'No, don't talk soft, come in, come in. I was just hoping to give the flat the quick once over 'fore your Royal Highness arrived.'

I follow him into the living room, my eyes pinned to his broad athletic back. His flat is large, airy and aspires to minimalist cool.

'What's changed?' I ask, flumping down onto the sofa, 'Looks completely different in here.'

He shrugs his shoulders, eyes raking over me for a second. He flings the towel to the floor then disappears into the kitchen. He returns with a bottle of champagne and two glasses.

'You've had Carol Smilie in here.'

He pours me a glass and hands it over. Cristal. Wouldn't be bringing *that* out for the lads. The bubbles spill onto my fingers which are still stained with ink from this afternoon. I twist them away from his view.

'I wish. That is one beautiful Judy that is, la. Beautiful.'

Boo-ri-full, is how he says it. He sits way back into the sofa, crosses his legs faux-casually and eyes me now with ferocious intensity.

'What's changed about *you*, anyway?'

I feel my throat tighten. Sean's a prick but he's a good-looking bastard – and he's fucking intimidating, too. I'm willing Jamie and co. to ring on that buzzer *now*! I make self-deprecating gashes to indicate eyeliner, lipstick, make-up and attempt to lighten the atmosphere.

'Carole Smilie, eh? Yeah, suppose I'm having that. A few nips and tucks here and there, she'll still be worth a wank. Wouldn't fancy going down on her though, eh? Not at her age.'

Sean's not quite so comfortable, now. I can see it – it's a real effort for him to stay languid.

'How d'you mean, kidder? Boss-looking girl, she is! Age ain't got nothing to do with it.'

'For sure, for sure – but when a woman hits forty she kind of tastes different down there, don't you think? Must be something to do with hormones, change of life and all that. You know, marriage counsellors put so much emphasis on the psychology of relationships when accounting for infidelity, but I reckon, that *that* is the prime causal factor for affairs.'

'Fuck you on about, girl?'

'Cunnilingus. It can break even the most steadfast of marriages.'

'Just run that by us again!'

'Think about it. Divorce affects most couples between the ages of thirty-five and fifty yeah?'

'And?'

'Well, man goes down on young bride. Young bride is happy. Young bride hits forty. Cunt starts to fester. Husband goes on cunni strike. Sex is reduced to basic and functional intercourse. Wife feels fusty and unsexy, denies husband of intercourse. Husband gets frustrated. Husband has affair.'

''kinell Millie, la! You're not a full shilling, you!'

'So everyone keeps telling me.'

He tops up the bubbles, pulls up a leather beanbag and settles opposite me. I decide I'll flatter him a bit.

'So? What did all this cost, then? Or did some hopeful little hireling acquire it for you?'

A smile tugs at the corner of his mouth and opens it wide.

'There's nothing new in here, girl. Just altered the lighting and shifted the furniture around and that.'

'Well *that* certainly wasn't here last time I came.'

I nod towards an ugly ebony sculpture of a genderless child.

'Oh, that little fella. Got that from an artist mate of mine down in London. What d'you think?'

'Nasty. Cheap. Vulgar.'

'You'll get on like a house on fire then.'

I stick my tongue out.

'What you doing knocking around with *sculptors* anyway, Sean Flynn?

'My mate and that, isn't he? Met him at that Home. Good lad, he is.'

'He sounds it.'

'Pierrot and that, the sculptist lad . . .'

'*Pierrot?*'

'He told us it's got hidden meanings and what have you.'

'Really?' I say, fighting back a grin.

'Oh yeah – like, he's left its bits out and that so's we can make our own minds up.'

He slumps back defiantly, waiting to be challenged.

'Sorry – about what?'

'*You* know,' he blushes. 'He left it without no thingio so's we can half sort of put our own meaning into it and that, depending how we're feeling. Like somedays I calls him Jimmy and somedays I calls him Shelley.'

'Right,' I say with big mock eyes. 'That's *so* clever! Very postmodern.'

He's delighted. Mad to think of thuggish Sean getting mugged by a sculptor's bullshit, but God moves in mysterious ways.

'Is though, innit?'

'I mean not just because it gives the viewer a heightened sense of autonomy, but because the artefact itself *transcends* gender altogether. It resists categorisation, bypasses the modernist mode of thinking wouldn't you say?'

'Oh yeah. Is right. Deffo and that.'

He eyes his androgynous friend with animosity. We

sit there in silence for a few seconds, then I relieve him from the ordeal by changing the subject. *Pierrot*, by the way!

'How's business?'

'Chocka,' he says, reverting to his usual overweening self. 'Barely enough hours in the day, truth be known. What with the new Sushi bar and that – fucken done in, I am. Did I tell you I've opened another salon up on Smithdown?

'Anne Marie's gaff?'

The words have slipped out before I even think. The smile drains from his face and for a fleeting moment, I feel the same crippling fear of an animal ensnared by it's predator – but then the grin returns, bigger, bolder and he starts talking to me *so* casually.

'Who told you that?'

'Dunno', I bluster. 'Just heard she was going to be looking after the new place for you.'

'Looking after it?'

'Managing it. I heard she was going to be the manager, like.'

'Anne Marie?'

He grins his big bold grin again and shakes his head in mock disbelief. He gets up and disappears into the kitchen and I down the bubbly in one, in an attempt to numb myself to the surge of uneasiness I've poured into the room.

It was Billy who told me. I met him after lectures – we went for Dim Sum. He'd been malingering around town all day, drinking like a paraffin. He finds it painful at the best of times to keep a secret Billy, and with two vats of lager gushing through his veins, it was a handicap he couldn't manage a minute longer. He had to unload. When I walked into the Mandarin that night he was like a kid who's dying for the toilet. He could hardly wait for me to sit down and order a Tsing Tao.

'Get a load of this', he said, jabbing his fork at me. 'You'll never guess what I just found out . . .'

And with a swift glance either side, he informed me in a conspirational whisper that his future sister in law not only has a demon beak habit herself, but has been enlisted by the Flynns to help run their empire. Billy's not arsed about her – said that in a weird way he's got a sneaking respect for her, for being *so* fucking stony cold ambitious. But he doesn't want anyone making a cunt out of Jamie, least of all his future wife and he's certain Jamie knows *nothing* of all this and he's ready to go round there and tell him everything. I surprised myself by talking him out of it – not out of any regard for Anne Marie, but because I know how stories get around in this city. An ice cream man can become a drug baron in the space of an afternoon and I told Billy that if he's going to tear the arse out of his brother's world he'd better make double sure of his facts first.

Sean returns, composed and moody, now. He cuts out a couple of ample lines. I wait, fearful he'll press me further about Anne Marie. He doesn't. He gestures to the beak and my heart leaps – Bonnie Night has started! I take a note from my bag, roll it into a perfect cylinder and swoop. My nose is stuffy and it takes two or three attempts to clean the table, but I feel the buzz immediately.

'Wow. Nice gear.'

'Clean, innit?'

'Yeah,' I say, topping up our champagne. 'No edge at all.'

We clank glasses. He stands, and pads over to an expensive looking sound system. I watch him all the way, watch his lithe, prowling movements – graceful, yet fearsome.

He feeds *Norah Jones* in and skips straight to 'Feelin' the Same Way'. I peel my fake fur off, sag down in my seat and let the music wash over me. I allow my eyelids to sink down for a while and when I open them again I catch him roaming my body. My cunt tingles and I feel my cheeks flush over.

Okay, Thing One – no way in the world am I attracted to Sean Flynn, right? But Thing Two – there's no denying he has one of the most beguiling faces I've ever seen. And that's not just the beak talking. His face is bewitching. I could stare at it for hours. It's his eyes – big brooding pools of mystery that can flame with such yearning, such intensity, yet with the blink of an eyelid abate into vacant recesses of tissue and matter. There's hatred in those eyes too, and when he's been drinking, his pupils contract into demented, dangerous pinpricks. But to be sat within such proximity of such impossible physical architecture floods my cunt with a woozy warmth – like pissing in the cold sea.

'Just out of interest,' he says, over-concentrating on the small mountain of powder before us. He sifts and chops and sifts again, then looks up at me. He smiles. 'Who spieled you all that shite about Anne Marie?'

'Fuck – can't remember!' I try to disguise my anxiety behind a ditzy smile. 'Is it important?'

He makes a big thing of smiling kindly, this time letting himself twinkle in unison.

'Not in the slightest,' he says, raising both palms to let me know the subject's closed. Slightly too eager, I reach for the bottle and pour the remains of the champagne. To compensate for my haste and my awkwardness, I raise my glass.

'To the lovely Anne Marie.'

'To the lovely Anne Marie,' he says. He swooshes the bubbles through his teeth and just sits there, watching me.

Our eyes linger in each other's and a sexual friction cracks wide open. I don't see Sean. Just a pair of savage eyes and perfect features. My head battles, a moral, deep-rooted instinct to walk away, flailing in the face of raw sexual desire. I take a deep gulp of air and feel his eyes pulling me towards him. He gets up, comes and sits next to me.

I flicker my eyes over his face, pausing at his lips. Moist and full and throbbing with desire. His lips. This is so wrong. I can't stop myself. I edge closer and surrender my mouth in utter despair.

Chapter 6

Jamie

Weird one, la. It's like we'd just walked right it on something. Now Sean is the last lad on earth that our Millie'd go for, but I know I'm not imagining it. The pair of em are acting double shady. I'll leave it for a while mind you – wait til she's had a gargle and that later on. I'll glean it out of her and I tell you now, I don't care who the fuck his brothers are, if he's laid a finger on that girl, he's dead.

I rally the troops and gets em moving.

Millie

Seffie park is pulsing with studes. A blur of bobble hats, southern accents and fluorescent sparklers. In spite of the fact that Billy has coloured his hair a garish blonde and Sean's two sidekicks Kev and Mally look like Big Issue vendors, I feel dead proud to be out with my pals. That incident with Sean, whatever it was, has faded along with the beak high. Every now and then, a furtive glance from him will drag it from my subconscious and I'll shudder. There is and never will be an *Us*.

We find Liam and his wife up near the hotdog stand.

Their son, Tony, is staring in mute amazement at the spectral showers above. Liam greets Jamie and Billy with bear hugs and Sean with a cursory slap on the back. Kev and Mally linger back, stiff and nervy – he always has that effect on blokes, Liam.

'You know Jackie don't you?' Liam goes, slipping an arm around me and ushering me towards her.

We exchange self-conscious smiles and I feel a lump of guilt lodge in my throat. Since the night I saw Liam in the Living Room, I've thought about him quite a lot. Stupid, harmless fantasies that aren't really to do with sex. Just me and him walking along the Dock front. Talking. Flirting. Getting to know each other.

'Hi, how's it all going?'

'Ah not bad love,' she says, 'And you? Have you finished with that Uni yet?'

'No,' I say, plaintively, 'final year.'

When you see Jackie you think of sucking babies, pendulous breasts and home-cooked dinners. She has warm, genteel features and a manner that is as effort-lessly compassionate as it is asexual. Kissable not fuck-able. She hasn't let motherhood pull her down though. She's looked after her figure through brutal aerobic workouts and pilates and her Clinique complexion is devoid of a blemish or wrinkle. She knows how to get the best out of that amiable reprobate of a husband of hers too. Ah, she'd probably be quite tickled if she knew I'd been thinking about him.

The night vault rests for a while and Tony springs to life, shifting his weight to the balls of his feet, and hurling a fusillade of punches which fall inches from my tummy.

'Ey, ey stop that will you,' Liam says, pulling him away from me, 'Remember what we said about all that? A time and a place ey son?'

I smile. Tony juts his chin out and folds his arms. I ruffle his hair.

'Neat little left upper you've got there Tony,' I say and slide my eyes up to meet Liam's. He holds my gaze for a moment and I wonder if I fancy him or if I'm just drunk enough to feel big feelings. The spell is broken by the lunge of Tony's fists as he shuffles around me, ducking and dodging like a stalked fly. Liam shakes his head despairingly.

'O'Malley's over there with that new lad,' he goes, 'Thingio. What's his name. Hornby. Must've seen him in the Echo last week?'

My heart sinks a little. The whole boxing thing has just gone stale on me. I loved it to begin with when O'Malley had the place on Granby Street. There was only a dozen of us back then, mainly friends of Jamie and Sean. Then he moved to a bigger venue in town and installed mirrors, running machines and a sauna and it quickly became a melting pot for doormen, mock gangsters and brassy women with He-man physiques. At Granby, I was the only girl, which meant I got to train and spar with the boys. I was loved and utterly indulged. Women though, they're vicious and ruthless – no attention to defence or footwork. All they're bothered about when they step into a ring is how quickly they can smear their opponent's nose across their face.

★ ★ ★

A belligerent succession of snaps and bangs signals the start of the main display of the evening. All heads lurch skyward and the night throbs in a thousand different colours. A gusto of applaud and drunken revelry follows. Students whoop and cheer loudly, hugging each other and grinning like phoneys. I detach myself, tilting my neck as far back as possible to catch the last dregs of my can. I let it fall discreetly to the floor and fire up another cigarette. Jamie quickly materialises with another cold can.

'Twice in one day, hey?' he goes, snapping the ring pull off for me.

'Uh?'

'Just seen your aul' fella there, queuing for a bevvy. With some girl. Here y'are, there he is!'

He points to a throng of people on the other side of the fire. A splinter of fear worries its way under my skin. Dad. I know it – I just know this is going to crush me. My eyes flit from face to face and lock right into him. He jerks away quickly, as though he hasn't seen me and tips his head towards a burst of colour in the sky that belongs to some other distant display. But his face is a dead give-away. He's been sussed. Before I can stop him, Jamie is trotting over. They embrace blokishly and laugh about something. Jamie swings round and points over to me. Dad crouches down and lifts his hand to his eyes as if trying to seek me out. He throws me a wave. I know what's going to happen before it even happens. A smiling radiant blonde skips up to Dad and hands him a hotdog. She kisses him affectionately on the nose. She's younger than me. Dad scratches the back of his head nervously and casts a quick glance in my direction. The girl is one of his first years — tall, blonde and pathetically pleased to be here, with him. She's making a big thing of being childishly, girlishly thrilled by a firework display. She's hunching her shoulders and simpering at Jamie. I want to launch a rampant rocket through her face. There's nothing weird about lecturers hanging out with their students. John Fenney takes his Gender in Literature mob on mad benders to Amsterdam, but it's something Dad has always snubbed.

'It's just not professional,' he'd say. 'How can you make an objective decision on a paper if you know the student intimately? Your students may *like* you more if they see you drunk, but they will respect you less.'

Dad shifts about awkwardly. Jamie tries to beckon them both over but Dad shakes his head and taps his watch. He throws me another wave and then disappears into the crowd. The girl gives me this look, and follows him like a puppy. I want to bite her face off.

Jamie jogs back, grinning apologetically.

'I did invite them over you know, but he said he was running late for something and that. I think he was a tad embarrassed.'

'He's well trained, my Dad. He knows better than to thrust students in my direction.'

'Yeah, but you'd make an exception for his bird wouldn't you?'

Not even by then am I prepared for the sting of hurt and bitter envy these words cause me. His bird. My Dad.

Back at Sean's, there's a mad scramble to use the bathroom. Jamie and Sean insist on performing their ablutions for the third time today and Mally and Kev remonstrate loudly against Sean's bedroom on the grounds that the mirrors are deceptively unflattering. Billy's decided he doesn't like his shoes and he's legged it back home for his Patrick Cox faves. I change in the kitchen. I've never felt comfortable in dresses – they render me feminine and vulnerable. I regret my choice of outfit but I'm too inebriated to throw a tantrum. I use the kitchen window as a mirror and dress as though a hidden camera is filming me, peeling off my clothes in a seductive manner, and lingering naked for a while before I pour myself into the dress. I smear on layer upon layer of black eyeliner and charcoal eyeshadow and smother my lips in two coats of red red lipstick. I step into my heels, run a hand through my hair and prance around the kitchen, pouting my lips, jutting out my hips and tossing back my hair like a disaffected drag queen. I open up the fridge which is one of those big swanky Smeg contraptions and pull out more champagne. I guzzle wholeheartedly, produce a very expensive belch then give my hidden camera the finger. I cork the bottle with a piece of scrumpled up kitchen roll and return it upright to the fridge. When I walk into the lounge, they've all changed and Kev is chopping out rows of white substance with a frantic earnestness. Different patches of aftershave conflict in the air. Jamie and Mally wolf-whistle in unison. Kev pauses and looks up. His eyes flicker seductively over my body and then he's back to the beak. I flash them a quick, coy smile and sit down beside Jamie who is wearing a grey shimmery turtle neck shirt. He looks clean and handsome. Kev and Mally look hideous. Kev is wearing a black Lacoste jumper four sizes too big for him, so that the neckline drags across the goosey white scrawn of his neck. Mally, although his outfit is sleek and composed, looks as though he is slowly decomposing. His face is streaked with a yellow nervous sweat. Almost as though his liver is mouldering, poisoning his whole body from inside to out. The pair of them are more mates of Sean's than Jamie's. Historical circumstances should have naturally thrust them apart but Sean just can't resist the symbiotic relationship they share. He provides them with beak and gratis entry into clubs and they afford him demigod status through cringing feats of sycophancy. It works.

Sean walks into the lounge, the top few buttons on his shirt undone, revealing a healthy chink of golden down. He looks right into me, gauging my reaction. His eyes are bold, lascivious and scarce of a blink. They scorch the air between us. I stare back neutrally, and for a moment he seems almost crestfallen. Taking a note from his pocket, he rolls it up with an effortless dexterity and hands it to Mally who hoovers up as much as his right nostril will allow in one sweep. Kev goes next, followed by Jamie who snorts with an exaggerated alacrity. He passes the note to me, but I decline and produce my own apparatus – a rolled up business card for Sean's salon.

The beak hits me straight away. It doesn't so much give me a high as it zaps the drunkenness away. I feel gregarious and magnanimous now, especially towards Sean. I tell him that I love his shirt. He drops his chin to his chest, eyes it up and down then informs me diffidently that it is a Donna Karan and he has one exactly the same in navy. He asks me if navy would complement his outfit better. I screw my face up this way and that way in a mock display of deliberation and then smile affirmatively. He takes the shirt off, tosses it over the back of a chair and disappears into the bedroom.

Mally and Kev can hardly spit their words out fast enough. Like kids on speed. And the fluorescent yellow sweat on Mally's face is starting to glow. No sooner has he wiped away one waxy layer with the sleeve of his shirt does another burst forth. His pupils are wide and wild and have swallowed the irises whole. I wonder if this is what people look like before they spontaneously combust. I saw this documentary once. It really freaked me out. Bodies melted down to the pelvis, lying forlorn in doorways, kitchens and on the stairs. Imagine coming home and finding your partner's legs on the floor in front of the TV. Perfectly unblemished. Still in a skirt and slippers. And where the torso and head should be, just a heap of ashes. Not even a rib cage or a skull. Just pure ash. I didn't sleep for weeks after seeing that. Every time I got palpitations, or I felt a little bit hot, I'd convince myself that I was about to implode. That my body was involuntarily mutating into a self-lighting furnace. That one day I would end up as an ankle which Dad would find festering in his study.

I tune into their conversation which is rudderless, like they're just spurting out every thought that rolls into their head and trying to procure some sort of discussion from it. Subjects which have absolutely nothing in common just glide into one another.

Beak has the exact opposite effect on Jamie. It silences him. He goes into himself, becomes a spectator. Just sits there, riveted, with a blissfully sanguine grin splashed across his face. I light a cig and we share it, inhaling deeply, kissing it quickly down to the stub and the nicotine and the beak beat my bowels to life. I race to the bathroom, passing Sean in the corridor. He's changed his shirt. He tosses me a quick nervous smile and when I open the bathroom door, I know why. It hums of shit. I pinch my nose, cushion the seat with bog roll and empty my bowels in one violent movement. I feel a stone slimmer. I check the contents of the toilet before flushing and feel gratified by the amount of toxins my body has disposed of. I wash my hands and spray the room with Calvin Klein. When I return to the living room, they're up and wired and raring to go.

We pull up outside Jamie's and Sean instructs the cabby to sound the horn a couple of times. The metronic throb of the diesel prises open curtains where televisions beat out their sickly light. I think about all the life going on beyond the cathode blue glow. Maelstroms of worries and ravaged dreams. Jamie and Billy grew up behind one of those windows.

'Fucken useless your brother,' Sean says, shaking his head, 'Worse than a fucken Judy. Go and get him will you?'

Jamie rolls his eyes gamely and hops out. I don't

want to be left in the cab with these three. I follow Jamie.

'Ay, where d'you think *you're* going?' Sean spits, accusingly.

'Say hello to the oldens.'

'Arr ay Millie, get back in will you. We've not got time for all that.'

I shrug my shoulders and turn on my heels.

A mob of young scals huddle a fire they've made in a metal drum. A couple of them slug cider from a bottle. They assemble into a neat line when they see us approaching, arching their backs, folding their arms and sporting choirboy smiles. Beyond them, on Jamie's wall, a girl sits smoking; fantastic little snarl on her face. We walk past the row of lads and I brace myself for some sort of boorish comment.

'Help the guy!' they chant in unison.

'Where's your guy?' I ask

'Down the knocking shop,' the oldest scoffs. His accomplices giggle loudly. The girl snarls on.

'Sorry boys, you know the rules, no guy, no penny.'

'Arr come 'ead, just give us a quid will you?'

Jamie is already half way up his path, shaking his head, muttering to himself.

'You should be in bed,' I say, quickening my pace to catch up with him.

'That an offer?' They all laugh again. 'Actually, you're not my type, girl.'

The snarl on the girl's face opens up into a smile. She's no more than fourteen. Plain common face with a graceless shock of yellow hair. But the tits, the tits are humongous. I try a seductive wink on her but it just bats straight through her. Shame, really.

The Keeley's live in one of those houses where the front door opens up into the living room and the first thing I see when I walk through the door is Mr Keeley sitting in front of a three-bar fire and the regional news flickering across his face. A billow of blue smoke sways above him. My tummy flips out with warm nostalgia when I see him. His face is ravaged and lined, and speaks eloquently of a life of hard work and delicate indulgence. His eyes are still bright and young and shine with an imperishable buoyancy that is replicated exactly in his sons' eyes.

'Millie!' He sits up, twinkling at me. 'I was just thinking about you girl. There's been a thing on the news about young girls like yourself drinking too much and that. EUNICE? Our Millie's here.' He calls into the kitchen but his voice is drowned out by the vicious hammering of a washing machine.

'Yeah, says them students are the biggest risk group, especially girls like. They're drinking over twelve times the recommended daily units apparently. Sclerosis of the liver and all sorts before they even hit twenty-one.'

He gets up and presents his lips, misses my cheek and lands a kiss of sorts on my nose. His shirt is unbuttoned to where the gentle swell of his belly begins. A soft blokey odour fans out from his chest.

'It's good to see you anyway. I were only saying to our Billy the other day that you hadn't been round for a while. Thought you'd fallen out with us.'

'Ah, sorry,' I say, flopping my head guiltily on his

shoulder, 'I've walked past a few times on the way back from Uni, but . . . well I'm here now anyway. Why don't you come into town with us for one?'

Beyond him, Jamie shakes his head and mouths a big belligerent NO.

'Or even better, why don't you and I go out next Saturday? What about that Cain's house, the brewery tap you keep telling me about?'

'The Grapes?'

'*That's* the one. We could start there, walk up to The Nook, have a couple in there, then if we're still thirsty we could stumble along to The Pineapple. Whisky doubles for a pound before seven.'

'Bloody hell Millie, you'll make someone a fine wife one day.'

'So I'll come for you at eleven next week?'

Jamie is tapping his watch madly, making eyes at me.

'I'll let you know. I'll have to consult with the Boss first.' He flicks his eyes over his head towards the kitchen.

'Ah, piece of cake, Mr Keeley. Tell her we're going shopping for her Christmas present.'

'Oh aye? And what do I tell her when I staggers in with no shopping, stinking of ale?'

'Won't matter by then, will it? Not to us, anyway!'

'You're too much you are — too much!' he says, shaking his head affectionately, 'I don't know how your aul' man copes. Eh James — go and pour us a couple of Scotches will you, son. Just frighten mine with a drop of lemonade will you and while you're there tell your Mam there's someone here to see her.'

James? Since when did Mr Keeley start calling him James?

'Sorry Dad – no time for drinks. We've got a cab running outside. We've only stopped off to pick up Billy. He calls up the stairs, 'Aye soft lad, are you ready?'

'Billy's not here son. He's been and gone.'

'What d'you mean he's not here? Where is he then?'

'Don't ask us lad. He was talking to that soft arse on his phone, what's his name?'

'Arr-ay! What a knob. Come 'ead, Millie. I'll see you later Dad.'

'Aye-aye – you not going to say hello to Anne Marie, then?'

A delicious silence fills the room. A nauseous tingling rises in my stomach and stops in my throat. Half trepidation, half excitement.

'Anne Marie? Is she *here*?'

'Yeah, she's in the kitchen with your Mam. Being measured her up for her wedding dress and that so you better knock 'fore you . . .'

Jamie flashes me a troubled glance. I pretend not to see it.

'Babes? Tell Sean I'll be out in a mo,' Jamie interjects. 'Don't let him go without us. I'll just say hello to the Missus and then I'll be out.'

His eyes practically spit me out of the door. It's quite obvious what's happened. He's not told her he's going out tonight. Probably fobbed her off with some half-arsed story and she's smelt it minging a mile away. So she's turned up at his unannounced, with some lame excuse about wedding preparations – the devious bitch.

Not that *she* would have been content with Seffie Park, Lady fucking Penelope. Would have regarded it as an insult. She would've wanted to be taken to some flashy display, throbbing with local celebrities, footballers and their tarts in leather coats freezing their plastic tits off. Finding him here in his glad rags is bound to spark a violent altercation. Finding *me* here dressed like a vamp is like dropping a nuclear bomb. And didn't Mr Keeley just call me 'Our Millie?' Delicious! The Saint in me is imploring me to walk out the door, quickly, and help lessen his chastisement. The Judas in me however, has other plans.

'I haven't even said hello to your Mum,' I say, with all the coy innocence I can muster. The washing machine starts to slow.

'*I'll* do that. Just GO AND GET IN THE CAR.'

The cycle finishes and the kitchen falls silent. The low drone of the television is not enough to absorb Jamie's rant. Mr Keeley frowns at him.

'Sorry,' he says, dropping his voice to an almost inaudible whisper, 'Didn't meant to shout. I'm just peeved with our Billy. That's all.'

The horn sounds from outside and I give Mr Keeley a valedictory hug, making sure my enthusiastic pleas for a drinking spree are soon heard from the kitchen. He squeezes me tightly and releases me with a contrite smile. I stare at Jamie. Guilt leaks from his face. I give him an injured snort and walk towards the door.

Too late.

Anne Marie bursts into the lounge in a white flannel dressing gown. In a series of montage cuts, her face passes from shock to bemusement to anger. She glowers at Jamie and then at me and then back at Jamie. I smile back, antagonistically. Stiffly, she lowers herself onto the sofa, still holding Jamie's gaze, her mouth like a slit. The same sofa that Jamie and I have curled up on many a night, watching videos, drinking wine from tumblers, arguing about the impossibility of monogamy, musing over memories, laughing, rolling cigarettes, trying to stretch the night out forever. I've never come face to face with Anne Marie in the Keeleys. It's something I always thought would flatten me. But is hasn't. Not me anyway. If anyone's hurting, it's her. And she's not as pretty as I remember her, either. Without the make-up and the sheen of a new hair do, she's nothing really. Trash in fact.

Mrs Keeley appears with a tape measure in her hand, a big smile annexing her motherly face.

'Hello Millie, love. I *thought* that was you I could hear before. Thought I was going round the bend!'

'Hello,' I say, planting a kiss on her cheek, 'We just popped in on our way to town to pick Billy up but he's already left.'

'He didn't mention anything to us did he Antony? Just dashes in, sees we're up to our eyes in wedding malarkey and he's gone! Can I get you a drink?'

'I've already offered,' pipes up Mr Keeley, 'There's a taxi waiting outside, better let them go, eh?'

'Yeah, come on Jamie,' I say tugging on his arm. 'Valuable drinking time you're depriving me of.'

Anne Marie stares at him, unable to absorb precisely what's happening, here. I'm loving it. He releases himself from my grip and bends down to kiss her. She jerks away from him.

'Look – why don't you stay here tonight?' he says softly, 'I won't be long. Wait up for me.'

'Don't you worry about her, son. We're watching *Key Largo* tonight after I've got her fitted, aren't we hon? Go on you scamps. Off with you!'

Anne Marie forces a smile for Mrs Keeley then abandons it as she turns back to face Jamie.

'Enjoy your *lads* night out, James.' she says, hissing out the word lads.

'*We* will,' I say cheerfully.

I give Mr and Mrs Keeley farewell hugs and peck Anne Marie on the cheek. She's too stunned to stop me.

Mrs Keeley smiles fondly and obliviously at the pair of us, but her husband has cottoned on.

'Have fun,' he says, smuggling a smirk beneath his moustache, 'You're only young once!'

Ah but Mr Keeley, if you only knew how happy you've just made me!

Outside the scals have dispersed into the night, but the fire still roars from the metal drum. We walk back to the cab, side by side, in silence, then just before I open the cab door, Jamie puts his hand on my shoulder and swings me round.

'Look, about before . . .'

'Forget it.'

'No, come on babes, let's sort it out before we head into town.'

'There's nothing to sort out. I'm fine. Honest.'

Sean raps his knuckles against the window, mobile phone glued to his ear.

'Let's just forget about it Jamie. Come on. We've kept them waiting long enough.'

'They can fuck off. Ignorant cunts. Beeping like that at this time of a night.' He flicks the vs at Sean. Beyond him Kev and Mally do camp wrist flicks and pull dramatic faces.

'I'm sorry for getting thingio with you back then. Really am. Especially in front of my aul' fella. But it doesn't take a genius to work out what's gone on does it? Just try and put yourself in her shoes, Millie. Me and you, like. It's difficult for her to get her head round isn't it? She don't see you as my mate. She sees this stunning looking woman that I chose to spend tonight with instead of her. And I lied to her. That makes me a cunt in her eyes wouldn't you say?'

If I was as good and as true as him and if I really believed she was a decent girl, and decent enough for my best friend, I'd send him back in. Tell him to forget tonight. Tell him to stop trying to please everyone and just please himself for once. Tell him to concentrate on the things that really matter. Them. Their future. But I truly believe she's not worthy of a slumbered wank, let alone the rest of his life. I swear, if you had to cash in her love for him, it wouldn't even buy you a shot of Scotch. Her masterplan's written all over her and it's about time *James* woke up to her. If he doesn't wise up, he's going to have to be told. She sees Jamie as nothing more than a stepping stone, a halfway house to bigger and brighter things. She's the girl that sucks off the roadie to get backstage then bags off with the singer. She's convincing though – so convincing that she's even

189

got wise old Mrs Keeley fooled. But not me, she hasn't
– and judging by the look on Mr Keeley's face, not him
either.

'At least she was civil to me tonight,' I say, and part
of me is being genuine here, part of me is being deadly
sincere. 'The way she speaks to me, Jamie, it hurts like
fu . . . well, it doesn't matter does it? She's your fiancée
end of the day and I'm not going to start slating her. I
just wish she'd give us a go.'

I climb into the cab, clamber over Sean and press my
face up against the window. The sky is sharper now,
almost as if the gunpowder has shocked it from its
reverie. The taxi swings into Park Road, presenting me
with a different view of the night. I attempt to arrange
the galaxy of stars into designs and patterns and in the
distance I hear the random sounds of gunfire. Gangsters
trying out their guns. Along Princess Avenue the barrio
falls silent as we pass through rows and rows of derelict
houses with haggard roof tops, yielding to the cycle
which will eventually lead to their recovery but as we
cross the junction that throws us into Catherine Street
and away from the Toxteth cavity it suddenly comes
alive with brass, their johns, drunks and looting teenagers
running from unknown locations into the lawless,
demented night. I love this city. I do. I fucking love it.

Chapter 7

Jamie

By the time we hit town it's after ten. Sean takes control of the night and hauls us into some trendy new bar in the financial district. All dim lighting, leather sofas and mad flavoured vodkas and what have you – fucken pepper vodka if you will! I used to drink in the place across the road with my aul' fella when it were The Rope and Anchor. Strange aul' pub and all back then – full of labourers, mainly from the docklands, nursing pints of dark liquid and watching their drinks like an egg timer – wondering whether to linger on for that extra half, if it were worth the aggro they'd get when they rolled in late and bleary eyed. And most of em played safe. Slunk home just past six, as the television in the darts' room reeled out the day's racing results. It was mad la, all these weathered aul' misfits, eyeing that TV with the same idiotic hopefulness of a man who goes to brass in search of true love. My aul' fella used to steer us away from that TV with the same silent finesse he used to coax us away from Sean's when we were teenagers but if the truth be known, I've never been a cunt for the betting. Fair do's and that, I have been known to slap the odd fiver on when we're playing the shite – nothing more than force of tradition I s'pose, but if I don't make it down to the bookies, I'm not gonna be pulling my hair out or nothing.

I'm just not in the mood for all this though, right now. Cannot even be arsed putting a face on for lil' Millie. I need to put things right with Anne Marie. The longer I stays out, the more time she'll have to stew and she's dangerous that one when she's been left brooding. Once she's made her mind up about somet, that's it. She'd rather fuck you off then back down, she would. *And* she's coming up to the rag la – fucken dementia, that is, at the best of times. What! Every cunt is out to get her! I become some depraved pervert who's shagging everyone from her best mate to my nieces. Throws all sorts at us, she does. And she rants. Fuck, does she rant la! Starts of in this low kind of half mumbling that drones on and on for hours, slowly feeding into this big mad tantrum where she tears the fucken house apart! Fair do's like, she always apologises in the aftermath. Pure ridden with guilt she is. And fuck does she more than make up to us in the bedroom if you know what I'm saying. Can hardly keep her hands off us round that time of the month. And I s'pose I'm half used to it now, end of the day – her rag. I've built up a resilience. Whatever she says floats in one ear and dribbles out the other. And if I'm being honest, it does half sort of tickle us, in fairness. Even when she's on one, she's adorable as fuck. But I could fucken *punch* myself for lying about tonight.

There was no need, neither. I told her I was having a lad's night in. That I was going to the bommie with the posse then back to Sean's for a bevvy. It's not like she would've minded if I'd've told her I was going into town neither, but I felt a bit of a cunt about it. She's been on at us for ages to take her out to that new bar that's opened on the Docks – The Pan. Says she's got a wardrobe full of classy clobber that's starting to collect cobwebs. I've tried to hint as subtly as possible that we shouldn't really be spunking our money on one-off indulgences. That we should be saving up for the wedding and the house and that. So you can see what a fucken hyprocite I must've looked back then.

The worst of it all, is the Millie thing though. Bad one la. Fucken bad one, that. Her seeing me in my gladrags when she's stuck indoors is bad enough, but knowing Millie's on board is like pouring paraffin on the fire. How the fuck do I get round that one? And she does have to choose tonight to suddenly start taking an interest in her appearance don't she? She's pure eye candy to begin with lil' Millie, but she's always been a jeans and no make-up type of girl. Nails bitten to stumps and soap-scorched hair that's never seen a brush. Christ la! You should've seen some of the knots I've cut from her hair! Fucken cig butts and all sorts in there. But recently, she's started making an effort and that. Just subtle things mind you. Clothes that hug her rather than hang from her. A lick of make-up here and there. Scent. Going to the hairdressers instead of her usual DIY job. None of which makes it easier on the Missus, end of the day. I s'pose if lil' Millie were nothing to look at then maybe Anne Marie could half handle it. My bezzie mate being a girl and that. But it is what it is, end of. Millie's been there, in the house, looking how she does and I've just fucked off with her. Bad one, la. I'm a soft cunt, I am. I'm a fucken knobhead.

Millie

Town is barren for a Thursday night, and we flit from bar to bar, often just poking our head around the door for any sign of vim. We finally settle at Revolution, a vodka bar on Matthew Street – a guaranteed full house. It is as well. It's fucking rammed with students, ostentatiously sinking slammers. Their presence puts a lump in my throat. Gets me thinking about Dad and that gangly, simpering girl. What on earth could he see in her? She's hardly his type. Dad's always gone in for elegance and restrained beauty – gypsy waifs. Andrea Corr, Catherine Zeta, Penelope Cruz.

Mum.

The rest of the crowd is comprised of single lads on the pull, and a few middle-aged tarts acting as reserves for a raucous hoard of schoolies. The sight of these brassy past-its, competing for attention puts a smile back on my face. Love it!

Nearly all of the schoolies are wearing micro skirts with boots, tiny fuck-me tops and layer upon layer of make-up but you can tell by their eyes that their sexual biographies would barely fill a sheet of A4. Most of them are still virgins and the ones that *have* ventured past tit and tongue have probably been driven by all the wrong

194

reasons – popularising themselves, keeping a boyfriend, impressing their peers or most likely of all, sheer misplaced curiosity. I doubt any of them have fucked for the sheer love of it. That's the whole tragedy of growing up. It's the one period in your life where there's so much pleasure up for grabs and no one's going to give you too hard a time for reaching out and seizing it. It's the one period in your life when you can behave like an absolute slut – and get away with it. But most teenage girls tear through adolescence oblivious to the epicurean world they inhabit. Their potency only reveals itself in the frustrated haze of hindsight.

Jamie and Sean pretty much shaped my understanding of sex. He's a funny one, Jamie – he's had his fair share of one night stands, but he seemed to accept them with a silent sorrow. He subscribed to an ideal which held love as a precondition for sex and he once told me that even if that love was ephemeral, even if it lasted all of five seconds, it had to be there in the beginning. If there was love, any sexual pursuit no matter how selfish or dangerous it was, could be justified. As a result he misspent a lot of his youth trying to negotiate between what felt good and what he thought was right. Sean was the polar opposite. He saw sex in its crudest terms – as something detached from any kind of emotion or meaning other than the physical. For him, sex was fucking – it was getting one's hole and getting as much of it as possible. He was ruthless, almost barbaric in his pursuit of women, especially those lacking in sexual experience. He slept his way through South Liverpool, leaving in his wake a bereft trail of ruptured hearts and hymens.

From Jamie I learnt that sex was as much concerned with psychology as it was with physiology. It was as much about the courting of anatomy as it was the meeting of two hearts, two minds. I also learnt that it was better to have done something and have regretted it, than to have not done it and spend your days wishing you had. Jamie spent a lot of his days reading books about things he wished he'd done.

From Sean I learnt that girls were divided into the bipolar categories of sluts and 'girlfriend material' and if I wanted to satisfy my voracious young libido than I had to act post haste. According to Sean you could be as promiscuous as you liked as long as you were under fifteen. You'd risk a reputation of being 'easy', but as long as you stitched up your knickers from sixteen onwards you could still qualify as girlfriend material. Girls who hit seventeen and were still doing the rounds would inevitably be branded sluts, and once past eighteen it was virtually impossible to transcend this stigma. If you were clever, however, you could bypass this labelling system through careful management of your sexual geography. A girl who fucked a hundred boys, a different one in every town could evade the moral flagellation reserved for girls who slept with more than one boy from the same school. As childish and dogmatic as Sean's suppositions were, there was a simple logic behind them, and they pretty much dictated my early sexual experiences.

My first sexual encounter was with a thirty-seven-year-old man. Philip. I was fourteen. I chose him because he was married. Because he had a nice car and wore a blue hooded Adidas top. Because he looked unhappy.

Because he lived at the bottom of our road but most of all because he was Dad's mate. I knew it would go no further. No one would ever find out. I could almost cheat losing my virginity. My name couldn't be added to the long list of slags that covered five and a half doors of the boys' toilets. I also assumed he'd be in awe of my supple, young body. His wife was a casualty of marriage – fat and dowdy and consumed by motherhood – and I just took it that Philip would be, well, grateful. If he was though, he never showed it. He broke down in tears within moments of stealing my virginity and then ignored my calls and threatened to tell Dad when I turned up outside his works one evening. And then he avoided me forever. He moved to Manchester and I never heard or saw anything of him again except on my seventeenth birthday he sent me his blue hooded jumper through the post. No card, no note – just a jumper that smelt of blokey aftershave. It's folded in a box at the back of my wardrobe along with the pair of silk gloves that Mum wore on her wedding day and I afford it far more sentiment then it deserves.

After Philip, I had a couple of relationships with lads my own age. Both were fleeting, prosaic encounters. The first was with a guy called Joey. We met in the State. He was dancing, bare chested, on top of a speaker. I handed him a bottle of water and he pulled me up to dance and slipped me a California Sunrise.

It was one of the best ecstasy nights of my life.

I could tell by the way he moved that he'd be a good fuck. He was fantastic, one of my best shags ever but he was also of limited intelligence. I was too ashamed to let him meet Mum and Dad, and after a week, I felt I'd learned everything there was to know about him. I took the dastardly route of finishing with him in writing. The other lad, Robert, I met at O'Malleys. Now, he *was* intelligent. Decent too. I flaunted him to my parents and I allowed him to meet me at the school gates. He treated me like a lady – spoiled me, adored me. He drove me to Cornwall just to see a full moon. He gave me money to buy my folks presents at Christmas and he wore rubbers cos he said the pill was bad for me. But he lacked Joey's sexual magnetism. He was careful and considerate and he frustrated me and I hated him for it. No matter how hard I hinted, he would never just fuck me. He saw my hankering for brutal, unrefined sex as something that needed to be corrected not satiated, and at fifteen I saw that as an unpardonable flaw. Sometimes, I called round at Joey's little flat and let him fuck me – and then I fucked them both off.

And then there were the girls. Which just kind of happened. There was no tumultuous path of self-discovery that preceded it, no traumatic decision or sacrifice, no introspective showdown. It was nothing like that. It just happened. It just happened the night that Mum left, the night I fled to the Keeley's – but the timing has no significance, nil, none at all. It simply happens to be the night I stumbled across two girls going down on each other in a porno mag. Of course sexologists would argue that there must always have been some latent biological yearning waiting to be triggered and the pornography served as a catalyst. That may well be the case, but all I know is that up until I pulled that magazine from under Jamie's bed, right up until I hit page twenty, I had no predilections for women of any kind, ever. Who knows, If I'd never set eyes upon Lara and Dawn I may have skimmed over such a moment of realisation and evolved into a healthy uncomplicated heterosexual. Maybe I'd be curled up in bed now with some young Paul Newman lookalike, supping coca, sharing a spliff. Planning languorous weekends away.

That morning, after Jamie and Billy had left for work, I did what I'd never done and went rummaging in their room. I found a box underneath Jamie's bed and my world burst wide open. Dismissively, more amused than titillated by its content, I sifted through a copy of Club International. There was some tart on the front with humongous breasts bursting out of a children's size footie shirt. The expression on her face said, *use* me. I locked the door and turned the page. The first few pictures made me giggle. There was a ginger motherly type with a bald fanny lying spread eagled on a kitchen floor – a big idiotic grin splashed across her face, a Chinese girl clad in Caterpillar boots and a cowboy hat, and then page after page of skinny airbrushed models pulling stupid faces. A spur of disappointment stretched inside me then faded quickly, leaving within me the dull throb of relief. My voyage into the arcane alter ego of men's sexuality amounted to a few burlesque women with average faces, advertising their accessibility as though their lives depended on it. That was *it?* Pornography? The boys club that had dared to exclude me. And that was what it amounted to? Those were the girls I had both revered and feared? I laughed out loud and flicked over a few pages, stumped as to what pleasure Jamie might derive from all this.

And then I met Lara and Dawn. And everything changed.

Dawn was svelte with the feline eyes, severe cheekbones and stony constitution of an East European hooker. Lara was flame haired and pale, made cheeky by an unruly army of freckles dusting her button nose. Her breasts were young and firm but the nipples had the rough and rampant protrusion that only greedy babies can bring. She was an eighteen-year-old fashion student from Hull '. . . who arranged lesbian orgies with her pals and with the right girls would do *anything* . . .'

If Dawn put a gun to my cunt, then Lara pulled the trigger.

There was a whole six pages devoted to them getting it on with each other in a living room which could have only belonged to a student. I masturbated right there on the floor and when I came it felt like all the muscles in my cunt had collapsed.

I split the rest of my stay between brooding and masturbating and by the time I moved back home, I was having difficulty pissing. My clit was so numb and spent that I thought it was damaged for good. I shaved my cunt, just like Lara's, so my thick glossy mane became a faint strip of central reservation, splitting my cunt perfectly into two naked halves and I fantasised constantly about meeting her. I even considered touring the canteens of the various fashion colleges of Hull. Soon, I became so consumed by the idea of sex with a woman that I could no longer padlock my fantasies to the realm of masturbatory expression and they seeped into my day to day existence. I suddenly saw women through the eyes of a pornographer. My school mates, my English teacher and the check out girls at Tesco's suddenly became candidates for Escort, Men Only, Mayfair and my favourite of all – Club Magazine. And all female activity, no matter how innocuous its intention became loaded with sexual connotations. A smile, a look, the way a girl wore her hair. Poise. They were all signals, conscious or unconscious, expressing sexual objectives. You could determine the Marys from the Magdalenas just by the way a girl wore her school uniform. Naked legs in the middle of winter; conspicuous lacy bras under see-through shirts, scuds of makeup and Lambert and Butler-hued fingers clad in junior Sovereign rings – they were the ones guaranteed to deliver. They were the ones who'd do *anything*. I reduced girls to bodies or bits of. I saw them in terms of tits, legs and arse. I undressed every girl that I met, bending them like plasticine – this way and that way into every possible position. No one escaped appraisal or categorisation.

I *never* saw myself as an object though. I neither identified with the women I objectified or the men that objectified them. I saw myself as something entirely different, as some sex-crazed genderless freak.

My love affair with wank mags and lap dancing bars lasted all of twelve months, and I'm glad in a way that it's over now. In hindsight I can see what a distorted view of the world it lent me. I don't buy into all that received feminist wisdom that holds porn responsible for every ill perpetrated on women by men, but there's no doubt that pornography impinged on my sense of reality. Implicit in its appeal is the idea that all girls are gagging for it, that they crave to be treated like filthy indefatigable whores as much as they crave to be pampered like princesses. That glamour models and lap dancers – they do what they do for the love of it. Not for the money. They *crave* sex. I truly believed that for twelve months. And when I discovered otherwise, the realisation crushed me.

I take Jamie's hand and weave us through to the bar. It's hot in here. I wriggle out of my coat and sling it over Jamie's shoulder then lean into the bar, jutting my chest out and flaring my lips in a way that is aloof but not entirely unapproachable. Within seconds I'm being served. A young girl with a heart-shaped face and a florid complexion. No tits. Literally, two gnat bites straining for recognition against a white Lycra vest. I am drawn to them in the same perverse way I am drawn to the disfigured faces of burns victims and I find it impossible to stop my eyes sliding off her chin. I can't stop myself. What do they look like – *really* look like? How would I respond to her naked body if I'd picked her up on the street and taken her back to a hotel room. Would I be repulsed or aroused? Would I make her leave her top on, or would I exploit her deformity? Shave her cunt and reinvent her as my hockey girl? But even through the deceitful lens of an alcohol swoon, I could never fancy her – not if she was the filthiest girl in the world. The skin around her eyes and lips have frayed a decade too early and her hips are too wide to evoke any type of schoolgirl fantasy. She just looks like a very average nineteen-year-old who's tits have skipped puberty. Fucked. I order three vodka slammers and offer her a consoling smile. She responds with a blank face so I fold my arms, squeeze my tits into an impressive cleavage and accept the drinks with a hostile eyebrow. I pass one of the glasses back to Jamie and he asks me why I've only bought three. I tell him that Kev and Mally can buy their own drinks. They haven't so much as dipped in their pockets all night. I know they're both hard up but if they've got no money they shouldn't be out – end of story. Saint Jamie is having none of it, of course. He slips past me and squeezes in at the bar. It's too noisy and crowded to expostulate, so in a gesture of silent protestation I down both the drinks in my possession, slam the empty glasses on the bar and then snatch the other from his hand and hurl it into the pits of my throat.

It takes a few seconds to hit me and then suddenly all at once I'm reeling from the surge and rock of a violent dry-retch fit. I can hardly get my breath. My guts are vaulting horribly. I lift my hand to my mouth to stop myself puking and concentrate hard on breathing, in-out, in-out. This is vicious. This hurts.

A skinny, wide-eyed thing with violent cheekbones flashes me a sympathetic look. I tear myself away from her tits and succumb to a querulous belch that scalds acid and vodka all the way up my nose. My stomach lurches into spasm, jerking me forward and my hand vaults up to my mouth again.

Concentrate. It's all about concentrating. If you don't think sick you won't be sick.

I think about Dad.

Dad reading the papers at the kitchen table.

Dad snoozing in front of the television.

Dad.

The images are malformed like an overtreated negative. My head goes blank for a while awaking the gripe in my stomach, but then a new montage of thoughts stumble into my head.

Mum. Brushing her hair.

Dad and that girl, having sex. I'm powerless to resist the image. I try to shove it away but it thrashes back, lurid and stagnant. She has tiny pink nipples and a smattering of ugly brown moles on her belly. A faint strip of mousy down trickles from her navel to her cunt. She smells of Gucci.

She smells of Mum.

Dad is on top, humping madly, his face all twisted and red. The image pulls back so their bodies only occupy two-thirds of the frame and some of the background detail slips into view. They're screwing on the floor. My bedroom floor. And on the bedside table behind them is a picture of Mum. Beautiful and smiling. And then the image blurs and fades like a cheaply edited movie and there's another void which is suddenly being filled with a familiar voice and the shock of a human touch. Jamie's hand is on my shoulder. He's looking right into me.

'Millie — you alright there babe?'

I nod wanly.

'You look like you're going to be sick?'

The word 'sick' triggers another bilious heave and this time it's impossible to contain. A viscous hurl seeps through my fingers and trickles down my chin. I clamp my lips shut to prevent any more leakage and then swallow hard, shuddering violently as the caustic liquid strips layers from my throat. Tears stream my face. I can just see me now. Charcoal streaked cheeks and a pungent gob slick with vomit. I grab the nearest bottle which belongs to a bloke. I don't see his face, just a hairy forearm that isn't Jamie's. I manage to down enough to swipe the evil taste from my mouth and quell the feeling of sickness before the bottle is snatched back. I stand there, suspended in a sickly vodka lethargy, my limbs heavy and limp, and I allow Jamie to guide me to a seat.

I blink the room into focus and the slew of beats and sounds become vaguely recognisable. I must be sitting with my head hung low for a while cos when I raise it, the tune has moved on and Jamie is placing a bottle of Volvic in front of me. I feel drunk — heavy and thirsty.

'Here y'are — drink this. I'll be over in a minute.'

His eyes are almost reproachful.

'I'll take you out for some fresh air. But you need to drink this first. Just take sips yeah? Little bit at a time.'

He lifts the bottle to my mouth and I sip at it gingerly at first, and then I give in to my puke induced thirst and polish off the bottle in big greedy gulps.

'Come 'ead then, let's see you stand up.'

I jump up and flash him a spunky smile. He raises an eyebrow.

'Now, d'you need us to escort you back to the table or am I alright to go and get these drinks in and that?'

'No, I'm fine,' I say, 'I haven't eaten all day and I think . . .'

Jamie doesn't even wait for me to finish. He's already making his way back to the bar. Even in my muffled state I can see he looks wretched from the back – stooped and tired and sapped of everything. He looks old. The strobe light from above picks out a thinning crown. He's thinking he's made a mistake. He's wishing he wasn't here – with me. He's wishing he was there – with her.

When I return to the table Sean's tongue, loosened by booze and beak is spieling Mally his well-worn anecdote about the Hollyoaks' bird he used to see. Mally's heard this story a thousand times before although he still manages to adopt the wide-eyed expression of a kid who's being let in on some big secret.

I think about hitting Sean with something sarcastic but abandon the idea when I remember the two parcels of beak lying neglected in his jacket pocket.

Kev is on the dancefloor and has somehow insinuated himself into the shimmying hub of schoolies. He's dancing like a muppet, punching the air madly, and snapping his pelvis to Kylie. The girls seem to love him though. Two of them are goading him into a sandwich, while the others form a circle around them, mimicking his moves, clamouring for his attention. The only one distancing herself from this whole shenanigans is a frail looking blonde with pipe-cleaner arms and an elfin face. She's sulking at the edge of the dancefloor, sucking a finger and making eyes with the room. I indulge myself watching her for a while, then grow bored and irritable. I *need* cocaine.

I breathe a huge sigh of relief when I see Jamie wrestling his way over with four bottles of Becks.

'I was gonna get youse a round of slammers but I thought better,' he says plonking the bottles on the table, 'Some girl throwing her ring up over there, in't that right Millie?'

I dart him an imploring face and it seems to work. No one is really listening to him anyway. Mally is still engrossed in Sean and Sean is still engrossed in himself. I slip him an appreciative wink and pull a chair out for him.

'Grazie,' I say.

I remove the cigarette from his mouth, eye it closely and inhale with great suspicion. I screw my face up and thrust it back in his mouth, almost singing his lips. 'Urrgh! Lambert & *Butler*?'

'Embassy actually.'

'Since when did you start smoking pov's cigarettes?'

'They're Anne Marie's,' he says.

I lean over and tap Sean on the shoulder. Resentfully, he plucks himself from Mally's cloying embrace. I make smoking signs with two fingers. He fumbles about in his jacket, turns back to Mally and raises his voice slightly.

'Anyway, can I fuck keep the bimbo at arm's length,

la! Was a bit embarrassing in all honesty. Her fella's in there and she just *can't* keep her hands off, know what I mean . . . That singer from the La's is fucken grinning his head off at us. Aye-aye lad, he's going, nice one and that . . .'

He extracts a pack of Marlboros and slides them across the table without even looking at me. I take out two cigarettes, hesitate, take out a third then slide them right back.

I flick my eyes from Sean to Jamie, Jamie to Sean. Things are so heartbreakingly different now. Even when we're out and having fun and on *bonnie* night too, there's this big dilating chasm between us. It was all so effortless back then – laughing, talking, absorbing and devouring every inch of each other's worlds. That's all we did. Drink and smoke and talk – long meandering conversations about anything and everything. I used to spend hours on the 'phone to Jamie – *hours*. And when either of us had done gear, we'd talk so long and hard that our mouths would blister with ulcers. Now, it's like there's nothing left to say. Everything's been said. We're here out of duty rather than want. Just treading time.

Kev swans over with a couple of his coterie, beaming like a simpleton. One of them is tall with a beautiful, exotic face but bad genes have distributed her weight unevenly. She has skinny legs, fat hips and a set of narrow shoulders pushed down into her ribs. The only thing going for her is her age – fourteen max. Her mate, the thumb sucking waif from the dancefloor is stunning. She's also very drunk. She collapses into Jamie's lap and allows her head to flop back on his chest. Instinctively he clamps his arms around her to stop her sliding to the floor. His face flicks from discomfit to solicitude. I imagine him growing hard beneath her.

Her legs hang within inches of my own. A subtle gesture from my left knee and we'd be touching.

Kev introduces them as Suey and Becky and the tall girl, Becky, says something that makes everybody laugh. Sean throws something back and they laugh even harder. I smile without hearing a word. My thoughts are consumed only by this girl sitting besides me. Our legs have made contact – young, warm, infallible skin breathing life into my groin.

Jamie loosens his grip around her and she tumbles down his lap. The sudden movement shocks her eyes wide open. He slips his arms underneath her shoulders and pulls her back up. Her skirt rides up unashamedly, exposing a flash of white panties. My clit pulses against my seat and I sit forward, shifting all the weight onto my cunt to intensify the pleasure. If I were a lad I'd be steel hard.

'State of her!' her mate shrieks, 'Always like this! Out of it on three fucken Metz.'

Sean grins a wide toothy grin.

'Pretty little thing though in't she?'

'I think this one needs to go home,' Jamie says, sharpening his glare and shifting it onto Kev.

'Be my guest,' he says gyrating his pelvis into Becky's arse.

'No – I think *youse* need to take her home. She's gonna pass out, here.'

Becky affects concern.

'Mmmaybe, I should put her in cab you know.'

'She'll be fine,' Kev says, nudging her off in the

direction of the dancefloor, 'She'll start sobering up in a minute. Just give her some water.'

He propels this instruction at me. I raise my eyebrows.

Becky twists her mouth to one side.

'O-kaay then, but if she starts voming or somet just come and get us will you?'

Again this instruction is directed at me. My eyebrows collapse with a snort. If Billy was here, he'd see the irony of it all. Thinking of Billy, where is he? I could really use his company tonight – fun loving and uncomplicated. Just how Jamie was, once upon a time.

Kev drags his shag off to the dancefloor before she has time to change her mind but two minutes later she's back again with a disposable camera.

'I've got to show this to the girls at school,' she says, snapping away clumsily, 'They'll piss themselves. Proper little goodie goodie, Suey here is. No one would belieeeeve she'd get in this state.'

'Here,' I say taking the camera from her, 'Let me.'

She hands over the camera willingly and I kneel down in front of Jamie, so I've got a bird's eye view of Suey's panties.

'Smile!'

Click. The flash goes off and my subjects spring to life. Jamie lifts his arms to shield his face and without his support, she plummets down his lap and her legs flop wide open. Click. Jamie grabs her at the ribs and lugs her back up again, dragging up her top to expose a hard white tummy. Click. Jamie's hands are all over her, pulling down her top and her skirt, trying to salvage what's left of her dignity. Click. Click. Click.

Sean and Mally are hunched over, great billows of lung-stripping laughter heaving from their chests. Even her ostensibly protective mate is finding it difficult to stifle her amusement. Jamie is livid.

Dizzy from the commotion, Becky neglects to reclaim her camera and rushes off to the dancefloor to relay the incident to her mates. I stash it in my handbag. Potential wanking fodder.

' 'kinell Millie, I knew you had a bit of a rep for getting girls to fucken thingio but that about tops it all!' Sean shakes his head devilishly. 'How the fuck's she got like that though, la? She's a fucken kid, look at the kite? No older than fourteen, that one.'

'We're gonna have to do something you know,' Jamie snaps, 'Can't just leave her here like this. I mean you can all see where this is heading can't you? Her mates are in no fit state to look after her? You heard about that girl that got pulled into a car last week outside The Allerton Towers?'

'Well, she's hardly ideal rape material is she?' I say.

'I didn't know there was a criteria for rape victims,' he retorts sarcastically.

'Well isn't it about the thrill of *forced* sex? I mean, she's hardly in a position to put up a fight? It'd be like raping a blow-up doll. Where's the fun in that?'

'Ah grow up Millie. That's fucken last that. I hope if you ever get in this state, you don't end up with someone as selfish as you.'

'But I wouldn't though would I? Get in *that* state? I mean that's the difference between me and girls like *that*. They get stupidly drunk and just expect their mates or some Mr fucking Samaritan like you to look out for them. *They're* fucking selfish – not *me*. Girls like that need to be taught a lesson.'

'That's rich coming from someone who was throwing her ring up less than ten minutes ago.'

'Yeah,' I say, snatching a quick glance to see if Sean has heard this. He hasn't. 'But I wasn't staggering around was I? I wasn't falling into strangers' laps was I? Tell me, have you *ever* seen *me* like *that*?'

The question hangs in the air for a while, and then Jamie lowers his head to her cheek.

'How you feeling little'un?'

'Ugh?'

Her eyes do an interrupted sleeper's stare.

'D'you want some more water?'

She mumbles affirmatively and then a glib of panic shoots across her face.

'Where ith everyone?' She's got a gorgeous little lisp. 'Have they got off without uth?'

She jolts upright.

'It's OK, babes,' Jamie soothes, helping her to her feet, 'Your mates are still here.'

She stands for a moment, then stumbles back into his lap again.

'I *need* to get home.'

'Well don't worry babes, we're not gonna let your mates go without you, are we Millie?'

I roll my eyes at Sean.

'You don't *underthand*. I need to get back. My Dad'll batter uth.'

'*I'll* take you home?' I offer.

'She'd be safer walking.'

'Pleathe!' She lets out a throaty hiccup. 'He'll batter uth. Me *and* my Ma for letting uth out.'

'Where d'you live?' I ask, reaching over and touching her thigh.

'Kirkdale.'

'Other end of town from me,' I sigh. 'If I get you home okay, will you put me up for the night?'

My hand is now sliding up towards her cunt.

'Yeth!' she says, clapping eyes on me for the first time, 'Are you one of Becky'th mateth?'

'Kind of.'

'I need to go now though. Before he geth home. Will you take uth?'

'Yep, grab your coat, you've pulled!'

Jamie flings my hand away.

'Fucks sake Millie – go and find her mates will you and stop acting a cunt.'

'She's not my type anyway,' I say, getting up and lobbing him a wry face, 'Too pale, too hairy and those Tuesday knickers? Nah, doesn't really do it for us you know.'

Our eyes lock over her head, pushing my heart into my guts. Something in his eyes is telling me this is it. Me and him are almost over.

I drain my beer and swan over to the dancefloor. Kev is dancing orgiastically doing this big daft sweeping movement with his arms like Mr fucking Motivator. His groupies have all opted for that risk free self-conscious type of dancing that belongs to the genres of upper-class girls and pre-chemicalites – arms in the air, hands draped loosely over heads, eyes clamped shut and head nodding from side to side in time with the music. Safe. Easy.

I manipulate my way into the centre of the floor taking full advantage of the melee by groping arses and then shifting the blame onto the nearest bloke. Becky spots me and dances over flicking her wrist to the beat. She looks absolutely ridiculous, like she's fending of a bad case of cramp.

'How's Su-ey? . . . She O-K?'

Her voice assumes the tempo of the music. I peer closely into her face. Her eyes are solid black and the whole of her lower face is twitching, but it's only when I see Kev's puckish face grinning dementedly in the background does the penny drop.

'Your mate's making a cunt of herself,' I say. 'She needs something to sober her up and quick.'

I extended the flat of a palm. She pulls her chin in and feigns ignorance.

'Now, Kev said, to hand it right over to me. A couple of doormen clocked you going into the toilets before and he thinks you're gonna get searched.'

Her eyes lurch with terror.

'Don't start panicking, you'll draw attention to us, just hand the . . .'

She practically throws it at me. I totter off, reeling with nervy excitement and good feeling for the night ahead. I'm done with this bar and I'm done with him.

I find her in the disabled toilet, wretching and slumped over the basin. Sheer fate.

When I'm out I *always* use the mens. Partly because there is rarely a queue but mainly because the toilets are cleaner. Girls are fucking monsters. This time though, I had an instinct that Kev might try and reclaim his goods, so I slipped into the disabled. And that's where I found her. Frail little Suey – spitting her guts out. Just asking to be fucked. She's left the door ajar so I lock us both in and kneel down beside her.

I rescue her hair from her vomit-drenched face and, twisting it into a low pony of sorts, fold it into her top. She looks round at me, foggy-eyed and helpless. The room spins in her face. She coughs up a long skinny stream of transparent bile and then makes all the ugly faces that precede vomiting. She stoops further into the basin so that a few stray hairs fall into the mire but all that comes out is putrid saliva. This seems to upset her greatly cos she starts crying and spitting and wailing. I move round behind her, and rub her back with the tips of my fingers in slow circular movements, a gentle, coaxing method Mum picked up in India, but rather than trigger a productive emission, the action has the opposite effect of placating her. The coughing and weeping subside and her shoulders loosen into a slump. And then she turns round and looks right at me. So I do what her eyes are telling me to do – I slide her top up.

The sight of her naked back shocks me stone cold sober. My head empties for a few seconds and everything tilts out of focus. Her entire back is blotched with livid bruises, dozens of them, so if you let your eyes fall lazy, her back is just one big bruise. Black and grey and green and red but mostly black. I wrench the top right down.

With my heart barrelling madly, I remove the package from my purse, and with my longest nail, scoop out a generous bump. Now think, Millie, think. I should go and get Jamie. Her mate, Becky. No Jamie – he'll know what to do. Maybe he's already seen it. Maybe that's why he was so adamant about making sure she got home safely. And on time. Before her Dad . . .

Her *Dad*.

An ugly swill spills into my guts. I should go and get Jamie.

I would have.

If I had not been within such close proximity to her warm narrow arse, so perfect and inviting. If she hadn't turned round with tears in her eyes and said what she said. If she hadn't asked me not to stop.

'Pleathe don't thtop that. Pleathe.'

That's what she said. I swear. And her eyes they were soaked with so many conflicting emotions – fear, guilt, relief, yearning, all struggling to gain momentum but the yearning burned hardest of all.

Take me, her eyes were saying, take me. So with gentle hands I take her.

I ease her skirt up over her slim hips and pull down her knickers. I cup a cheek in each palm, two tiny globes, and pull her apart gently. Her tiny fawn-coloured hole nestling under a diaphanous veil of ginger down hits my eyes like a soft explosion – unblemished and soft, and too lovely to encroach. Even my tiny slim fingers. That would be wrong. That would be violation. So instead I let my tongue press against the warm skin of her arse hole. I can smell the wetness beyond, ready to swallow me. Slowly I release my tongue in her and her snuffling subsides into an affirmative moan. I plunge deeper and feel for her cunt lips. I tug on them softly, rubbing them between the tips of my fingers, making her dribble all over my hand and all down her thighs. The beak has erased all reservations now. This feels good and right and natural, and as my tongue snakes her cunt and laps her eager hole I abandon myself to the depravity washing over me. I suck hungrily on her flaps, burying the whole of my nose inside her, devouring her, smelling her, swigging on her wetness, wanting to be as far up her as possible. She tastes of teenage fanny. Treacle – warm sticky treacle, unsullied by spunk and rubber. Lovely young fanny. I slide my tongue back up and all over her tense little arse, dipping at her hole again. Her sphincter pulls like a whirlpool and there's a soft strain under my tongue as it reaches and stretches, deep, deep inside her. And now I begin easing my fingers in her cunt, one by one, 'til apart from my thumb, my whole fucking hand's in there, wearing her tight young fanny like a glove puppet. Never felt a fanny so tight before. So tight and wet. And noiselessly she moves with my hand, rocking to and fro, swallowing it like it's the most normal, natural thing in the world. And this is what gets me. My whole cunt just floods at the sight of her, this young slag, loving it, *loving* the whole thing, just letting me do whatever the fuck I want. That's what gets me. She's part of this – she's letting me. And as the beak takes holds of me, my thoughts trip out to some dark sordid place and I'm helplessly thinking about her father's coarse lumpish hands feeling her too, feeling the wetness between his daughter's legs, inhaling the sweet odour of fresh cunt. I begin to fuck her really hard and soon she's shuddering and the whole of her insides are contracting and spasming around my hand. She comes wildly, all over me and I jam my hand inside my saturated kickers. The beak has stripped my fanny walls of all feeling but my clit is on fire. A few strokes and Jesus I'm going to come, I'm going to come with my whole hand inside this dirty teenager who is letting me. She's letting me do this to her.

My orgasm is muted by the chemicals and I withdraw from her feeling empty and cheated.

I pull my dress down and I remember the camera in my bag. I *need* a picture of her cunt. Wet and spent. I *need* to see this sight again. The flash goes off and the camera whirrs and dies. She looks round and her face has me gasping again. It's wide open with terror and shock and hurt. She buries her head in her palms and slumps to the floor

No! She *loved* it!

She did – she enjoyed it.

You made her come. She *came*. And now she's killing herself with all the weapons she can turn on herself – guilt, self-hatred, denial. But she *did* enjoy it.

I let myself out and catch a glimpse of my face in the mirror which is all flushed with regret and sex. I wash my hands which are drenched in thick fanny paste and blood. I dry my hands on my flanks and walk outside into a blast of music and flashing lights and everything in my head is safe and calm once more – but my cunt still aches and burns with unslaked orgasm. I trace our table through the sea of bodies. Sean and Jamie's heads are bobbing about in conversation. Mally and Kev are nowhere to be seen, but Billy has materialised at long last. He throws me a big wave. The stinging in my cunt intensifies, so it is almost impossible to walk. I locate the men's toilets which are situated on the other side of the room and skulk into a cubicle where the air is stained with the smell of weed. There is no lock on the door, so I stand with my back against it and yank my dress to my hips. I come quickly with the image of her young exposed cunt emblazoned on the insides of my eyelids. Not a very nice orgasm at all. Just a necessary purge.

I plonk myself down next to Billy. He's all over me about the schoolies.

'D'you get photies?' he's going. 'The lads was saying you've got some boss photies and that.'

Jamie is biting hard on his bottom lip. Sean's gaze is stabbed with sex.

'Have fun?' says Jamie, his eyes burning moodily beyond me. I leave him to it – I'm not getting in there, with him. Whatever it is that's eating him, he'll come round. I take a cigarette from a nearly empty packet and Sean leans forward and produces a flame. Our eyes crash above the long slick flame and tear into each other for a second. Jamie sees it, susses it. He's on his feet.

'I'm off,' he smiles – but it's a hollow smile.

I suck myself away from Sean's gaze and turn and face Jamie.

'Early start and that,' he winks, slipping his jacket on.

Sean looks at his watch and offers a sympathetic smile. Billy tries to blag him to stay for one more but he says goodbye, sweeps his eyes over me in one last, crushing strafe and is gone.

I leave moments later. I have to sort this out. He won't have gone far – the Lobster Pot no doubt or the taxi rank at worst. Outside, the temperature has dropped right down and the air hangs sharp and raw in my lungs. The city shimmers across the horizon, luminous and majestic. The streets are filled with familiar detritus – giddy voices, broken glass, fast food packaging and the drunken lurch of sodden bodies. I travel quickly against the flow, drinking in every pulse of my surroundings. I head up Church Street and pause at the junction with Hanover, unsure whether to try left or right. There are no cabs, only a long, disorderly queue. Jamie is nowhere to be seen. I wait. I reach for a smoke and realise I've left my bag in there. Fuck! Just can not be arsed turning round and going all the way back for it. Billy'll look after it, for sure. I didn't have any cards on me and I've got enough in my coat pocket for a few drinks and a cab home. I wait some more but then the cold takes hold of me and I'm fucking off Jamie for the warm, dingy safety of a pub.

I head up towards the Cathedral. The Nook'll still be serving, I'm certain of it.

It is. It's buzzing with solitary drinkers all smoking with gusto. I wrestle my way to the bar, feeling myself sucked into a dozen conversations. I settle patiently beside a man with a bull neck and beady eyes. He clutches his glass tightly to exaggerate the muscles in his arm. I order a shot of Jameson and a pint of Stella. I stand at the bar, drain the whisky in one slick gulp and order another. I rest it on the bar and stare at it, allowing it to be weakened by the melting ice. The man with the bull neck gives me a benevolent grin. The Jameson seems to have softened his face a little. I ask him to watch over my drinks while I go the bog. He beams back a big soft smile. I lock myself in a cubicle, wanting that clear chemical feeling back. I squat on the cold, dank floor and scoop out a voluptuous bump with a key. And then another one for good luck. It hits me immediately, stamping out the whisky swoon and replacing it with something bigger and more beautiful. I check my kite in the mirror, pull a few moody pouts then return to the bar. I buy a packet of Embassy from some scabby faced bag head that's doing the rounds. Two quid – can't complain I s'pose. The crowd at the bar has dispersed a little now and the man with the bull neck has struck up conversation with a barmaid. Feeling all lovely and gregarious I offer them both a cigarette and tell the barmaid she is gorgeous. She smiles coyly but the eyes are too assuming and I feel like snatching the compliment back. I tune into their conversation for a while but it's nothing – going nowhere so I look around for other conversations to latch onto but most of them are too far gone for an inquisitive third party so I just stare at my fathomless golden pint, so placid and beautiful. Too beautiful to disturb. I smoke a couple more fags, leave the pint untouched and leave. I say good night to the man and he drags my gaze down to the foaming lager and shrugs his shoulders dejectedly. On Upper Duke Street I latch onto two paraffins and walk with them as far as Hope Street where I pause to offer them a pound. One of them informs me with a befuddled face he's not homeless. The other just stares at me with these big see-through eyes, like some switch has flicked off inside for good. I shrug my shoulders and insist they keep it anyway.

I walk up towards the Cathedral, in awe of the night ahead – an open canvas and a thousand colours in my pocket. I paint a picture. Deranged sex with a hooker, quelling the ceaseless burn and anguish in my groin – then hours and hours of coke-fuelled conversation with any willing participant. I continue up past the Cathedral and turn onto Huskisson Street where a shrill search-light floods the busy street in its dazzling beam. People are everywhere, congregating in small groups. My first thoughts that this is a murder scene, right on the cusp of the red light district. I walk quickly towards the commotion, a strange knot of thrill in my solar plexus and I'm disappointed to learn that it's a film crew, churn-ing out TV's latest tight breeches and décolletage clas-sic. Hope Street and Percy Street, the mouldering lungs of my brassland, have been turned into a Dickensian slum. I contemplate walking home through Toxteth but then an idea enters my head.

I press the buzzer. There is no reply but I can tell by the jaundiced hue penetrating the curtains that there's activity within. I step back onto the road, pick up a small stone and, losing my balance slightly, hurl it at the window. A couple of blokes in Oliver Twist garb wolf whistle as they pass me by. I shake my head, embarrassed for them. I lob another stone and the window gasps open. Our eyes crash awkwardly.

'What d'yoh want?'

The voice is angry and as classless as ever.

'It's me Millie. Remember?'

The figure at the window casts a furtive glance over her shoulder then leans right out. Her hair is scraped back, accentuating the earthy jut of her cheekbones and the wild black eyes. She is thinner and more beautiful than I remember. My vulva is stinging for her touch.

'Millie today, is it? Well yoll 'ave toh fock off, what-evoh yoh name is. Do one!'

'Oh, come on, let us in will you? It's fucking freezing!'

'Are yoh not listening, kiddoh? I'm focken *busy*.'

'Too busy to spend the night with your favourite punter?'

Curtains flutter and part in the windows above and the haunted faces of decent folk glower down at me.

'Ah've told yoh nice girl. Now fock off, will yoh – leave us be.'

She slams the window shut. I hurl another stone. It bounces back and falls to the road with a thud. I throw another and this time the window quivers with the impact. She re-appears at the door in a dressing gown. The one that I wore. Her eyes are pure eyeball, shot forward in her skull. My confidence takes a dip.

'Sorry,' I say, 'I just wanted to know if you wanted some company. We don't have to do anything. We could just have a smoke or something.'

She's not having it though. Her head begins to twitch

dementedly. Ok, one last stab, and I'm off, I'll give up and settle for a mag. I try some humour on her.

'Anyway, it's the least you can do after giving me a dose.'

'Get the fock out of e-yoh or I'll rip yoh focking face off.'

She lunges forward and I turn and run. Run and run. Past the gobsmacked film crew, down onto Catherine Street and straight over Upper Parliament street, deep into the Toxteth sprawl.

Jamie

Bang out of order, she is. Don't know what gets into the girl – I really do not, la. It's like as though she can't let things get too smooth, too easy. We've had a hard time, we goes to Wales, we sorts it out, yeah? We half comes back stronger than we was before. So that's like an open invitation to Mizz fucken O'Reilley in case any of us makes the mistake of thinking she's a nice, regular girl that you could have as a mate and that, have a laugh with and come to rely upon – she fucks all that. She pure will not have none of it. Me? Nice girl, good heart, good soul – fuck off! I'll show you! I'm dragging this poor kid in the bogs and I'm beasting her right in front of you just in case any of you thinks you knows us too well. Well, I'm fucken done with it, la. I've got my own priorities now, and they don't extend to running after lil' Millie whenever she wants a bit of attention. I'm in no way doing cartwheels for the girl anymore. She's on her own. Finito.

Chapter 8

Millie

Toxteth has a dozen faces and just past midnight is my favourite. The streets are silent and empty of danger, peppered with inebriated old men, gleefully ambling home – letting life slip naturally away from them, with dignity and with grace. Even the huddles of guttersnipes which collect under street lamps like fireflies are placid and unsuspecting. All anticipation of violence and danger flees from their bodies leaving them slack shouldered and heedless. Toxteth is sleeping.

I flop down to the pavement and soak it all in. It's bothered Dad for years that these mean streets hold no fear for me, but it is what it is. I can't feel afraid when I know no bad will befall me here. I know that.

I dig in my pockets, scoop out the beak, take a finger nail's, and spark a cigarette. I throw back my head and exhale way into the blue-black dome, aglow with pin-wheeling stars.

A gentle wind skids a newspaper to my feet where it flaps for a while then leaps off behind me. Time passes. I light another fag.

A belching black cab ruptures the dead calm, slowing to shed its load. Silhouettes stand and confer, then dart across the road, gone. The taxi pulls off, as abruptly as it arrived, swings a bend and is swallowed up by the night. Toxteth is silent once more. I take another bump, commit the night sky to memory then pull myself up.

By the time I hit Smithdown, I'm out of fags so I head for the Twenty Four Hour. Streams of students lumber home, flush faced and garrulous, laughing self-consciously in that stupid student way. They spill in and out of fast food joints like stunned bats, whilst on the pavements gangs of teenage girls in trackies and pyja-mas, some no older than ten, lurk for stragglers.

The queue at the garage stretches out onto the road. There are students, scals and impatient taxi drivers but mostly there are teenage girls with faces tragically wise beyond their bodies. I march to the front and thrust a fiver into the hand of a young Somalian lad, chemi-cally overconfident that he will not abscond with the money.

'Get us twenty Marlboro Lights will you, please.'

He drags an exasperated eyebrow aloft but takes the money anyway. I wait for him on the wall and make eyes with a baghead on the skank — all bones and faded eyes, but the mouth and breasts still full and defiant. A hardened nipple strains through a fleece top, sending a shiver through my cunt.

'Hey girl,' she croaks, inching nearer, 'Lend us a quid, get home and that?'

The wraith is unprepared for what comes next.

'I can do better than that,' I beam, 'I'll take you drink-ing if you like?'

A flicker of something enters her faded eyes.

'Wha?'

'We could go to that Jalons across the road there, have a laugh and something to eat. You fancy it? Come on – we'll have a scream.'

Her face falls wide open.

'You taking the piss?'

'No! I'm asking if you fancy coming for a drink. *You're* on your own. *My* pals have fucked me off. And being absolutely honest with you, I really can't face going home. I've just found out that my old fella's got a . . . ah, don't matter. I won't bore you. But come on, what d'you think?'

'Fucken mental,' she interjects, 'Off your fucken head.'

She's on her feet now, scrutinising me with those glassy eyes. The realisation that she's about to fuck off fills me with panic. I don't want to go home. I want to stretch the night out forever.

'OK – I'll pay you,' I whisper, 'I'll make it worth your while. Come on, we can go down to the park, me and you. I'll make you feel nice.'

She thrusts her face into mine and I recoil at the stench of her breath. Her eyes seethe in their orbits. My chin slumps down to my chest and in my tummy I feel the gnaw and anguish of something bad and familiar.

She stumbles off, muttering and shaking her head, her bony arse jagging at her trackie.

'Your loss,' I shout after her, 'Your loss.'

I delve in my pocket for a cigarette. I don't have any. I'm about to go and join the queue but I remember the Somalian guy. I look up and he's next to be served.

'Fag buyer?' I holler over, 'Get me a top shelfie as well if you will. Club or Escort will do.'

My chest tightens with the effort reminding me how much poison I've poured into my lungs tonight. It'll take days to recover from all that fagging – *days*. The whole queue is suddenly looking in my direction. *Grinning* at something behind me. A couple of lads wolf whistle. I snap my head over my shoulder, anticipating a newly acquainted couple eating the face off each other, but all I see is the empty road. And then it hits me. They're looking at me. Why though? I dig my chin into my chest and concentrate on the floor. Moments pass. And then I'm wondering what the fuck I'm doing here and I'm up on my feet. A lad with dark skin strides over and hands me a pack of fags and I'm remembering again.

'Ehm, didn't have no mags love.'

He can hardly look me in the eye.

'Yes, they did. I always get them from here. It doesn't matter though.'

Head down, he hands me my change and turns on his heels. He can hardly get away fast enough. I shrug my shoulders, fire a cigarette and carry on up Smithdown, where the noise and colours slowly fade out into stock-still blackness.

I walk on. Time passes. I light another cigarette and toss it prematurely into the gutter, chasing it with a ball of catarrh.

I turn a bend and there is the purr of an engine. I swing round slowly. A set of dimly lit headlights lurks a hundred yards behind. I walk on with my head held high and my shoulders pulled back, assuming an air of manufactured confidence, but no matter how much distance I put between us, the glare and volume of the engine remain constant. Someone is following me. Instinctively, I leave the main road and veer into a residential street, scanning the rows of tightly packed terraces for signs of life. Everyone is sleeping. I scud headlong into the next street and my tummy dips with relief at the yellow light spilling on the pavement from people's living rooms. Still the headlights follow. Not wanting to risk reaching the end of the street and being thrust into another row of slumbering houses I slow right down but instead of shadowing my pace the engine draws closer. It's the deep, diesel thrum of a four wheel drive. I delve in my pockets and make a tight fist around my keys, fitting my thumb and forefinger around the body of the sharpest to make a knife of sorts. A prick of fear penetrates the cocaine haze and my heart begins to bang like a jackhammer. Underneath my coat a puddle of sweat forms in the dip of my collarbone.

The vehicle is crawling alongside me now and the driver is looking right at me. He's leaning across and he can see my face stretched tight with panic He can see the rise and fall of my flailing chest and my rapid, shallow breath spuming in front of me The whiz of an electronic window rends the night air and I almost pass out with fright. I stall and hover outside a brightly lit window and, very slowly, light a cigarette. From the corner of my right eye I see a slice of exposed face caught in a band of light from a house. It's the face of a white male.

'I wouldn't though would I? Put myself in danger like that. I mean that's the difference between girls like me and her. They go out, get off their head and then walk home and expect their pals or Mr fucken Samaratian to look out for them. Girls like that need to be taught a fucken lesson. Isn't that what you said?'

I swing round. Sean is leaning across the empty passenger seat of his Shogun. From out of his chiselled face, two green eyes laugh in their sockets.

'You *ba-stard!* What the fuck are you . . .'

'Get in.'

He opens the door. I climb in, slam it shut.

'You . . . You utter cunt!' I finally spit out, 'What the fuck are you playing at?'

'What am *I* playing at?' he says, eyes dilating in shock, 'I think it's me that should be asking *you* that question. Fuck was you doing walking home through Tokkie this time of a night?'

His voice is husky from chemicals and fags.

'Er, hang on a minute! You've been following me since *Toxteth*?'

'We passed you in the fucken cab remember? Me and Kev. You was in fucken la-la land weren't you, splayed out on the fucken pavement like a meff.'

The black hack. The two silhouettes. That was yesterday wasn't it – or the day before? Thinking on it makes me feel dizzy. I try to zap it from my memory banks and look away. My breath blurs up the half-opened window.

'Fucks sake girl, what was you thinking?'

A tight clot of anger swells in the pit of my throat,

sucking the breath from my lungs and firing streams of adrenaline into my limbs and up to my head. I pivot round, slowly, and stare right into him.

'Don't you fucken lecture me like some student imbecile,' I say feeling the anger tense and twist my face, 'I fucking *know* that barrio as well as you do soft cunt.'

He flinches involuntarily and his mouth falls open. He doesn't know what to say.

'And even if I *was* being a dick, what gives you the fucking right to try and teach me a lesson?'

'Teach you a lesson?'

He composes himself now, disguising the shock of a moment ago with a mocking belligerence.

'Yeah, trying to prove a point by freaking me out back then?'

'Millie – what are you on about, girl?'

He pulls his head into his chest and holds his hands up.

'You. And your fucking games.'

'Games? Lessons? You're starting to sound like a bad fucken beakhead. I mean that's pure paranoia that is, babe.'

'Paranoia?'

'Is right, girl – and I'll tell you another thing shall I? If I didn't know you'd been caning it like that tonight, no fucken way in the world would I be letting you sit here in me Danny like this, giving us all that fucken attitude.'

He slumps back again shaking his head and trying to look wounded. I sneer at him.

'Just slow it down a bit, eh – and accept that not every cunt is trying to get one over on you. I seen you

231

slumped on the pavement back there looking like some roughed-up crack whore. I didn't want to inflict Kev upon you so I got rid of him and come back for you. I was fucken worried about you, weren't I? Girl got raped last week. Does that not mean anything to you?'

He shakes his head despairingly.

'*And* I'm about four times over the limit, la. Risked my fucken licence to come and find you and all you've given us is abuse.'

There's hurt in his eyes now, real hurt.

'And I'm sorry if I scared you and that – but I had to make sure didn't I? Can't just be pulling up on birds and frightening the living shite out of em, can you?'

I flop back in my seat. No way am I conceding, here. There's a long silence, punctuated only by the sound of my breathing. And then he nudges me.

'Great little swagger you've got there by the way. Almost thought you were advertising for business.'

He lowers his headand runs a playful finger along the bridge of my nose. I want to stay mad at him but I can't. He squeezes my chin, coaxing a reluctant smirk from my lips.

'Come 'ead,' he says, slipping the vehicle into gear, 'Let's get you home. We'll shoot back to mine and I'll get you a couple of sleepers. Can hear your heart racing from here.'

No, I want to say, take me straight home but I shrug my shoulders and let him drive me.

The car picks up speed.

'Don't suppose any of you grabbed my bag?'

'No, hon. Not that I know of, like. Any cards you need to cancel?'

He hands me his mobile.

'Nah, never take them out with me.'

I feel a genuine pang of regret that I'll never see those photos. Other than that, the bag was worthless. Outside his apartment block he shuts down the engine and invites me in. I decline with a 'I'm really fucked and need to get to bed' voice and his face twitches for a second. He tightens his lips and jumps out. In the sudden dark silence of the empty vehicle, flashbacks of the night collide in my head, flooding me again with a tremulous paranoia. All Sean's crap about saving me from the wrath of the streets is just a fucking front. There was no need to come looking for me. He thinking he should have had me when we were alone in his flat this evening. He could have had me, if the boys hadn't come up when they did. That's just the way it goes. But there was no need to come looking for me. He saw me sat on that pavement and thought he'd been given another chance, end of story. Well here's the news – he's got *no* chance.

I climb out and the cold slaps my bare legs like a wet towel. I walk to the front of the car and lean into the warmth of the bonnet. I spark a cigarette and think the situation through. If I just walk away now, I'll come across as nervous – at worst, intimidated. But if I let him drive me home then that's exactly what I'm doing – letting him, saying okay to him.

Time passes. I find myself wondering whether little Suey got home okay. I hope she's alright. I shouldn't have done those things to her, no matter how badly she wanted me to. That was wrong. I light another cig. Lights flick on and off in a window high above, then moments later, Sean materialises. He struts over self-consciously, a half-smoked spliff hanging from the corner of his mouth. And fuck does he look gorgeous. I swear, if it wasn't Sean, if it was someone else, some stranger I'd kidnapped in a club, I'd rag him all over this city. A feeling of absolute yearning swells in my cunt. I clutch it and contain it. There's no way that animal's getting anywhere near.

'Neck these,' he says handing me two tablets and a bottle of ice cold Volvic. Bastard. Does he really think I'm *that* dense? I wait til he turns away and slip them in my pocket.

'Sorry, I took so long. Forgotten where I'd put the little bastards. Might take a while to kick in, but you'll sleep like a baby. Zopiclon. Straight from Rodney Street. No hangover or nothing. Fucken clean as, la'

He hands me the spliff and jumps up into the driver's seat.

'Come 'ead,' he shouts, craning his head out of the window, 'Finish that in here.'

I open the passenger door and linger. His eyes scorch the air between us.

'Look – thanks for all this Sean, but I'm gonna walk. I'm wired. I need to walk off some of this energy.'

I gauge his face for signs of demur, but there's nothing. Relief if anything.

'OK babes. If you're sure like. S'pose it's safe enough round here. Go Rose Lane way, yeah?' He glances at his watch. 'Still be chocker with students this time of a night. And anyway, I shouldn't really be driving in all honesty.'

I'm in shock. My heart is lurching. What the fuck . . .

'Are you warm enough? D'you want to borrow a coat?'

'No. I'm fine, ta.'

'Keep your mobile switched on babe?'

I nod. I take a final drag on the joint and toss it into the night. Reflexively, I huddle against the cold.

'Listen la, I'm giving you a fucken fleece whether you like it or not . . .'

He swings out onto the gravel and walks round to the boot. It's uncharacteristically messy for Sean, stuffed full of CDs, maps, waterproof coats and fleeces.

'You've never struck me as the outdoor type,' I say, pulling a compass out.

'Ahh you know . . .' he says, looking slightly embarrassed, 'Good for the quads and that.'

'And the soul.'

He shrugs away from the remark and hauls out a heavy tarpaulin coat with a hood and thick fleece lining. I slip it on over my own. The sleeves are almost touching my knees.

'No chance.'

'What d'you mean no chance?'

'I look like I've just escaped from Park Lane.'

'Exactly. So if you decide to go philosophising on pavements again, potential rapists and what have you'll probably think twice.'

'But Sean, just say if I spot some piece of jailbait

staggering home – drunk and gagging for it? Do I have permission to lob it?'

I pull the hood over my head and Sean dissolves into peals of laughter at the absurdity of the spectacle. I wrench myself from the coat, fling it back into his boot and fold my arms defiantly.

'No way. There's no way I'm walking up Rose Lane wearing that. I'll take the risk of being kidnapped and bummed within an inch of my life, thank you very much.'

He just stands there giggling, appraising me affectionately and then in one seamless gesture his eyes lapse into carnal slits, distorting all sense of time and place, ripping all reservations from my body. All I am is a vacuum – exposed and needy and yearning to be filled.

He moves closer. I feel my eyes dilate and suck him in. He kisses me, deep and powerfully. He pulls back as the beam from a passing car lights up his face and then he kisses me again, sucking my lips into his mouth like he wants to inhale my whole fucking soul. I want this to stop. I want to stop this so badly – but I'm helpless. All sense of right and wrong has been lost in the pure resin of desire. All I can do is hand myself over. Give in.

He slips an arm around me and whispers, 'You're fucken beautiful,' and he explores the small of my back and the jut of my hips and rib cage, expanding with the lunge and surge of my dilating heart, pumping sex through my veins, everywhere, across my scalp and down my spine, swooping round my belly, girdling my solar plexus and exploding in the damp of my armpits and Christ, it's too much. It's too fucking much. All these sensations and bodily emotions, overwhelming me and stupefying me, reducing me to just a feeling, a ball of pleasure. He releases me suddenly, leaving me stooped and wordless, panting like a dog. He steps back and our eyes crash savagely and the need to fuck devours his face, then fades quickly and is replaced by something else that is impalpable and so fucking distant that for a moment I think he might turn and walk away and this horrible chasm snaps wide open in my guts. He has stunned me with a yearning so profound and danger-ous that if he leaves me now, like this, if he turns and walks away then my mind will crack. He moves close again and I sigh unabashedly and once again his hands are wrapped around me, gripping my frame as if he wants to crush it and his tongue, probing every inch of my mouth, thrashing over my teeth and gums and the wrinkled roof of my mouth and I can taste me on his lips – beak and booze and cunt, and then he pushes me back against the car and my face slams sideways into the cold of the pane and even though I can't see his face, I know what it's filled with as he drags the flat of his palm across the other side of my face, pulling my cheeks into my ears and blurring my vision. His tongue snakes the naked length of my neck and he thrusts his fingers into my mouth, digging into the moist flesh of my cheeks and stretching them back like he wants to tear my fucking face apart and I can feel my cunt collaps-ing and contracting, jet wet streams shoot down my thighs, absorbing the night like a damp sponge and just as I think I can't take any more, that my body might implode, he pulls back and kisses me softly on the mouth, spinning me out into a different junction and we are calm and intimate for a while, like familiar lovers.

His grip tightens once more and he's pulling clumps of hair into his palm, dragging my head back so my eyes hit the sky where wisps of clouds drift aimlessly in the twinkling vault and I can't swallow and once again I'm vulnerable and tiny as this tall, strong man presses his steel-hard cock right into me and unzips his jeans and Jesus, I'm gonna get fucked right here and now, under the glare of a broken street lamp. But then he slides his tongue across my cheek and into my ear and tells me:

'Get in the car.'

His voice is stripped of all emotion and I feel it resonate deep deep in my cunt and I start to panic cos if this pleasure intensifies, I might black out. Black out and miss the fucking fireworks.

I'm on the back seat with my legs dangling out of the open door. I'm lying here, spread like a whore, bare legs wide open, wide open and waiting for him. He's standing there with his hands on the roof, drinking it all in, his eyes mad, his breath rapid and steaming in front of him and I'm totally fucking naked, naked and shivering with my legs open for him. He looks in awe at my body and at my cunt glistening under the mellow street light and fuck but I'm powerless and utterly everything is nothing apart from this split moment of corrosive impossible desire.

The need to be dirty and depraved swells quickly now and the need to be fucked, fucked hard and fast has taken over my everything. I pull him into me. He resists a moment, steps back again and peels of his jacket, cool and composed and sexy as fuck but I can't hold back for much longer. I don't want a fucking strip show. I want his cock for Christ's sake, deep inside my cunt. So then I'm on to him, tearing off his shirt and wrenching, tugging his jeans down. His dick springs free and I gasp instinctively at the sheer fucking beauty of it. I catch his eyes and drag them down to his groin, shaking my head in mute awe as it twitches and throbs in the light from the broken lamp above which picks out the swell of veins striating it's impossible length and the shiny velvet complexion of a swollen head. He goes to touch me and I knock his hand away, aggressively.

'Wait,' I tell him, 'I want to watch you a while longer' and I settle on the seat with my back against the cold windowpane and soak him in from a distance while the stench of my cunt rises like a fog. I take the flat of his palm and hold it to my cunt.

'Look what you've done,' I say and smear his come-drenched fingers over my lips and under my nose and all over his face.

'Jesus, Millie!' He lurches towards me, 'I've got to fuck you, girl. Please. Let me fuck you.'

I hold him off a second longer, eyes pinning him back, drinking him in.

'Oh I'm gonna fuck you, Sean. I'm gonna fuck you like you've never been fucked before.'

I straddle him and swallow his dick whole, every

pulsing rigid inch of it. I buck him hard and urgently and he groans and growls with his hands and teeth stuffed full of my tits, pulling and squeezing and biting, sucking and bruising. I slam down harder and harder on him til my legs begin to buckle beneath but then he grips my waist and slows me right down, taking the lead and moving me with the thrust of his hips, fast and skilful, and things are starting to blur now, but I'm not ready to come. I need him deeper, I need dirtier. I need absolute fucking depravity – to be fucked and used in every orifice, in every way, like some cheap street whore. I want him to hurt me.

I lift myself off him and clamber back onto the seat. The windows are steamed over and the car is heavy with the stench of our sex.

'You OK there,' he says, catching his breath.

'Fuck me the other way,' I tell him, 'Fuck my arse.'

He runs a hand over his sweating scalp and mumbles something, low and dirty. He steps out of the car and frees his legs from his jeans. His face is frenzied and wild. I lie supine and pull him on top of me, his thick rigid cock gouging into the soft of my belly and the sheer fucking strength and beauty of this naked male is like nothing I have ever experienced before. I have never wanted anyone so badly. I would kill for this. I kiss him deep and urgently and with my left hand reach down to his cock and guide it to my anus. No spittle, no moisture – the pain is almost unbearable and I recoil violently. It feels like my whole body is being torn in two – like he's plunged a red-hot blade inside. He withdraws and apologises, kissing me softly on the cheek. He feeds his way back inside my cunt, but

I seize up my muscles and spit him out. I wrap my legs around his broad athletic back and reaching down again, coax him back to the neck of my backside. I want that pain. I want more of it.

'Fuck me,' I whisper in his face, 'Fuck me like a whore.'

This time there's no stopping him. He lets out a low guttural groan and rams me hard and selfishly, without feeling or sentiment. Nothing between us but raw physical need and theft. The pain scalds through my whole body, like a chainsaw scouring out my insides and I can't take much more of this pain, this tearing and burning and violation but then slowly, inexorably, it relents and dissolves into something alien and needy and so fucking lovely that it brings tears to my eyes and from nowhere, these explosions in my head, one after another and I forget where I am and when I remember, he's coming inside me. Fast hard jets of cum spray shudder and stab my insides and I'm coming too, spurts of pleasure gushing from some inner coil and then it's leaking away, deflating quickly like a balloon worried loose and the sobering aftermath creeping upon us so suddenly. And how empty and sullied I feel.

We're sitting a foot apart, staring ahead into the falling sodium light, panting and sweating and I can feel myself plunging into a desperate, dull, deadly vacuum. He must sense it cos he drapes an arm around me and pulls me close. I recoil and look away, fighting back big quivering torrents of tears. Something horrible is happening to me. It's unfathomable. The moment he withdrew his cock, he sucked my soul out too. I dress quickly and self-consciously, shielding my body like he's a stranger. I meet his anxious gaze and a tear trickles down my cheek. I pull my coat on and open the door.

'Millie,' he says, 'It don't have to *be* like this.'

But it does. It does. Another look and I'm gone.

I pour myself a tumbler of Scotch, snort a long draft of beak and run myself a hot, foamy bath. I perch on the toilet lid, pull my knees into my chin and sip cautiously at the whisky. I hate Scotch and I fight hard to suppress a gag reflex but once in my guts it sparks and smoulders like any other whisky. I slide into the bath and add more foam so I don't have to look at my dirty, refracted body splayed out before me. I let the cocaine rob my head of all thoughts and feelings. Nothing left now but a vague sense of buzzy contentedness. Time passes. The water grows cold. I add more hot. I drain the whisky, doesn't taste so awful this time, and the slow burn glows through me.

I close my lids and forget. The water softens and caresses my swollen holes, cleansing me, absorbing the steady emission of spent fluids with reprieve and discretion. And then I'm slowly, seamlessly, drifting into strange, disjointed cocaine dreams.

A bang bang bang in my chest jolts me awake. I bolt forward, clutching my heart and a great whoosh of air screams through my lungs. I take deep, controlled breaths and the palpitations subside. The water has gone cold and my skin is pricked with goosebumps. I haul myself out of the tub, lungs lurching at the effort, and as I catch sight of my bleary outline in the steamed up mirror the realisation hits me like a clenched fist.

SEAN.

YOU FUCKED SEAN.

The palpitations thrash back, hard and fast.

Christ, Millie, what have you done? I drag the flat of my palm across the milky width of the mirror and my reflection confronts me like some ugly foreboding. Why, Millie? Why?

I pad myself dry, slip into Dad's towelling robe and fumble my way downstairs. Dad has left a light on in his study. I pour myself another whisky, slump on the couch and lie there for a while, staring out at nothing. Gradually the darkness and silence, punctuated only by the ticking of a clock, begin to estrange me. I feel disconnected from my surroundings, like I'm viewing the room through a window. I slide my eyes across the room in search of an object, an image, that will jolt me from this abstraction but everything recedes further and further away. I change seats, snap on a wall lamp, and am flung into a different juncture. Now my surroundings are suddenly crowding in on me, demanding attention, cluttering my thoughts. I pull a newspaper from beneath a cushion and throw my head into my lap, drinking in every picture, headline and sub-headline, not daring to look up at the ever-shrinking room. I read the paper a second time and then I place it on the floor and slowly, timorously brave the room. The walls glower back.

I cross my legs and uncross them. I cross them back again and then flinging myself to the floor, allow myself to succumb to the fact that I don't *feel* right. It's nothing to panic about, though. Deep breaths. And it will pass.

It gets worse.

My head starts to reel with irregular thoughts. Sex with Mr Keeley. A severed child's ankle floating in the Mersey. Melted skin, sliding of cheekbones. I smack my face hard. Get a grip – I tell myself, keep yourself busy, Millie – and don't think. I flick the TV on and focus heavily on the faces of two men, the husband and the lover of some absurdly obese twenty-year-old and things abate for a while but then the faces suddenly melt molten yellow and my heart is flapping like a trapped bird. I vault up and take a deep drag of air. It's okay, I reassure myself, you're okay. I drain the rest of the whisky, perch on the window ledge and concentrate on acting and thinking as normally as possible. I manage to keep it together for a few minutes but then I catch sight of my reflection in the mirror above the fire, eyes all wild and alien, face a decade older. I am *not* OK. I'm losing it here. Something is very very wrong.

I pace the length of the living room, five steps forward, four steps back, deliberating whether or not to wake Dad up and confess. Confess *what* though? That you're about to overdose on cocaine. No! Don't *say* that. You're fine.

'I'm fine,' I tell myself out loud, recoiling from the harsh scratch of chemicals in my voice. I pace some more. Five steps forward, four steps back.

'I'm O-K. I'm O-K. Left right left. Left right left,' I chant out loud. I realise with blessed relief that the movement is slowing me down, tiring me out. At last.

At long fucking last. Sit down. Have another drink. A fag. That's what I need. One cigarette and I'll be just fine.

My jacket is hung over the banister in the hall. I delve in the pocket and pull out an empty cig packet. My heart bang bangs in the crux of my solar plexus. Where are the fucking Marlboro Lights the lad at the garage got me? I swoop again, dig deep into the lining of the jacket, utterly desperate, now. Nothing. In flashback I see myself tearing off my clothes, ready to lie back in Sean's car with my legs splayed open for him. I see the pack of cigarettes fly out – fuck knows where. Who cares? Serves you fucking right Millie. Serves you right.

But I need a fag, quickly – a cigar even. I flounce into Dad's office. I know where he keeps them. Clutching my skull to stop it splitting in two I kneel at his desk. The bottom draw is locked but I know for sure he keeps his Chobitas in there and without even thinking I force the lock with his paper knife and now it's open and I've found the cigar box and it does not contain cigars. I empty it wildly on the floor, still expecting a secret stash to reveal themselves but instead I see papers. I'm dazed and faint as these letters and photographs take focus and slowly, so slowly, I know what this is and how dearly, badly I wish I had not come in here. And then I'm prone and gasping on the floor, swamped by a flickering side-show of words and truth and lies and I'm giving in to this sharp crackling wave moving up my body, pushing me out to some place black and empty.

CHAPTER 9

Millie

The first thing I see is sky. Acres and acres of sepulchral pasture. I hoist myself up and squint out of the bedroom window. A dozen blocks of concrete foreboding loom in the distance. Two armies of high rises split between north and south, sizing each other up across the no man's land of the city which is slowly uncoiling beneath the morning light. In the street below nine to fivers are pouring boiling water over their frost-slapped cars. A postman lumbers across the road with his head hung low. The whole of the city is flat and hungover.

The first thing I hear is Mum. Fighting with Dad.
MUM.
She's back.
Downstairs in the kitchen.
Dad is pleading his love for her. I can't fathom what she's saying but the tone is stoic and unfamiliar, all sapped of Mum. I hear the sound of crockery smashing. And Dad sobbing. Mum shouting. Dad sobbing. Mum shouting. Sobbing and shouting. Sobbing and shouting till their voices curdle and clot into a crazed cacophony — a high-pitched screaming which grows louder and louder then collapses into stock still silence. The only thing audible now is the jerky throb of my

heart, sore and inflamed as it bangs against its cavity.

I bite into the nowhere of my pillow and will the silence to end and the fighting to continue and the house to be claimed by the same ghosts that wrenched us from our last one.

Please. Mum. Say something. So long since I've heard your voice Mum. Don't leave me again. Stranded in this silence. Don't leave.

My pillow's damp with tears and the back of my neck sticky with sweat. A weak, powdery sunlight is bleeding through the curtains. My eyes stretch and fasten onto a grey lightening split on the wall. Beyond the plaster, Dad is snoring passionately in the next room. And Mum is not by his side.

My bladder is full, my throat sore and a cocaine depression is hollowing its way through my head. I fumble my way to the bathroom, head thumping behind my eyes groaning inwardly at the sudden explosion of daylight from a curtainless bathroom window. I slump to the cold seatless basin of the toilet. My arse is tender and swollen and my piss stings – a horrible lacerating chemical sting that is replicated in my throat and nose. I blow the surplus of last night's excess into a tissue – blood and beak and all the vice of the city. I wipe my cunt from front to back, smell the tissue and retch. I fill the sink with hot water and lug a steaming flannel across my face. Then I brush my teeth 'til they're flecked with blood and spit the foamy gunk into the sink. I plunge a hand in, free the plug and stick a finger in the eye of a whirlpool. The tornado spins away from the suck of the drain, tumbles and quivers and clings to the sink before it's dragged down the plughole with a bellicose gurgle. I dry my face and brave the mirror. My reflection leers back, white and ugly, cowering under my scrutiny. I trudge downstairs.

I slob out on the kitchen table and, with my chin buried deep between my palms, endeavour to make sense of the night. My dreams pretty much determine my mood for the day. The boundaries in my mind separating the subconscious from the conscious must be bleary eyed, unsure, because my dreams often seep into reality with such a seamless sincerity that often I inhabit a world whose foundations are entirely fictional. Sean though – that was no dream. He fucked you. He had you. The cunt had you.

I down two mugs of sour tap water. I blow my nose and flick the kettle on. Absent mindedly, I prepare two cups of tea. The depression intensifies.

Staring out into the gloom of the yard, a spate of meaningless thoughts crawl through my head. Sean's crass sculpture, the fireworks, the three-bar fire in Jamie's living room, Dad's groupie, the cluster of bruises on that young girl's back.

Sean.

Fumbling for my key at the doorstep, taking a bath, opening the bottle of Scotch, snorting myself into panic attack, drinking myself out of one, routing for fags . . .

Another burst of memory rushes in on me, colliding with a wave of liquid panic rising somewhere, deep in my guts.

Oh Jesus. No. Please let this be another dream hang-over. An image starts to crystallise in my head – Dad lying naked with a faceless woman. I try to let it flow but it stays unformed like a foetus. I remove myself from the cold grey yard and with a floundering heart advance to the study.

Everything is as it was – the broken drawer, the cigar box. I black out.

I have no notion at all how long I'm out. Seconds? Minutes? I drag myself to my knees. All around there is evidence of me, prying. The snooping daughter. I've even chipped a drawer. Mum would be mortified. She rescued this little fella from a tip in Southport. The most cher-ished of all her foundlings. It was damp, snapped at the spine and denuded of drawers.

'You're wasting your time love,' Dad had said.

And behind the dissenting smile I threw Dad, I was thinking exactly the same. Months she spent nursing it back to health. Invested so much time and effort. Time, I used to think, she'd denied my father of. And now in hindsight I see the ugly irony of it all. That the resus-citation of mangled bits of metal and wood might some-how fill an emotional hole that Dad had dug with his own bare hands.

That's what she was best at Mum. Being a Mum and a wife. Put her everything and beyond into looking after us.

The cigar box is empty, all it's contents strewn across the floor. A lethal kaleidoscope of lies and deceit, unearthed in an accidental discovery. My eyes fall lazy and listless as I toil through the painful heap of blurs and dots. The sunken pall in my guts has been preparing me for something much much worse, and now it caves in on me. Mum wrote to me. I remember removing the letters from the pile, isolating it from the rest of his filth, not wanting to believe it. I was going to burn them. I couldn't read them.

Certain things I was too stunned to see last night now become apparent. The postcode on one envelope is rain smudged and incorrect. It belongs to our previous address. The envelope is from a Mont Blanc set I bought her one Christmas. She always opted for the quill and ink method, Mum – even for making Doctor's appointments. But she never used even a sheet of the paper from that set.

'They're too nice!' she'd protest. And so they lay supine on her dressing table like a piece of inordinate jewellery. Just bits of paper. Profound and sentimental in their nakedness.

I stare at my name on the front of the envelope. I can't open it. I open it. I take out the letter and am shocked to tears – not just by the familiar neat hunch of her handwriting, but by the date – 19th June. She sent this less than six months ago.

June 19th

Darling Millie,
I wish more than anything I were looking into your eyes right now. These are things that should be spoken,

not written. I love you. I love you so much and each and every minute of this silence between us, is killing me. I put that distance between us. I walked out, walked away from the thing I love most in the world. I've called and I've called and waited for you my darling. I'm begging you to give me a chance — please let me explain.

How I miss you, Millie. How I wonder still whether I did the right thing. I wanted so much to wait til I'd seen you through University. I wanted to <u>be there</u> when you got home from lectures, when you brought your boyfriend home, when you stumbled in drunk! I wanted to be there when you got your first assignment marked, when you learnt to drive, when you came back forlorn from an exam or a date that didn't meet your expectations. I want to be there when you graduate.

Did Daddy speak to you, Millie? Did he explain? We agreed he'd judge when the time was best for you to hear of our horror, but two years have dragged on my baby, and I'm dying here without you. I can't go on like this for much more. You won't answer any of my calls, you tear up the train tickets I send you. You turn and run away from me in the street. Oh my darling, I have hurt you so badly haven't I? Maybe I should have stayed, stuck it out like so many others do. Maybe your father has been cruel and selfish to keep you in the dark for so long. But darling you were so young, so very young — If I'd have told you the truth you would never have recovered from it. I hung on for as long as I could, until the day you passed your exams — and that's the day I cracked. I'd waited seven years darling but if I'd have known I wouldn't see you in all this time, I never would *have gone. I would have stuck it out like the other wretched mares whose men tear their lives to shreds. I'm so sorry Millie.*

I've enclosed some money for a train ticket. I need to see you Millie. I'm begging you now. Please don't hate your father. In spite of what's happened between us he's a good man and he adores you. He lives for you. I know that. And I know that hiding behind these lies has hurt him almost as much as his silence has hurt me.

Please forgive me for walking away, but I can't ever regret it. If I could turn back the clock, I still would have run but I would have taken you with me. Forgive me little darling,

I miss you so much it hurts

With love from your loving mother

xxxx

I fold the letter in two and slide it back in its envelope. I try not to cry but it's hopeless. I'm helpless. I sob and sob and if I had a gun I swear I would blow myself away. I drag the back of my hand across my face and blink my vision free and work through Mum's letters in order. Fuck. Fuck. This has been . . . I can't come to terms with this. How could he? How could he do that to her? How could he keep this from me? I sift through the rest of the poison – Dad's pathetic keepsakes. Letters from love-struck students, pictures, so many pictures – so many faces. Matchboxes. Train tickets. A handmade card with a Penzance postmark. The writing is faint and almost identical to Mum's.

Migod Jerry what have I done to you?
Going away. Going far, far away.
I'm so sorry — sorry for all of you
Can't stop. Won't stop loving you.

Mo? Auntie Mo?

My heart bloats then vanishes.

It returns with a sharp needle sticking through it.

There's another card. New Zealand. She's in New Zealand. She'll wait for him forever. Auntie Mo is not dead, then. I am ecstatically crushed.

Jesus, what *did* you do Dad? Please no, Dad. Please tell me you didn't fuck her sister? Was I there? Were we all there, on holiday together? What have you done to my Mummy, Dad? Your students, these other faces, these smiling, pretty virgins — I can square all that. In my treacherous fucked up logic, I can almost applaud you for that. I'd take your side. I would. But her sister? Oh God no. Fuck, Dad — what have you done to her?

I tear back upstairs. His door is slightly ajar. I can see his body rising and falling, sweating against the white powdery sheets and I can see his left cheek, loose and pulpy against the pillow. The sight of him slumber-struck and oblivious fills me with rage. I want to hit him so much that my arm is almost rising in a fist by itself. I could take him right now. I could. Just walk right over and press my thumbs down on his scrawny windpipe and squeeze and squeeze till his face drains of all life. And then walk away. I could leave him there, white eyed and cold.

But then he coughs and turns on his side. It's a feeble,

vulnerable cough, an old man's cough – and I'm small and helpless again and in my sudden smallness I'm paralysed with fear.

I throw on clothes and start to pack with a fitful urgency – bank cards, underwear . . .

His bed creaks and my heart takes a deep, long pause. It returns with a thud, disorientating me, spitting tiny fragments of my head all over the wall.

Fuck. My phone. Where did I leave my phone? My eyes snake the room, pausing at the window where they're lulled momentarily by the careless rhythm of the sky.

Phone, money, beak . . . *beak?* Dressing table, bedroom floor, kitchen, study? Think. Think.

I hear him fart. He coughs self-consciously and then the bed creaks decisively – he's awake, now. I can hear a great whoop of air being sucked through his yawn. I can feel him sitting there, collecting his thoughts, fuzzy headed and not a clue. Not a fucking clue what's happened.

Jesus, his feet are on the floor now. Heavy, uncoordinated and stumbling towards my bedroom. I tiptoe to the door and hook the lock in its latch. I drop to my haunches, cowering beneath the handle. Easy, Millie. Get a *grip*. He won't come in. He *never* comes in.

His feet are at the door now. He's outside the fucking door. I can hear his Marlboro breath, wheezing softly, almost drowning out the hammer of my heart.

I begin to hyperventilate. The metallic bite of adrenaline stings my mouth raw.

'Millie? You awake?' His voice is all distorted, like he's speaking from inside a radio.

Using the flats of my hands to steady me, I lower my buttocks to the floor, then shuffle back towards my bed.

'Millie?'

Fuck, off you bastard!

'If you need me to hand that essay in for you, give us a shout, love.'

You drove her out and you let me despise her and you kept her letters from me. You gutless bastard – you kept it all from me.

I bury my face deep into my pillow and seize my ears, shutting of his voice, so all I can hear is the thud of my heart. I lie there motionless, too scared to breathe or blink.

Time passes.

'Millie, are you OK in there?'

I gulp deeply, trying to swallow down as much oxygen as my battered lungs will allow. The room blurs.

'You've not got lectures today have you?'

You bastard. You've just carried on, haven't you? You've just gone on like nothing's happened, like you're a normal, decent, loving man. Like you're my Dad.

'Millie?'

Dad's voice grows clear.

'Are you OK in there? Do you need me to get you some Alkaseltz or something?'

'No, Dad, I'm fine.'

'D'you need me to hand anything in today love?'

'No.'

'You sure you're alright in there? You sound like you're having an asthma attack.'

'I don't have asthma. Leave me. I'm sleeping'

★ ★ ★

He pads off to the toilet, and I wait for the sound of falling shit. And then I slide my legs over the bed and using the side of the wardrobe to steady me, slowly, I haul myself up. I wait for the sudden rush of vertigo to subside, then grab my bag and steal onto the landing where the smell of shit hangs like a fog. I slip downstairs and on the kitchen table I spot the beak. I stuff it in the back pocket of my jeans and exit the house via the back door. I sprint down Glovedale, and turn left onto Bridge Lane where the shrill winter sun screams in my face and causes me to bounce off a lamppost. I spin but don't fall and continue running all the way up to Allerton Road, 'til I'm safe in the hub of the morning rush hour. Outside Tescos, I flag a cab down and realise I don't know where I'm running to. At Catherine Street, in a half trance, I murmur for the cab to put me out. Where do I go now? Where? To Mum? Not yet, not yet – I need to think. I need to think this whole thing through. I wander, bleary headed and rudderless all the way down Parlie.

I stumble into a phonebox and call Jamie.

Jamie

'Can you come and meet me?' she goes. Fucken sobbing, she is. Better little actress, I'll give her that. 'Something terrible's happened.'

Oh I'll come and meet you alright girl. I gives it my sternest voice – let her know and that.

'I'm in work Millie. Don't break til twelve. What is it, like?'

'I, I can't really say over the phone, darling. It's . . . it's bad.'

Bad is it, hey? That what you calling it? Bad don't even come fucken near, la. Sick is more like it. Nasty, she is – nasty and evil. Pure fucken messed up, she is. Too fucken right I'm meeting her.

'Do you think you can meet me at the Number Seven, then? Twelve thirty-ish?'

'Oh aye – I'll be there.'

Counting the fucken minutes if the truth be known. And she's gonna wish she'd gone for somewhere more discreet when she hears what I've got to say. Not one for public showdowns Millie. Remember when me and her folks went out for her Seventeenth – some swanky Chinky up in Parkgate along the waterfront. Her folks started having some big mad row about whether she should be allowed to drink or not. Jerry was in favour of course. It was placid enough like, wasn't the vicious plate throwing efforts you see round our way, but Millie were pure mortified. Never seen so much colour in the girl's kite. Excused herself to the toilet and did a runna. Did a runna from her own fucken birthday party.

'Jamie?'

'Yep?'

'You alright?'

'I'll see you half twelve.'

I kills the call and fingers the package again – the package that has kicked the arse out of my life.

Millie

By the time I reach the Seven the sky has clouded over – grey tinged and non-committal. I settle at a window table in the smoking section and stare into the cobbled street. I've never loved anyone enough to know the trauma of betrayal – not even Terry, but what Dad's done to me, that's what it feels like. My body seems to have skimmed through all the orthodox responses – jealousy, hatred, anger, grief, self-worthlessness and what I'm left with is something entirely new and terminal.

I'm just fucked. I'm drained with it.

A couple of off-duty pro's march past the window with rapid jerky movements. Crack heads on a mission. Dirty tracksuits and cadaverous faces. One of them sucks confrontationally on a joint. She has a hideous unnatural confidence about her. They pause and leer in, pressing their faces up against the pane, their eyes strident yet glazed, infected with the miasma of the streets. Whatever they're looking for is not to be found and they slither off, all skeletal legs, horrific in the harsh sobriety of daylight. A young studenty waitress wiping down the next table looks at me apologetically. I lob her a half smile then look away quickly before she tries to ignite a conversation. Students. I fucking hate them. That Dad could stick his dick inside those girls is bad enough, but to spend time and money, *our* fucking money, dining them in *our* favourite family restaurant is unfuckingforgiveable. Even kept the receipts and a napkin impregnated with a lipstick kiss. A spent match. The twisted fuck – what thoughts were swimming through his head when he was shooting his fat in them? How dare he fucking cheapen our memories with some chinless bitch who's probably lying in her room now, head over heels in awe of the idea that one of the most esteemed professors in the University and in the field of Criminology has chosen her. How superior she must feel next to her guileless pals, all splayed out on the conveyor belt of the student one night stand. Oh, Daddy – what a wanker you are. And Mo, dear gorgeous, untameable Mo – what the fuck were you thinking of?

Jamie

Half feel sorry for her when I walks in and sees her bunched up at the window like that. Looks terrible she does. Stone white skin and eyes rubbed red raw. Does my head in that, birds crying. And fuck knows, I've seen my fucken share this morning. Still can not take it in, la. One minute I'm snuggled up to the love of my life, her body all velvet and warm and next minute I'm stood trial for a crime that – and I've got to hand it to her – lil' Millie has planned to perfection. Almost had us questioning my own innocence, she's done us in so good. The lengths she's gone to though, la. Down the 24 Hour Tezzies to get em fucken developed. Back down here to shovel her shite through the door. No wonder she looks fucken wrecked, the bitch.

Worst of it though la, I thought it was the thingios. The mock-ups of the wedding invitations when I first seen the package. Never even stopped to think why's it hand delivered and that – never give it a minute's thought. Little package plops though the door addressed to her and to tell you the truth I'm half made up. It's like she's one of the family now – people's dropping stuff off for her cos they know she'll be here and that.

So when I've come back from the bog and I finds her sat at the kitchen table all glazed over and what have you, staring out the window, the last thing I'm thinking is it's anything to do with the envelope. I think she's found something, know what I mean, a bluey or a photie of an ex.

So I drape an arm around her and ask her what's up and she just jerks away from us. Throws us this look which puts goosebumps all over us. Even though it's at the back of my mind that she's coming up to the rag, there's something crazy in her eyes that I've never seen before. She just sits there, looking right into us, and then she gets up, puts on as good a dignified face as she can muster and walks out. I goes after her, in bits I am – I haven't got a fucken scooby what's going on – and she kneels down by our front door and just places the envelope back on the floor, like as though she's winding time back. Fucken does my head in seeing her like that, la. She's fucken broke, man – she's finished. And then she stops dead still at the door and I can see her take a mad big deep breath and she tells us ta-ra and she's gone.

I want to go after her, bring her back, sort this out – but my limbs are like liquid. Like they've been given a local. Can not fucking move for the life us. I just stand there, la, pure fucken paralysed. I'm staring at this envelope on the deck and after a fucken eternity I walks over and picks it up. The handwriting I half know, even though it's capitals. I know them capitals. I opens it up and it hits us like a lump hammer in the face. I just drops to the floor – I cannot believe what I'm seeing. But it's real la – it is happening to me, here and now. And when I looks again I can only think one thought. Millie.

Kite just lights up when she sees us. Like a kid in a supermarket, laying eyes on her Mam when she's thought she's lost her. Rattles us a little bit if the truth be known, the way she's looking at us. It's like she actually believes that she is in someway the victim of all this. Maybe she's finally cracked – done too much of the other and just lost the fucken plot. Like that lad our kid used to knock around with – Ste Rigby. Dead nice lad and all he was – lovely folks, normal upbringing – all that kind of thing, and one day he goes out clubbing, gets home and murders his aul' fella. Said some voice in his head told him to do it. And maybe that's what's happened to Millie, maybe she heard voices in her head and she was too far gone to try and argue with em.

I settle down opposite her. I've played these next few moments over and over in my head since she called us this morning and I've gone though the whole thing, watched it from a distance, as though I were a spider splayed out on the ceiling but now that I'm sat here, face to face with them big forlorn peepers, floundering in their orbits, I'm struck with stage fright, la. Billy's always telling us that I let people walk all over us, that I'm too eager to see the good in everyone. Even when they blaze pure badness I still want to slip a halo over their heads and hope that the light from it will pick out the stray specks of good. And he's right as well. I root for the good in everyone. Even with the likes of James

Bulger's killers, pure messed-up cunts that they were, I find myself delving back to when they were just embryos, harmless bits of cells, shielded from this big mad world and all the stuff that might impel em to do such evil. Like now for example, even though I'm sitting here knowing full well what she's done, the fucking irreparable devastation she's caused, I'm still choked for words, still looking for ways out of it. Making excuses for her, trying to see it from her perspective. I simply cannot believe that this girl who I love with such a fucking wild intensity, my alter ego, my soul mate, would just kick us in the head like that. I hate myself for it, but I've got to do this.

A waitress with a posh face walks past. I grab her attention and ask for a freshly squeezed orange juice. She pulls this arsey expression and tells us that I'll have to go to the till to place an order. Millie's face storms over and as the waitress turns away, she vaults up, veins bulging at the neck and temples. I reach for her wrist, slim and fragile in my hand, and pull her back down.

'Students,' she spits, shaking her head, 'Fucking hate them.'

A couple of girls on the next table glance over and Millie stares into them aggressively. They flinch away, a streak of fear leaping from face to face like lightening, then return to their coffees, silent and defeated.

The whole incident puts a big mad lump in my throat. None of that were done for show. It were pure genuine. Done on instinct like. She loves us she does. Can see it in her eyes. Don't like anyone making a cunt of us and always has been like that. Always taken my side even when she half suspected I was wrong. Always stood by us. And our Billy too for that matter. Floored an ex of his in the State once cos she were gobbing off to her mates that our Billy was knocking her around. And that's what she wanted to do with that waitress just then – slam her one for making her best mate feel a cunt. Ahh, I don't know, this is pure madness all this. Us sitting here like this. The odd fucken irony of it all. That she loves us enough to die for us yet could do something that has as good as killed us.

I inhale deeply and delve inside my jacket pocket. I pull out the photies and without taking my eyes off her, I don't even blink la, I place em in the middle of the table. I sit there half expecting an immediate and tearful confession to come tumbling from her lips but instead she scoops them up and eyes them with a half cheeky grin.

'Who are these dogs?' she goes. Her eyebrows furrow over at the first three pictures and on the fourth and fifth a look of confusion crawls over her kite. She shuffles through them and when she claps eyes on the final picture – which I've stuck there for maximum fucken impact – she's all shock and horror. She's fucken good, la – it's a very convincing hand of cards she's playing.

'That's you.' She goes, all matter of fact, 'And that's Suey, the girl from last night. How . . .'

She flicks through them again pausing on the last one and then pushes them aside, like they don't mean nothing to her. Then she folds her arms and slides towards us.

'Jamie – have you any idea what's going on in my life at the moment?'

Her face wrestles between tears and anger.

'Do you even care?'

'*Wha'?*' I snort, unable to believe what I'm hearing.

'Sorry, stupid question. Of course you do,' she ploughs on, 'It's just that something's happened in my life that's *changed* everything and I haven't got a clue whether I'm fucking coming or going. I feel like I'm going mad. Seriously. I feel like I'm losing it Jamie and I'm fucking terrified. I *need* some help here. I need . . . I need someone to tell me what to do.'

I can't believe her. If she was a fella I'd deck her. I shove the photos back in front of her.

'These came through the door this morning. Addressed to Anne Marie. She's left us. Know what I'm saying?'

She withdraws her elbows and picks them up.

'*What?* Someone sent these to Anne Marie? *Why?* I mean *who?*'

I watch her very carefully, makes my mind up and that's it. I goes for it.

'Fucken sick you are, Millie, la. Badly need your swede sorting out, girl. I mean it. Get fucken help, la. '

I snatch the photies back, straightens em into a pile and slips em back in my pocket. She looks into us, wide eyed and ashen. Her mouth opens to say somet but she just makes this sputtering noise instead.

'Seriously Millie,' I say, throwing my hands on the table and pushing myself up, 'You and me are done.'

She staggers after us, knocking a cup off the table and a dozen pair of eyes burn into us. I can almost hear her heart clunk to the floor. She's shaking now, proper fucking tremors. Half gets to us, it does – I half want to throw my arms around her and tell her I forgive her, but she just keeps on after us giving us this what the fuck you on about spiel, don't know what you're talking about Jamie – just *lying* to us. Lying to us like a cunt. I turn on her.

'How could you do that to her? I know you never thought she were good enough for us and that. Oh aye – you fucken looked down on her didn't you? But I fucken *loved* that girl, Millie. She made us happy. We was *good* together. You never saw any of that. You never saw what it was like when it was just me and her. It was perfect. I was so fucken happy with her Millie. How could you, girl? How could you do such an evil thing?'

She's crying now. Tears just teeming down her face. Everyone's looking at her. That posh waitress gawping, making it into a scene and a half. Millie's fucken crushed la – eyes all glazed and shattered. Just like Anne Marie's this morning.

Millie

I follow him out and a room full of heads lurch after us. Tears of anger tumble down my cheeks – so much unbridled anger coursing through my veins, driving me after him. And it's weird – I'm not bothered about what he's said. I don't give a fuck – I know I've done nothing wrong. I just don't like him walking out on me like that.

I go after him. The studenty waitress rushes over with this hateful sisterly expression and asks if I'm alright. Rage rises in my throat and explodes into another flood

266

of tears – I'm not sad, but I can't help it. I can't stop myself from crying. I flounce out into Falkner Street straight in the path of an oncoming van which swerves and screeches away from me. Jamie's head swings round, his mouth clamped in an anguished oval – but he grimaces again as I reach the other side unharmed. He quickens his pace, breaking into a trot across Hope Street. I see his car, parked outside 60 Hope Street, *our* restaurant. I step into the road again without looking, and more cars swerve and screech but this time he doesn't look round. He is anxious to get in his car and fuck right off. I sprint the last few yards and dive into the passenger seat, slamming the door behind me, before he even has chance to get his keys in the ignition. Our eyes crash stonily.

'Get out, Millie! Get out of the fucken car!'

My eyes burrow into the familiarity of his physiognomy – his clean hard jaw, the gentle creases around his eyes and mouth, his soft browbeaten skin – vaguely almonds and olives. Features that don't correspond to the stranger skulking within. I inhale deeply, swallow back another teary outburst and launch right back.

'You think I sent those pictures.' The sound of my voice – calm and composed, shocks me a little. Inside I'm quivering demonically.

He opens his mouth in aggressive protestation but a huge bank of pigeons swarming on the pavement in front suddenly twists up. He follows their progress, and when he swings back his expression has moved on and the look of anger has been replaced by something far, far worse. Jamie's face bleeds of utter hatred.

'I *know* you did.'

'What?'

'Why can't you just come clean you gutless bitch?'

'Jesus,' I quake, 'You really believe I did *that*?'

'Well isn't that what you brought us here to tell us? It was just a joke and that? You thought she'd see the fucken funny side? What happened, then? Lost your fucken bottle did you?'

A high-pitched wailing sound forms in the pits of my guts and skews out from my mouth.

'Sorry, girl – you're not crying your way out of this one. You took them pictures. You got them developed. And you sent em to Anne Marie so's me and her'd be finished. True?'

'*Ja-mie*? I don't know anything *about* those pictures. I asked you to come here cos I *need* you.'

'Ah do us a favour will you? Don't talk to us like some dickhead. I might not have them letters after my name like your aul' fella but don't treat us like some soft cunt yeah?'

A huge gulf yawns open between us.

'You bastard.'

I open the door and swing a leg out but his hand pulls me back in.

'And another thing,' he spits, tightening his grip, 'Even if I'd never met her – you never could've had me. If I wanted to bang you I would've banged you like every other cunt. Know what I'm saying?'

Stunned and frightened, I release myself from his grip and rub my arm. His eyes are big and remorseless and swallow me whole.

'D'you think I held back cos of morals do you? Think I'm some lovely dumb cunt that wouldn't even think of knobbing a schoolie? Think again, girl. I never fancied you, end of story. And if you want to know the whole of it, I only kept things going with you cos I feel last. DO you read me? I feel fucken sorry for you. Or I used to. Now fucken do one and don't ever, ever call me or knock on my fucken door again.'

A mawkish tear rolls down my cheek. I'm beaten now. There is no worse than this – I can go no lower. Like this is the place where it all ends. From this moment on, there's nothing he or Dad or any other bastard can do to hurt me. I'm beyond injury. I will never ever be the sum of completeness I once was – these last hours, months even, have ripped and snatched things from me that will forever leave me incomplete.

I stand in the middle of Hope Street, watching him disappear, forever. I feel lost, alone and utterly worn out. I don't know which way to turn or what to do next, so I just stand there.

Chapter 10

Millie

I don't know this pub. I don't remember getting here. I perch on a tall bar stool and order a Talisker and a pint of Stella. I neck the malt as soon as it's placed in front of me. I order another – a double this time which I slug slowly, stretching it for a cigarette and a half. I leave the Stella foaming and perfect. The pub is already strewn with early morning drinkers, a mosaic of hard disobliging faces musing under thick billows of smoke. I take a few sups of my pint. It triggers the kick of the second whisky and I suddenly feel gregarious and sparky. In spite of the lovely haze the whisky has thrown on everything there is an uncompromising air of reticence about this place that shows no signs or relenting so I turn my thoughts to me. I flirt momentarily with the idea of calling Jamie but deep down, I'm beyond caring. I really, really don't give a fuck. I don't want him, any of them in my life. Him, and Dad and Sean. I'm through with the fucking lot of them.

I sup the rest of my pint and order another whisky and gradually, inexorably my head begins to sag under the weight of an impending depression which swells and radiates through the room as a shoal of lunch time suits spill in, reminding everyone that life still bores on outside these four walls. I gulp down the whisky then stumble out into the cold, sharp day. Chinatown sits within throwing distance. Perfect – next port of call, The Nook. I walk past a gang of students, huddled on the pavement, smoking tampax-sized roll ups, parading their idiosyncrasies like their lives depend on it. They laugh self-consciously. They probably don't even know why or what they're laughing at. Some crap student joke that no one really gets but will no doubt get relayed over and over again. I brush past them aggressively, knocking a couple of girls off balance and I smile inwardly as all idiosyncrasies leak from their face and they shrink back nervously into one faceless mass. Outside The Nook, I hear the over confident braying of suits from within. I turn on my heels and walk – away from town, not knowing, not caring which way I go – crossing roads, turning left, making my mind up at the last possible moment. Left or right? This way or that? I feel like I've just stepped out of an all night rave and I desperately need to be showered and warm, curled up in some place familiar with someone familiar. But who though – who do I have? Nobody. So I walk – away from the crowds and down to the water where the air smells sour and dank. Receding even further from civilisation I walk past vast episodes of industrial deterioration – fortresses of magnificent buildings lying prostrate under a gloom which has solidified them like gel.

The sky is changing now – dark and savage and full bellied. Not yet dusk, but no longer daylight. I spot a pub, just on the cusp of a timber yard and I quicken my pace, craving it's dark and dingy comfort like a drug. It's empty apart from a young barmaid with a hard face who doesn't want me there. She doesn't want anyone in here, but she double doesn't want some shambolic student bird telling her please and thank you and keep the change. That's what I am to her. A fucking student bird.

I down a couple of Jamesons. My guts churn and my limbs fall heavy so I order a Stella and hope that the bubbles with pull me from the stupor. Instead, my vision fogs over and the accumulating drunkenness hits me in a big muddled flush. I sit at the bar and leer at the woman. She is plain and skinny with fat tits. She settles at the opposite end of the bar and turns away slightly, masking her chest from my gaze only to expose a distended gut. An image flashes through my head — a pregnant whore I once saw at the top of Parliament Street sliding into a car, trying to ignore the swelling and kicking in her bloated belly. She looked so sad and utterly alone, like she had no one in the world. And now there was this thing growing inside her, stunting her business — another fatherless mouth to feed.

The barmaid is looking at me strangely now and I wonder if I've been talking out loud but I'm too drunk to give a fuck anyway. The room is starting to sway a little and my bladder is painfully full so I stagger to the toilet, slipping her a little wink on the way past.

I'm sat on the bog with an empty bladder and my head hung between my legs and the cubicle is spinning. I wish I hadn't drank that last whisky cos it's put this horrible syrupy taste in my throat. And then a shudder of joy as I remember the beak, and I'm fumbling in my pocket and pulling out a fat little wrap. I squat and tap out a small heap on the cistern. I snort then clamp my hand over my mouth and swallow hard to suppress the gag reflex as a chemical bile lunges up my throat. My stomach settles quickly and I start to feel normal again. Not high, just level. I return to the bar and there are two barmaids now and they're both glowering at me like they've been watching me in there on CCTV. I check over my shoulder to see if this look might be directed at someone else but the pub is perfectly empty. I order another half and sit near the window and try to act as normal as I feel but the barmaids keep on glowering and a creeping paranoia forces me out into the glare of streets which scratches my eyes like a razor. I walk and walk.

Stumbling onto Lambeth Road now – the malignant bowels of the city where teenagers in pyjamas walk self-consciously past cars, parked up on the pavements, all rumbling with the buzz of competing sound systems. Two bagheads with faces of starved intensity pass me and laugh. I'm starting to fall again. More beak. More liquor.

Into another pub, small and packed with fruit machines chunnering away. I stride straight into the toilets to refuel and then settle in a dark corner. I stare at the table and tear a sodden beer mat to pieces. A drink sits in front of me that I don't remember buying and fuck this place is seething with hard faces – weaselly scallies in trackies. I take big gulps on my pint. I feel safe in here. Safe and protected. I'm just another wretch, spinning another day away.

The clock above the bar reads four thirty and the pub is filled with different faces. Just blurs – moving smudges but their eyes clear and lucid, watching me like hyenas. My mouth is dry so I take a deep swig on my bottle. It is empty, along with the three pint glasses sitting on the table. I start to feel anxious cos I know I didn't drink all that and someone or something in this bar is trying to fool me. This whole fucking bar is evil and corrupt and trying to fuck with my head. I've got to get out. I stumble to the door, boring my way through a sea of reedy voices and random arms which are trying to stop me from leaving and then I'm out onto the cold, dark street, boarding the first bus that comes my way.

Back on Hope Street now, watching the sky sag and collapse above the city's topography and this line from a song floats into my head:

. . . *safe in the womb of an everlasting night, you find the darkness can bring the brightest light* . . .

I tell this to some paraffin slumped on the pavement and his face splits into a smile. I slump down next to him and share a cigarette and we muse over days gone by, silently, independently.

Dusk deepens into blackness and I'm hopelessly hammered, bursting into the Blackburne Arms, collapsing at the bar, necking whisky after whisky. I'm so fucking happy to be free of them all – those gutless

275

cunts. And Jamie and Dad especially, they're gonna pay, I'm gonna hurt the pair of them so bad that they'll *never* forget what they've done to me, those bastard gutless cunts. And then I'm on some bloke's lap, looking into a chiselled brown face through glazed eyes and he's telling me to go home and Van Morrison is swirling out of the juke box and I'm on my feet, swaying to *Brown Eyed Girl* and no one's really looking, and the brown man is shaking his head and smiling in this amused yet slighting way and maybe I'll just let him fuck me, cos he's looking at me thinking I'm a nice decent girl and if he only knew what filth festers in my head and I go over to tell him but I'm paralysed by this burning aggression in my windpipe which has come from nowhere trying to bring me down and *ruin my fucking night* and the music must've stopped cos the guy is guiding me back to my seat and he's skinning up and we're sharing a spliff. I offer him some coke and he absconds to the toilet but doesn't return but I'm not too bothered cos this spliff is sooooo fucking lovely. This is where I've been heading all day. Sitting here with this lovely spliff and all these lovely people who wear the constitution of the city and behind their deadpan eyes slither such despair but if they could only have some of this spliff . . . And then it's time to move on, cos a change of atmosphere will mean a change of buzz as I'm starting to feel weird now, but not bad weird, I just don't like the way I'm smiling at people, like for show, to prove that I'm normal, this stupid fucking elastic smile to stop them staring. I'm stepping outside into the felt black night which is sharp and cleansing yet unmistakably intoxicating. Fuck, the winter's air is getting me more stoned so I clasp a hand over my mouth and hold in my breath and then I'm lumbering through Bedford Square with the germ of a plan in my head and the noisy strum of the city has withered away to an eerie murmur. My mouth is dry and my body's rancid and my lungs are infected with the filth of the night. The burning aggression returns and I'm in the Eleanor Rathbone building where Dad is based. I'm staring into the mirror of the girls' toilets and I don't recognise the reflection and I'm looking for beak but I can't find it and fuck I really need something to help me see properly because I don't like that person in the mirror. Not one fucking bit and Van Morrison is humming in the background in this reedy freaky way which hurls me into a fit of giggles and I'm out on the corridor, bumping into people and almost falling to the floor with laughter and Dad's not in his office and this woman with glasses and a hideous face is staring at me, really fucking staring at me which isn't funny but I can't help but laugh and she says something but says it in code which is fucking nasty cos she knows I can't understand, not unless I find the beak. I'm looking for Dad now, bursting into offices and toilets and classrooms seething with shocked molten faces. Where the fuck is he? And I'm pushing past students and grown ups with pasty faces and people are speaking in this code and I need to find the beak now and then I remember my germ of a plan – I remember that it's Dad big lecture, last thing on a Friday, that's why I've come, that's why I'm here. Things seem clearer now.

★   ★   ★

I burst into the lecture theatre and I want to shout something cutting and brilliant but I'm speechless. I see him, a man who is revered and all I can do is laugh at him. And then I'm crying, passionately, and I'm out of there, running, running. Dad's running after me with his sleeves rolled up and he's sobbing too. He's caught me and he's trying to help me but he's dragging me by the arm in the wrong direction and everyone's shouting in this code. We're outside and he's holding me up against a wall and I'm screaming at him and telling him that I know all about Aunt Mo who's face I can no longer evoke and then I'm telling him that he's sick and evil and pathetic and then I'm telling him I love him, even though I came here to tell him I hate him and suddenly he's staggered backwards and more and more students have spilled out on the grass. He's pulling this crumpled face like screwed up newspaper and he's shrinking or maybe I'm moving backwards and it's starting to rain. The air smells of industry again, dank and sour and I'm stumbling out of the grounds now and into a whole new juncture. I'm running, desperate to get away from it all. Running and bowling headlong into the city's core, sucking in great lungfulls of the demented night air, my head thundering with the voices and evil liqoured faces of whores and tramps. Running and running and running. A rising terror driving me.

Chapter 11

Millie

I wake cold and disorientated to the hiss and spatter of rain. My eyes are crusted shut and the left side of my body has been numbed stiff by sleep. I'm huddled on some damp, hard surface, frozen cold to the bone. My first thought is that I've fallen asleep on the kitchen floor with the window open but the sizzle of a passing car tells me otherwise. Fuck. I'm out in the open. How on earth . . .

I prise open an eye and blink my surroundings into view. It's dark, but I can make out shapes. I'm lying on a bench in a grassy park of sorts, its square marked out by iron railings and skinny trees. Beyond stands a terrace of grand Georgian houses. It's all so familiar – and so, so alien. I knuckle a gritty wedge of sleep from my eye and swing my legs to the floor. The square spins and slides into focus and that cloying panic clings to me again. My neck is stiff and sore and my throat is raw with some vile infection. I cough and hawk and swoop in my pocket for cigs but all I find is a damp and empty packet.

Suddenly, a voice pierces the void.

'Sleeping beauty. She wakes,' it says.

I spin round and confront it, toppling sideways and hitting the ground with a slap. Blurred beneath the veils of rain a young bloke in a Parka, hood pulled up, is walking towards me with a mug in his hand.

'Sorry,' he says. 'Didn't mean to scare yer or anything.'

'What the fuck are you doing creeping up on me like that!' I shriek.

I shuffle back and try to stand. With a hundred aches and cramps my knees buckle beneath me, forcing me back to the ground. The stranger pulls back his hood. A grin wriggles across his face.

'Thought yer might be able to use a hot drink, like.'

He squats down in front of me and hands me a mug which smells of Sunday dinner.

'Drink this and yerl feel better.'

'What d'you want?'

I eye the drink with extreme caution and his face splits into another grin.

'Here' he says, taking the cup and sipping on it. 'It's perfectly safe.'

I lower my head to the broth and inhale its warmth. Steam rises, gently burning my lips.

'I brought yer this as well,' he says, producing a Mars bar. 'I know, doesn't really go with Bovril does it?'

'What are you – a travelling tuck shop or something?'

His eyes twinkle and flirt with me. I take one sip, then another, then I give in to my gnawing hunger and drain the mug in a few greedy slurps.

'Where am I anyway?' I ask, handing back the mug. 'I sort of know it round here.'

'A small quaint square, situated within walking distance of the city centre,' he offers in Queen's English. 'Stan, by the way,' he says, producing a slim firm hand. 'I'm staying at the Embassy there. I saw yer staggering round the park before, screaming obscenities at pigeons.' He pauses, awaiting some kind of reaction but my face remains expressionless.

'I went into town, came back and yed collapsed on the bench. I've been trying to wake yer fer ages. Didn't want yer getting pneumonia, like – not here on me doorstep.'

I manage a smile. He hands over a bar of chocolate, warm and squishy from his pocket. I tear the wrapper off and cram as much of the sticky parcel into my mouth as possible. The sugar hits me immediately, sobering me, sharpening my vision.

'Yer must have one stinking hangover. The park smells like a fucken brewery.'

I ignore him and continue chomping on the chocolate.

'I was tempted to go and hire a camcorder when I found yer cavorting about before. Funniest thing I seen in ages. What, did yer just go on one or something?'

'Do you have a cigarette?'.

He dips in his pocket, pulls out a packet of Regal and a box of matches and tries to produce a light. After the fifth damp match is snuffed by the wind, he disappears with the cigarette into his hood and reappears with two lit cigs.

'So, what was it? Bad exam or something?'

I raise an eyebrow and take a deep long drag.

'Do I *look* like a student?'

'Ah suppose not really, but then yer don't look like the type of bird yed expect to find paralytic on a park bench.'

'I wasn't paralytic – I was sleeping. And I wasn't drowning my sorrows, either. I was celebrating.'

'Celebrating, eh? And in solitary, too. I like yer style. And what was yer celebrating, might I ask?'

I shrug my shoulders.

'A new life.'

He throws his head back and roars with laughter as though this is the funniest thing he's ever heard. I throw him a bemused expression, but I can't help laughing with him. I like him. I take his hand and pull up his sleeve. His watch has fallen asleep at midday.

'It's late' he says, wiping away a solitary tear of mirth. 'And yer snore like a trooper.'

'I've got a cold,' I snap defensively.

'Yerl have more than a cold if yer don't come inside and dry off.'

'Where's inside?'

He nods over to The Embassy, the hostel across the road.

'Friendly little gaff. Cheap enough, too.'

He stands and helps me to my feet.

'Coming then?'

I give him a noncommittal shrug, which he takes as yes. We trudge through the park in silence. At the gates, he pauses and points to one of the white terraces. A crescent of a moon pours down on his head. He looks gorgeous, angelic almost, and I know right there and then that I can recover from this sickness.

'There,' he says childishly, as though it were his own home. 'That's the Embassy.'

The white stone façade, the big red door and the sign emblazoned above it are all etched in some distant memory I can't quite possess. The adjoining houses are grand enough for dons or barristers, but the Embassy looks folksy and inviting and conjures up images of weary travellers huddling a table, exchanging tales late into the night. A moment ago I might have wallowed in the shelter and warmth that such a place might offer but suddenly I feel strong again. I know what I need to do.

'Look — I'm gonna do one,' I say, conscious of the guilt inflecting my voice. 'Thanks for rescuing me and that, but I should really be getting home.'

'Suit yerself,' he says. A glimmer of disappointment flickers across his face. 'Would yer like me to walk yer to a bus stop or something?'

'Nah — safe as houses round here.'

'Yer know where yer are then, now?'

'Yeah-yeah. Red light central, borderline Toxteth. Another hour and these streets will be swamped with hookers, pimps and crack dealers.'

He stifles a gasp. I laugh at his wide-eyed face.

'Well, thanks for the local info.'

'And just so you know, the going rate round here is between fifteen and twenty.'

'Oh really? I got it fer ten last night with an Indian head massage thrown in fer free.'

I raise a playful eyebrow and we both sway into self-conscious laughter.

'Well take care of yerself Millie. It was lovely meeting yer.'

'You too. And thanks. For the drink.'

I give him a stiff hug of sorts and depart with vague sensations of fear and strength and resolution. I walk in the direction of the Cathedral which, like the moon, stands as a permanence within the mercurial passage of the night. How ironic that a place which radiates such beauty and sanctity should fester such vice and corruption. How many of the tourists that flock here en masse would return if they knew it served as a beacon for whores and their punters? If they knew that its very graveyard was a makeshift bordello in which the most precious of all human interactions are exploited and capitalised – reduced to a meaningless exchange of fluids and cash.

I walk no more than a few yards when an isolated thought crashes in on me.

'Hey,' I shout, swinging round. '*I* didn't tell you my name.'

His face blisters into a huge grin.

He pats the left pocket of his coat and then gestures at mine. I swoop down and pull out my bank cards and keys. I stare at them, then back at him, bemused.

'Yer looked too beautiful to rob,' he says.

I flash him a huge smile, and mean it.

'Well, thanks once again. For not robbing me – or raping me. You're a real gentleman.'

'Pleasure's all mine.'

He salutes and turns on his heel and I watch him disappear up the path and into the hostel. For a second, no more, I wonder what life holds for Stan. And then I think of me.

I walk quickly along Canning Street; teeth chattering loudly, clothes clinging to my skin, the wind whipping swatches of hair across my face. My head is banging, now. I need food, I need to wash, I need to speak with Dad.

I head for *Jamakalicious,* the Jamaican on the front line. It's always busy and the queue spills out onto the pavement bringing with it the sweet smell of goat curry and the hiss and sizzle of sweet cakes. The queue moves forward and I'm inside, out of the bitter wind and into a warm smog of bubbling pans. I order a tray of curry and black-eye rice. I buy some fags from the offie next door, then squat under a flickering street lamp and wolf down the food. I eat quickly, barely chewing. I lick the gravy-streaked tray, cast it aside for tomorrow's pigeons and reach in my pocket for fags. I realise I'm without a light so I haul myself up and trudge back towards brassland in search of smoking strangers. I approach a tall bloke with a punter's face. He grimaces but produces a flame anyway and as I stoop to embrace it, he sniffs the air and recoils. I back away with an embarrassed 'thank you' then as soon as I'm out of sight, I drop my chin to my chest and take a long hard draft of myself. Even with a stuffy beak nose, the smell is vicious. I fucking stink – booze and sweat and drugs and all the filth of the city.

I pad along Hope Street with my head hung low, shielding my face from the gnawing wind and onslaught of prowling headlights. The need for food satiated now, I need to press ahead. The possibility of a hot bath, a warm bed and fresh underwear hurls me headlong to a bus stop on Catherine Street.

I've been walking for hours.

My limbs are hot and heavy, my calves tight and painful. And my head aches with emptiness. He wasn't there. The one time I needed him to be in, to hold me, to tell me his story, Dad wasn't there. I took his money and left him a note.

The sky is boiling blue black, dragging a storm across the horizon and I can feel it, sucking me into the hinterlands of it's madness as my body buckles and revolts against me. I'm so, so tired now, I'm losing it. Irregular thoughts and strange flashing lights hammering my head. The cold demented night air clinging to me like unwanted skin. And my eyes, so sore – so heavy and sore. I need to sleep. Need to lie down. Got to rest before this madness consumes me.

Walking quickly now. Across the park and past my bench where two paraffins cackle like fairground ghouls, their faces thrown up to the rain.

Out of the gates and across the road.

Almost there now. The sound of drunken laughter bubbling beyond the red door. Humans. Warmth. Comfort.

Stan.

All fear and anxiety slowly ebbing away.

Through that door and into the warmth and everything will be just fine.

Jamie

I've been sat here on the dock for hours now, watching the lightening leap across the Mersey. Six years ago it all began. This exact fucken spot. And there was a storm brewing that fucken morning, too. The river was off its head, la – howling and screaming like a mad dog. We was sat on a bench, me and her, just over there, right by the water's edge.

Her face was all raw and pink from the rain. She was coming down badly, eyes all dreamy, proper done in. Me, I was fucken ruthless la – dog tired and hungover. Been on the ale all night with our Billy, hadn't I? Didn't get home 'til after daybreak and no sooner has I drifted off than I'm getting woke up by this little waif at my door. Just turned up out of the blue she did, after disappearing out of my life for over a year. No explanation or nothing, man – it was like she'd only been gone five minutes. Tell you what though la, she fucken took my breath away. In that year she'd gone from being a kid to an absolute stunner. My stomach somersaulted when I opened that door. I did – I fucken swooned, la. Her hair, her lips, her little slender waist but more than anything her eyes. Them eyes, man – I was gone. She give us this look and I was thirteen all over again, head over fucken heels.

She dragged us down the docks, right here where I'm sat now. This is where it all began. This is where I knew I was in love with her.

Should've told her there and then. Should've just followed my heart. But I never. I done what I thought

287

was the *right* thing to do, didn't I? And doing the *right* thing become the blueprint for me and her. It is what it is and it's all down to me.

I watch the storm brewing and I think back on this moment, this second when our eyes collided, just before the storm split the sky in two, and I knew what her eyes was telling us. She was aching to be kissed and held, and how I fucken wanted so badly to wrap my arms around her frail little body and suck her, eat her, kiss her so much. But I never. I took a deep breath and let it go. Couldn't do it, la – would not have been right. The girl was coming down, weren't she? Her mind and her body is out of control. It would've been like getting into someone that's been sedated, la – it would've been wrong. It would've been theft. I wanted her to look at me like that when she was straight – when her mind wasn't spangled by eckie love. But that moment never come back again, and if the truth be known, I don't really regret letting it slip by. I wouldn't change a thing about me and her – not a single chink of our history. I love it just the way it's worked out. I would have failed miserably as her fella. I'd never met anyone quite like her and I wouldn't have known how to handle her. She saw life in the purest terms, la – that you don't put nothing off, you do it *now*. In Millie's world, any fucken thing was possible. I would've only turned them possibilities into problems. I would've held her back. No, I don't regret how it all turned out. But if I lose her, that'll be us, fucked. Done for. And it looks like I've lost her.

I won't say I'm not arsed about Anne Marie – but

I'll get over her. Being honest, I'm half over her already. But lil' Millie – how could I?

It all happened so sudden. I'm sat in The Globe, recovering from my showdown with Millie and our Billy bursts in, wired to fuck. News has got back to him about me and Anne Marie and he's been looking for us all over town. I've told him I don't want to talk about it, but once the bevvy's worked a few knots loose in my chest, it's all come gushing out. *Everything*, la. Millie, Anne Marie, Sean, the wedding – all this stuff that'd just been festering inside us just come pouring out all at once. I don't know what I was expecting, but I never bargained on what come next. He's got his head in his hands.

'Fuck kidder, I'm sorry. I'm so fucken sorry.'

He's crying, la – crying bad, he is. And when he comes round he just looks us in the eye and tells us it was him that sent the photies. It was him – my own flesh and blood. Started off he was just beaked up on Bommie Night, got into a stay behind, ends up going the Tezzy 24 for a big mad breakfast at 5 in the morning. He's got Millie's bag and he's half caned and the next thing he's getting her pictures done for her. This is what he tells us – he wants to do something mad for her, for lil' Millie, one of them. He's going to get a Joe Baxi round to hers, slip em through the door and sit back while she's trying to work out how come these photies that she's only took a few hours ago are now sat there on her kitchen table. That was his plan, yeah – but then he sees the fucken pictures and an altogether different idea comes into his head.

Now our Billy has known about Anne Marie's

involvement with Sean right from the start – the business arrangement and what have you. He's known that she was much much more than a fucken beautician. He's known that that was all a front. He's known how she's fond of the beak and all, too. And he's known that I know fuck all. The long and short of it is he knows she's gonna break my heart, but he don't think it's down to him to run snitching to me. He's in bits, la. He don't know *what* to do. So when these photies drops into his lap he sees an easy way out, don't he? He don't give it a second thought – he's full of ale and beak and he just does it.

Things I said to Millie, la. I'm tearing the fucken flesh off my hands just thinking on it. That's us done, now. That'll be me and her finished. Can't stand it, man. I pure can not stand it.

Millie

Fuck, but I've slept! I can feel it deep in my bones when I waken – I've slept long and true. The other beds are empty. I stare up at the peeling ceiling and sniff the smells of cooking from below. From another room, three voices chatter in Spanish. I find the little bathroom down the corridor and steam myself sensible under the jet of the shower.

I'm momentarily unnerved to find them all in the kitchen. A tall redhead offers me some Scouse from a big pan. Eva Cassidy purrs from a lone speaker which sits on a bookshelf bursting with ravaged books. In the corner, an ochre-skinned girl with waist-length braids sits cross-legged on a rocking chair smoking roll ups whilst a gang of student types sprawl round a big oak table strewn with Guinness cans and spliff paraphernalia. One of them crumbles resin evenly along a rizla. An intense-faced girl is pouring her soul into a journal, her fingers scribbling quickly in a graceful blur. Stan has already moved on. The girl in the rocking chair introduces herself, prompting an onslaught of friendly exchanges. Most of them are travellers or graduates on gap years. I reveal as little as possible about myself without appearing deliberately enigmatic and all of them seem happy not to probe any further. I feel bad about just coming and sleeping and taking and going, but I need to get moving. I'd expected to be up and half way there by now.

Outside the street is littered with storm debris and deep puddles of ink. Yesterday, last night; it all seems so far away. Almost as though it didn't happen. Head down, I make it to Lime Street in fifteen minutes. I purchase a one-way ticket to Glasgow Central then join the queue for the payphone on the platform. I slot in fifty pence and punch in his number, feeling my heart sink as it runs straight onto answer machine.

'Hi,' I say. 'It's me. I really wanted to talk to you. I'm going away for a while. I didn't do any of that stuff. You got me all wrong. I miss you already.'

Jamie

My mobie goes. A local number that I don't recognise so I lets it run onto answer and carries on driving. Feel fucken wretched I do. Haven't slept a fucken wink.

Stomach's pure been in knots, it has – hardly ate nothing since yesterday and anything that passes my lips, just rips right through us. All's I've done is drive la, just drive around in circles, hoping against hope that I might see her.

The mobie goes again and this time it's Millie's aul' fella. I feel a bit thingio about picking up, but I takes a deep breath and goes for it. He might know something.

He doesn't. He's in bits himself. Never heard him like this, la – the fella is pure battered. Tell you what kidder, I can sort my own thing out in good time. Aul' Jerry sounds fucken mental, there. I'm going round.

The ansaphone claxon blurts out. I play back the message straight away. It's her. Oh, baby! It's her and she's sad but her voice, la – her voice is fucken radiating with something that not even soft-arse here can mistake. She's mellow and tender and I swear to you man, there's love in that voice. I mean it. There's love. I don't know what to do with myself. Anyone driving past would think I've just had a baby boy or something, just won on the Lottery. I'm just fucken ecstatic, la – and this time I ain't fucking it up. I drive on to her Dad's and whatever it is, I'll try and make it right for him.

Millie

The train hits Glasgow Central just after seven. The station's heaving with drunken Celtic fans – a belligerent blur of glazed eyes and red faces etched in defeat. I weave my way through a mob of green and white shirts, too weary to respond to the groping hands and leery comments, dribbling from upside-down smiles. I spot a guard up by the Left Luggage and ask if there's another train to Inverchlogan this evening. There isn't, and there's only one Sunday bus service tomorrow, leaving at 6.55 a.m. I can't miss that. I ask him if there's a hotel nearby. He screws up his face, drags a weary hand across his brow and directs me to Lola's.

Lola's is seedy as fuck. The reception is full of bagheads on the nod and homeless lads arguing in sleep-starved gibberish. The receptionist sits behind a shield of plastic scraping the sweat from his skull with a beer mat. His eyes are fixed to a pair of silicone breasts filling the whole of a portable TV screen. I ring the bell.

He lurches his head round, absorbing me in one lingering sweep.

'I only have a double left,' he says before I can speak. 'But yer can take it for single occupancy.'

He simpers at me as though he's said something impossibly funny.

'Thanks,' I spit and push the money through a gap in the shield. He pushes me a key and offers to show me up to the room. I decline with a firm face and once in the stairway, bolt up to my room and lock myself in. The air is fat with cigarettes and stale bodies. I prise open a window, shove a chair against the door, then collapse fully clothed onto a steel-hard bed. I sleep fitfully, lurid apparitions of angry invisible insects upon my skin and evil men entering the room creeping in and out of my dreams. The sound of scratching beneath the bed finally jolts me awake around five. My eyes ache and hammer, but no way am I going back to sleep.

It hurts to swallow. I empty my bladder, splash cold water on my face and stumble bleary-eyed to reception. John Wayne is straddled across the backs of two galloping horses firing a pistol at the fat guy who is snoring like a pig. I hand a homeless lad my key, tell him to take my room then plunge out into the fuzzy black morning. In spite of the chill damp of the early winter's morning, I am euphoric. Today is a new day. I spark a cigarette, draw deep on it, and head to the bus station.

It's filled with night people. Homeless, drunks, insomniacs, the unclaimed, the unloved and the unlovable. Was I one of these people? Would I have been? I find my platform and settle on a bench beside a shivering teenager, all peroxide and make-up – a boil in the bag kind of pretty that'll be gone for good in a year or so. I flirt with the idea of firing up conversation but there is something volatile in her eyes. All I want is to talk, to while away the time.

The journey is long and dark. The girl sits behind me snoozing gently against the window while I stare wide eyed and manic into disconnected flashes of scenery. Battalions of new-build houses squashed onto wasted city land. Massed council estates overhanging infallible swathes of beauty – hills, lakes, valleys, slowly revealing themselves under the shifting inflections of morning. We snake deeper into the countryside, far, far away from the madness of the city. Somewhere, out there, way beyond the frost-bitten greens and amphetamine-plated mountain peaks is my Mother. This is my Mum's land. My head becomes light with her memory. Her soft hands and shy smile. Her brilliant, fiery eyes – Mum's eyes. Bright and trustworthy and forever.

Following the bus driver's instructions, I walk through a dawdling village, veer left at the church and then down into a dip specked with small, cosy cottages. I am bewitched and emotional. All previous fears and apprehension of my unexpected arrival are made nothing in the presence of such beauty. I clock the house numbers and make my way to number ten – it is almost too much for my eyes to drink in.

Her house is small, very plain, but pretty, decked with holly and a tangle of creepers. I pause at the gate and my heart starts to flip. Birds bicker in the eaves above. A pure white winter sun glows majestic beyond the peaks. I wait and watch. I'm not fearful now – I only want this moment to last. I want to remember the minutes before I found my Mother again.

And then a light at the kitchen window and she's filling a kettle from a big brass tap. It's her. She's right there, even more beautiful than I remember. A big maelstrom of emotions are thrashing through me now – excitement and fear and a mad, mad thrill that I can see her there and she doesn't know I'm here. The very act of her filling the kettle floods my heart with so much love that I can't hold back my tears. I push the gate open. She's yawning, running a hand through her hair. And her hair has grown so long! I'm down the path now and Christ, there she is, so perfect and beautiful. She moves away from the window and the sudden absence pangs sharply in my stomach. I shuffle to the door and the crunch of my feet on the gravel brings her back to the window. Our eyes meet and she stares into my face and all thoughts leak away, so my head is just white and empty and filled with nothing else but the vision of her.

Mum. My beautiful Mum. Look who's here.

Acknowledgements

Mum — my lifeline and bestest friend, thanks for believing I could write one of these things and for supporting me through every high and low; Dad, thanks for each and every sacrifice and for a childhood that not even Enid Blyton could cook up.

Jamie B, David G, Stan and my lovely editor, Colin 'method' McLear — thanks for backing me and Millie; Dr David King — gentleman and genius, thanks for nurturing my 'queer'predilictions; Dr Storrar, thanks for pulling me from those deblilitating lows and for your advice and encouragement over the last two years; Peter C — my fun buddy and ally, tar for indulging me and my Tockie jaunts; and Deena, thank the Lord for Deena and her deliciously skewed take on it all.